More praise for
MURDER IN GRAY AND WHITE

"A satisfying and engaging tale . . . Just plain fun to read."

Austin American-Statesman

"Sawyer has written this novel with wit and a sharp eye for whimsical detail. . . . The energetic and humorous plot has enough twists and red-herrings to make it puzzling and fun."

Tallahassee Democrat

"Idiosyncratic personalities, witty remarks, and pertinent details flow through the narrative with few impediments, as Angela Benbow and Caledonia Wingate conduct surreptitious searches and interviews. Spry fun."

Library Journal

"An exciting investigation and adventure . . . A lighthearted and amusing mystery."

Booklist

Also by Corrine Holt Sawyer
Published by Fawcett Books:

THE J. ALFRED PRUFROCK MURDERS

MURDER IN GRAY & WHITE

Corinne Holt Sawyer

FAWCETT CREST • NEW YORK

For the best of friends:

CAROLYN and NED WILLEY, who urged and prodded, scolded and cajoled, teased and encouraged—because without them, there would be no books at all—

RAY BARFIELD, the fourth member of ''The California Four,'' and his rare sense of humor—

and the first and closest friends of all, my sister, MADELINE CAMPILLO, and my mother, GRACE UELAND HOLT.

Chapter 1

UNTIL THAT fog-grayed early morning in June when she was
found beaten to death, Amy Kinseth could have won any
contest set to choose the most disagreeable of all the residents at Camden-sur-Mer. From her ice blue eyes (which
matched the color of her ice blue hair) to her crocodile-skin
pumps (which matched the knobby toughness of her soul)
Amy was an unyielding, self-centered, and insensitive rod
of the purest steel.

Thus the irony was all the more keen that someone had
been able to bludgeon her so cruelly with mere wood.

A week before Amy's arrival at Camden-sur-Mer, the elegant old hotel—now redone as a retirement complex—was
peaceful and serene, as befits the last home of people moving
toward the close of their lives. But even contented people can
get bored, and even the most enfeebled sometimes welcome
a diversion that can break through all that stupefying serenity
to offer a temporary focus, a point of interest—always provided, of course, that nothing in that diversion might endan-
ger their personal status quo. Spectator sports, not
participatory activities, were what most Camden residents
really wanted.

Amy Kinseth's arrival at Camden had furnished exactly
that moment of focus, and if she had been heralded by trum-
pets and accompanied by an array of dancing elephants, she
couldn't have created a bigger splash. To begin with, there
was the move itself. Many people taking up residence at
Camden-sur-Mer were brought by solicitous friends and

family, with perhaps former neighbors bringing in a sofa, a brother-in-law carrying the lamps, a granddaughter struggling along with a little sewing table, a nephew hoisting a rocking chair. . . . Only a few (those who came from a distance or those who had no family) hired professional movers, and none of those had a personal decorator to supervise the furniture placement. None, that is, but Amy, who was attended not just by a crew of moving men, but by Jacques LaChaise himself of LaChaise, LaChaise et Cie, Limited— a very expensive firm from the town of Camden (in which the old hotel stood and from which it took its name, a town about thirty-five miles north of San Diego, on the kindest stretch of ocean coast in North America).

On her moving day, Amy stalked into the Camden lobby and seated herself bolt upright in a stiff-backed chair, a chair designed to complement the decor but never to be occupied by a living human. From that vantage point, she ignored the whole moving process. There she was, right in the middle of the most upsetting experience known to modern man— moving day—and she was apparently unconcerned and perfectly calm. Anyone else might have rushed anxiously down the hall to see if the movers had remembered which was the living room, which the bedroom of the little apartment that was to be hers. Amy looked off into space and let her decorator worry about all that. And when the young decorator dashed up to consult her, his dark, curly hair plastered to his sweaty forehead, she granted him audience with regal hauteur.

"Dear Mrs. Kinseth"—he panted slightly and pulled out an already damp handkerchief to mop his brow—"forgive me. . . such exertions . . . Dear lady, I told you that *semanier* just is not *right* for the bedroom. It makes everything terribly overcrowded. It simply will *not* fit where the men are trying to put it. I can't think why you insist on keeping it."

Amy looked at him with the same distaste she'd have shown if he'd pulled out a toothpick and started to clean his lunch from between his back molars. She said not a word. He blushed and went hastily on. "If you'd just allow me . . . I think I might be able to fit it in beside your dear little bathroom. It will crowd the doorway just the teensiest bit, but I'm afraid that is the only practical location. . . ."

Amy nodded a quarter inch and looked away again. LaChaise mopped his forehead once more and hurried off, presumably to tend to the placement of the lingerie chest. The onlookers stirred with interest. And there were onlookers.

It was nearly lunchtime, and Camden's residents had slowly gathered in small groups throughout the lobby, waiting for the silver sound of the Westminster chimes (albeit only on tape over a loudspeaker system, rather than real chimes) that would signal the opening of their common dining room. It was one of the times they all liked the best, a time to share a little fellowship and a lot of gossip. Today they had more to gossip about than Camden's resident drunk, Mr. Grogan, who sat blearily on a couch near the dining room doors, humming a little Victor Herbert melody and trying to figure out whether he was there for lunch or for supper. Today the residents had something new and exciting to look over: Amy Kinseth. And they were enjoying every minute of the show.

"My, my," little Mary Moffet whispered to Tootsie Armstrong. "Florida modern, she's got . . . All that white and flowers . . . I don't think anybody else has things like that!"

"It's all new!" Tootsie whispered back. "Or most of it is! Imagine. She bought new things to move here. I don't know anybody else who did that."

Down the lobby a little farther, Angela Benbow and Caledonia Wingate stood side by side and pretended not to look while they registered every stick of Amy's furniture, every shred of her clothing, every carat of her jewelry. . . . These two women would have attracted attention anywhere, even if they were not acknowledged leaders among Camden's nearly two hundred residents: widows of admirals, both of them, and as unlike as Alice's Red Queen and White Queen.

Angela stood just less than five feet if she stretched herself up hard, and her silhouette was distinctly barrel-shaped. Spoiled by her late husband, she had possessed a wicked tongue and a distinct air of snobbery when she arrived at Camden some years before, and because she said what she thought, she had in those days been much feared by the other residents. But she had mellowed with the passage of time.

Furthermore, Caledonia Wingate had adopted her. And with the other residents, what Caledonia said usually went, for she was the most forceful and the most admired of all of them—not to mention the biggest. Caledonia stood nearly six feet even without her size eleven shoes; she weighed well over two hundred pounds, and she increased the impression of size by wearingly only flowing garments modeled vaguely on Arabian caftans. These she had in a variety of rich fabrics and vibrant colors, and she invariably dressed them up even more with a rope of obviously expensive pearls.

Besides being a true friend, Caledonia had gradually molded Angela's behavior so that Angela's gift for living had blossomed. As little Mary Moffet put it to the group in the lobby one day, Angela was incredibly *alive*. She found things interesting; she looked for challenge; she thought young! Or, as Mary quavered, at least she didn't think old.

So while Mary Moffet was still a little in awe of Angela, and while Tootsie Armstrong was still too nervous about Angela to play bridge at the same table, most of the residents no longer avoided her. They even took her a bit for granted. And a few even liked her (sometimes, like Mary, in spite of themselves).

Now Angela watched with Caledonia as Amy sat and waited for the moving of her possessions to be finished. One by one, various residents drifted past her "throne" and introduced themselves, perhaps offering a welcome; one by one, Amy Kinseth appeared to dismiss them, with a smile that stopped just below the tip of her nose and no more than a word or two. "Look at her," Caledonia Wingate said, amused. "Reminds me of you when you came here."

"Oh, surely not, Cal . . ."

"Oh, surely yes, Angela," Caledonia said, grinning

wickedly. "She doesn't waste words getting rid of people, does she? I bet that next to her, Calvin Coolidge would look warm and cuddly."

"I wonder if she's just shy, maybe? Not as antisocial as she seems."

"Well, if she's shy, she's in for a rough time now. Look who's arrived!"

One of the nurses from the health facility across the street was bending over Amy now, and a sphygmomanometer had been set up on a side table, while a large inflatable cuff had been attached to Amy's arm. Angela recognized the nurse with amusement. "It's the Monstrous Maddox, Cal," she said. "Do you suppose our new woman can get rid of her as well?"

Connie Maddox was one of the senior nurses on a generally excellent staff who tended both the residents in the main building and those who, temporarily or permanently, had taken up residence in the little hospital–nursing home across the street that was an adjunct of the main retirement complex. Residents generally tried to get one of the other nurses in preference to Nurse Maddox. Though not a big woman, she was perfectly capable of lifting a patient without help while she changed their bed linen with one efficient hand, and word was that she was not always gentle about it. The residents also whispered that she was quick—far too quick—to tie into his wheelchair some patient whose balance was poor, or to clamp a heavy and sometimes bruising hand on the shoulder of a senile case who was pouting and refusing to eat his dinner. Nurse Maddox with needle in hand was a menace before whom the strongest man had been known to flinch.

"I believe she actually enjoys giving shots," Angela had grumbled on one occasion. "Why doesn't somebody nominate her the next time there's a vacancy for harpoon expert on a whaling ship?"

"Actually, she's more efficient than cruel, if one is to be fair about it," Caledonia had answered.

All the same, now they both looked with curiosity toward

the far end of the lobby where Nurse Maddox was ministering to the Ice Queen, Amy Kinseth. There was a minor tussle over the inflatable cuff; there were low, fierce words exchanged which no one else could hear; and then to the residents' delight, Amy jerked her arm away from the hand with which Nurse Maddox was trying to find her pulse and said, quite clearly, "My dear woman, surely you could find some more convenient time for all this." She clamped her mouth tight, and as Nurse Maddox sought to insert a thermometer, thwarted the effort by turning her head aside.

"Almost got the thing into her ear doing that," Caledonia whispered gleefully. "What a pair they are! The irresistible force and the immovable object."

The immovable object apparently won the skirmish, for Connie Maddox suddenly picked up her little medical kit and headed abruptly for the door. "If she weren't wearing rubber-soled shoes, she'd be making a noise like a flamenco dancer! Boy, is she mad!" Caledonia said. "I've never been able to make Nurse Maddox pay the slightest attention to anything I said! I'm going to have to ask this new woman how she managed that. . . . Oh-oh . . . get a load of this!"

Caledonia nudged Angela, who turned where her big friend was pointing and saw Olaf Torgeson, his face glowing crimson in token of his high blood pressure, puffing his way out of the main office toward Mrs. Kinseth. Torgeson, known to the residents either as "The Wart Hog" or as "The Toad," was the highly efficient and much-hated manager of Camden-sur-Mer. The very economies that made him successful in the eyes of Camden's owners made him an object of loathing to the residents. His latest excess was to declare that residents could not feed leftover bread to the birds. It was to be saved, cubed, toasted, and served at another meal as croutons.

There was very nearly a revolution over that, since several of the residents fed the birds regularly, carrying their napkins away from the breakfast table full of crumbled toast and bits of muffin. After numerous petitions and angry letters, Torgeson had reluctantly rescinded the ruling. But he glared at the flocks of pigeons and seagulls that swarmed in to feast on the leftovers the residents carried into the garden, and Caledonia swore he was plotting vengeance of some sort on those birds. He was, in addition to being a sore loser, a snob and a sycophant, a transparent hypocrite and a habitually bad-tempered man. But he ran a tight ship—which was why he was kept on, over the frequent protests of the residents.

Torgeson seldom left his office during the working day except to take meals—or to hold an assembly to announce a raise in the monthly fees. But obviously he considered Mrs. Kinseth's arrival an event meriting an exception to his rule. He advanced beaming, with a smile so broad and white against his red face that it reminded Caledonia, as she said later, of a streak of Cool Whip spread across a slab of Shoney's strawberry pie . . . and he extended his hand as he came.

"Welcome to Camden. Welcome dear, *dear* Mrs. Kinseth," he gushed. "I cannot tell you what a pleasure it is to have you as one of our little family. . . ." Amy's eyes were bright and impersonally cold as she held her own hand up parallel with her sternum—and parallel with an enormous ruby and diamond brooch, on which Torgeson's calculating eyes had focused from across the width of the lobby.

Amy held her hand close to her body and limp from the wrist, palm downward, as though she thought he meant to kiss it. Uncertainly, Torgeson took the hand in his, and she pulled it away sharply. "Was there anything else?" she asked, and she half turned so that he faced only her profile. She appeared to be examining a hedge of Mexican gardenia that grew just outside the lobby window, blocking the sunlight and keeping the lobby cool and cavernously dark.

For a moment, Torgeson groped for something adequate to say. Finally, all that came out was, "Well . . . well . . ." And unable to improve upon that, he slunk away, his face even redder than usual, his daily headache well begun.

The residents sprinkled around the lobby, earnestly pretending not to watch or listen, were hugging themselves with delight. For her putting Torgeson The Toad in his place, they were predisposed to accept Mrs. Kinseth as one of their own.

Whether or not they might have gathered around her throne to offer her congratulations was destined to remain moot, however, since the Westminster chimes rang through the lobby at just that moment.

Now, Murphy's Law is perfectly sound: it's as sure as death and taxes, maybe surer, that if anything can go wrong, it will. But right up there with death, taxes, and Murphy's Law for inevitability is the fact that older people care about their meals. They really care! One of the most interesting speculations during most mornings at Camden was what would be on the menu for the rest of the day; among the favorite topics of conversation among the residents were restaurants they had visited and gourmet dishes they had eaten.

When the dining room doors swung open, all the residents turned away from Amy Kinseth and headed for their assigned tables and the beef stroganoff their superb chef, Mrs. Schmitt, had created for the day's lunch. The Ice Queen sat alone. But if she cared one way or another, no one could have told.

And that was the famous entry. . . . Two weeks later, it was just a pleasant memory, as residents nudged one another when Torgeson passed through the lobby and muttered among themselves, "Say, did you hear how that new woman Kinseth gave the needle to Torgeson?" And when the novelty was gone, things settled down into their usual rut.

It was another pleasant lunchtime, and the dining room was bright with the little bell-sounds of silverware touching china and crystal, against a background hum of easy conversation. Angela and Caledonia sat at the table they shared, happily remembering an entree of lamb shanks followed by a lemon pie that would have made Escoffier weep with jealousy. Angela was having just one more cup of coffee while Caledonia finished off the almond-cherry muffins that had accompanied the main course. "All right, all right," Caledonia growled as she buttered her third muffin. "I give up. Just who is T. Albert Pockmark?"

"J. Alfred Prufrock," Angela corrected her primly. "Prufrock."

"All right, all right . . . I never was very good at names,"

Caledonia said. "Who is this guy anyway, and why should we spend a whole afternoon listening to his love letters?"

"It isn't going to take the whole afternoon, and it's his love song, not his love letters," Angela said, patting her snow white chignon—as though a hair would have dared to slip out of place on that neatly groomed head of hers. Being a widow of an admiral had given Angela the sense that she too had command of things. "Cal, why on earth do you pretend you don't know T. S. Eliot's poetry? You're an educated woman . . . you're sophisticated . . . you recognize the name of the reading for today's tea every bit as well as I do . . . Please pass the cream."

"Mmmmph . . ." Caledonia popped the whole of one more muffin into her mouth and reached for another with her left hand while she deftly speared a butter pat with the knife held in her right. "Iffs thaff Mffs Ffsainsferry . . ."

"Mrs. Stainsbury?" Angela interpreted. Caledonia nodded. Angela slid the bread basket from the far side to the center of the table, where it was easier to reach, and continued, "Oh, I agree. She's terribly tiresome with her constant announcements—and why she doesn't learn to control the public address system . . ."

She shook her head as though to clear the last bit of the ringing sound that had afflicted her ever since Trinita Stainsbury had picked up the microphone at the beginning of that same lunch hour and had fought the electronic howls and crackles to announce: ". . . we will have a special treat at today's silver tea in the lobby (*SCRE-E-E-CH*). Sorry ladies and gentlemen . . . this system needs some repair. I started to say, that charming local poet, Elroy (*WHO-O-O-O . . . CRACKLE*) Carmichael, has agreed (*POP-SPLUTTER-POP*) to read aloud from 'The Love Song of (*SQEA-EA-EA-EAL*) J. Alfred (*WHI-I-I-NE*) Prufrock.' This will be followed by a general (*BLA-A-AT*) discussion of Mr. Prufrock, led by (*WHE-E-E-EEK*)—I say, is this getting worse? Let me try again . . . (*BLOW . . . TAP . . . BLOW*) It seems to be all right. Let me (*SQUEAK-SQUEAK-SQUEAK*) let me finish quickly . . . thediscussionwillbeledbyMr.Carmichaelwhose commentsIamsurewewill (*SKREE-E-E-E* . . .) findmoststi-mulatingand . . . (*SHRE-E-EE-EEEK* . . .) Doesn't *anyone* know how to control this . . . this *THING*!!!'' There followed a sharp pop and absolute silence. The microphone was completely dead.

Trinita Stainsbury, resplendent in pleated, silvery-lavender crepe that matched exactly both the shade of her hair and the rims of her glasses, laid the mike down across the amplifier assembly, whose lights still shone bravely with empty promise. She cut off the switch and stalked, head held high, to her seat across the dining room. She had done her best, her rigid back said plainly, and they would have to make do with that.

"Cal," Angela was insisting, "you know very well who T. S. Eliot is . . ."

"Maybe so," Caledonia said jauntily. "But I don't have to waste my afternoon listening to Elroy Whatsis talking about J. Alton Popsicle's love songs, do I? There's a ball game on TV, there's a sale at the May Company in the mall, the dolphins are feeding regularly in the kelp beds offshore and I could enjoy standing on the cliff and watching 'em out there. . . . Anything but Elroy. You go if you like, Angela. Though why you'd want to . . ."

"Well, to tell you the truth, Caledonia, I'm bored. I mean, it's the same old thing here every day, isn't it? Oh—*do* reach over and pass me the cream, please. I get up, I come in here and I order the same things for breakfast every day, and then I always go back to the apartment and watch some TV. Then it's change clothes and come to a sewing morning or a discussion group or a bridge game . . . always with the very same people. Then lunch and finally supper—the only thing different is the menu. That's novel, I'll grant you that. But it just seems like day in, day out, everything else stays the same and . . . Frankly, it's desperation thinking, I know, but the poetry program might at least be a change."

"Well," Caledonia said, at last laying down the butter knife and brushing the crumbs from her ample bosom, "you could try the exercise class. You haven't done that, I'll bet . . ."

"Spot of butter on your chin, Cal. No, the other side . . .

there, you've got it. Now, why on earth would I want to go to an exercise class?" Angela said.

Caledonia laughed. "Well, personally, I'd rather be horse-whipped. But maybe you might . . .'"

"Have you watched those people? With their funny little sticks clutched in their hands? They're so earnest, marching across to bend and stretch . . . What are those little sticks for anyhow?"

"You'll never know if you don't try the class," Caledonia grinned, heaving her bulk upward. "I think I'll watch the last of the noontime news on TV before I figure out which of today's exciting activities I want to be involved in—oh, drat!" She sat down again with a groan. "I just remembered! I have bridge this afternoon with Tootsie Armstrong and Hazel Hanson . . . and that new woman, Mrs. Kinseth . . ."

"Ah, Mrs. Kinseth," breathed Angela. "Now, there's a lady I mean to get to know a little better."

Caledonia snorted. "You would. You would! You're incurable, Angela. I watched you eye her the day she moved in . . . You took one look at her armload of gold bracelets, and you were a goner!"

"That's not true," Angela defended. "And pass the cream, please. I admit she dresses awfully well . . . and she has some marvelous pieces of jewelry . . ."

Caledonia just laughed. She and Angela were both extremely well off, but that was no novelty at Camden. The high entrance fees and monthly payments made it out of reach for those who had not put money by for their retirement. (There were a few exceptions. For example, Mrs. Schmitt, the chef, had exchanged a low rental for her mother for a long-term contract for herself in the Camden kitchen, at an extraordinarily good salary—and the exchange made the daily menus one of Camden's biggest selling points for prospective residents.) In fact, you'd say that most of Camden's residents were "comfortably off." Caledonia's point, of course, was that Angela was reverting to her snob's view of the world.

"Hand me the butter, will you, Angela? Thanks—I think

maybe one last muffin . . . I saw you eyeing Mrs. Kinseth's luggage, too.''

"Well, it was unusually attractive. All matched leather . . . and so many pieces. I do hope it's well stored in the basement, not getting all damp and moldy . . . I must ask her if she's seen to that.''

Caledonia snorted. "Well, that's as good an excuse to get acquainted as any, I guess." She lavished the butter on that last irresistible muffin.

"Cal, it's no use saying you weren't impressed. Everybody was. It's not just what she owns. And it's not just her putting down The Wart Hog that way—though I heard some say they were thinking of striking a medal. It's—it's the way she carries herself, you know what I mean? You just know she's somebody. . . .''

"Ah, but who is that 'somebody,' is more to the point, isn't it?'' Caledonia, clutching the butter knife in one hand, freed the other hand by popping the eighth muffin into her mouth, whole. She swallowed once, hugely, and then reached over and patted Angela's arm. "Well, girl, you be as snobbish as you like. I love you anyway.''

"Cal!'' Angela pulled her hand away, annoyed at being called a snob. "Oh, go play your bridge. I'll go and listen to Elroy, thank you.''

"Okay.'' Caledonia peered under the cover of the bread basket and sighed to discover that the muffins were all gone. "I can't imagine you'll have a fascinating afternoon. El Wimpo has come here three times this year already to thrill us with his talk about poetry, and I didn't even like the first lecture! So I wouldn't go to the other two, and I won't go to this one. Tell me tonight at dinner what Elroy says J. Quentin Popfork found to sing about, will you?'' She tossed her napkin down on her empty plate, heaved herself upward, and rippled out the garden door toward her cottage, the sun glinting fire on the satin of her flowing caftan as she went.

Angela glanced hastily around to make sure no one was watching, held her own sleeve back against her elbow to be certain it didn't drag in the butter dish, and "made a long arm" to get the cream pitcher—at last.

The afternoon passed lazily along, and it was a quarter to five before the phone in Angela's apartment rang.

"Come on down for the sherry hour, Angela," Caledonia's voice boomed from the receiver. "I want to bend your ear a little."

"You already have," Angela said, rubbing her phone ear. But she came. It was always a pleasure to have sherry with Caledonia.

Caledonia's apartment stood to one's left in the first of a line of bungalows; there were two lines of these low buildings (each containing four or five individual units) extending down either side of the garden from the hotel toward the sea. Unlike many of her contemporaries, Caledonia had been raised to believe that wealth was for spending, provided one had it, and she had rented and combined two of the modest apartments (by the simple expedient of having a builder knock down the wall between them, giving her extraordinarily gracious quarters. And whether there were guests present or not, between four-thirty and five o'clock Caledonia brought out the most exquisite cut-glass sherry glasses in fine European lead crystal and poured into them a good, pale amber amontillado that warmed the eyes before it warmed the palate. She served thin, dry English "water biscuits" for those who had learned to enjoy them, and Triscuits for those with more plebeian preferences; Caledonia had her own strong preferences, but she was relaxed enough about them to make allowances for others.

"Well, what's up?" Angela said, when she was seated in a rose velvet chair, the only chair in the room that allowed her to touch its back and the floor at the same time. Caledonia had bought most of the furniture for her double-sized apartment to be proportional with her own statuesque build ("Statuesque?" she had once snorted, when her late husband, Herman, attempted to compliment her with the word. "Where did you ever see a Budweiser Clydesdale immortalized in a statue!")

Caledonia brought Angela her sherry and settled down on the love seat, which disappeared beneath her, engulfed in the waves of an aquamarine moire caftan trimmed with a small cluster of grass green stones at the vee of the neckline, stones that Angela suspected might be real emeralds. Surprisingly, they looked quite handsome—glass or genuine stones, whichever—contrasted with Caledonia's inevitable very long rope of very real, very large pearls.

"That Kinseth woman!" Caledonia said, inhaling deeply and setting the green stones to sparkling in the lamplight. "That woman! Angela, if I ever scolded you for your sharp tongue, I want to apologize. She's—she's—"

"Tell me about it. What did she do? What did she say? What happened?" Angela leaned forward, her eyes snapping. Good gossip was a treasure not to be underestimated.

"Well, first of all, she had on so many diamonds it's a wonder she could lift her hands to hold her cards!"

"That's not so bad," Angela retorted. "You know we wear our stones, Cal, if we have 'em. There's no time left to save things for special occasions . . . every day is special, at our age." Angela, who had difficulty seeing herself as old at all, could still be realistic about old age in general.

"No, this is different. Wait till you see. She had to be doing it on purpose to show off. She had two rings on each ring finger, right and left. She had a pinkie ring on each hand. She had a middle-finger ring on her right hand—and the only reason she didn't have one on the left, too, was that the diamonds on the left ring finger were so lumpy she probably couldn't get one on. Lumpy? Listen, there wasn't a stone under one carat—and the main stones were anyhow two or even three. Set in platinum I'd say, by the look of them. She had to be showing off for us."

Angela nodded. She thought she understood the impulse. Before she'd known Caledonia really well, her friend's obvious wealth had brought out the competitive streak in Angela . . . and Angela had gone overboard with jewelry. "She probably was. But that's not so—"

"Oh, I haven't got to the bad part yet. Just the gauche

part. Wait. We all sat down at the table and Hazel Hanson put out the dish of nickels . . .''

All the residents at Camden played bridge for money. Players brought to a game twenty-five cents in nickels and put the coins into a saucer set near the bridge table. They played six hands with one partner—then, regardless of the score, they changed partners and added up the total at that moment. The partnership that was ahead in points each took a nickel out of the pot—and their points were entered on a master scorecard under their names. In addition, each time a slam was made, both partners took out a nickel. This went on all afternoon. At the end of play (that is, eighteen hands, six with each available partner, or suppertime, whichever came first) the one player with the highest point score took the remainder of the unclaimed nickels. "Winning the nickles" was cause for much crowing and celebration.

Obviously, it wasn't a high-stakes game, but the residents vowed it was the only way to make the game "interesting," and perhaps they were right, for the standards of play were erratic. There were near-experts, and there were beginners; there were adequate social players . . . and there were those whose expertise was hard to judge because they were becoming extremely forgetful and finding it hard to concentrate. It was a rare bridge afternoon when one's partner did not trump one's ace; when one wasn't left in a cue bid to play in an impossible suit; when someone didn't forget how to answer a Blackwood bid; or when at least two people didn't forget to count trump. And for every hand that was played, at least one voice was raised with the cry, "Whose deal is it?"—followed shortly by, "Oh, is it my turn to bid? Sorry. . . .''

"Hazel put out the dish of nickels," Caledonia was reciting, "and that Kinseth woman said, 'What's that? You're not playing for money, are you? I *never* gamble. I consider it a kind of cheap thrill; there are much more exciting things to do than gamble. And if you need the money, there are surer ways to get it than that. Put that thing away!' I tell you, Hazel was so shocked I thought she was going to cry.''

''Well, I never!'' Angela shook her head. ''What a strange way to behave. Cal, did anyone think to mention the nickels to her when she was invited?''

''That occurred to me—that maybe she just didn't know. I asked Hazel. She said she told Kinseth quite specifically.''

''Then I don't understand. What . . .''

''Personally, I think that Kinseth woman waited to object till she could embarrass everybody and make a fuss. And you don't know the half of it yet,'' Caledonia went on. ''We played for about a half an hour, and suddenly Kinseth said, 'What time is it?' We told her it was just after two and she said, 'Well, it's been fun, but I really have to run. I told someone I'd meet them down at Beach Lane at two-thirty. See you all at supper.' And she just dropped her cards and took off. And yes, before you ask, Hazel says she'd made it quite clear that we usually play most of the afternoon. No, that Kinseth woman just didn't care whether she ruined the party or not. Of course, Tootsie thought it was something she'd said or done . . . she's so insecure . . .''

''She has good reason to be,'' Angela said tartly, with a touch of her old acid. ''She's not the brightest woman in the world, you know. Maybe she *had* said or done something. I know I never enjoy playing with Tootsie. Maybe . . .''

''No, trust me Angela, she hadn't. Tootsie'd been on her best behavior. And anyhow, you ought to give her another chance. She's been reading up and taking lessons—she's quite a respectable bridge player now, at least compared to a lot around here. No, Tootsie had nothing to do with it. That woman just never intended to play long at all. She spoiled Hazel's little party, gave Tootsie nervous indigestion, and riled me up—all in one short afternoon.''

Angela shook her head. ''Well, did she actually go down and meet someone?''

''I guess so,'' Caledonia said. ''At least, she came up the garden walk from the direction of Beach Lane about an hour ago. . . . And here's what I wanted to tell you about, even more than about the bridge game. I had stayed on with Hazel and Tootsie to talk and kind of calm them down, so I was just coming back to my apartment when I met her face-to-face in the middle of the walk. And I thought 'Cal, you'd better say something. Maybe she doesn't know how she upset the girls.' So I stopped her and I said, 'Listen, Mrs. Kinseth, I think you should know Hazel felt awful about you leaving her party today.' And what do you think *she* said?"

"What?"

"She said, 'So what? I really couldn't care less what that woman thinks. She's obviously not someone I want to know any better than I do right now. She's not—' and I want you to get this, Angela, she said, 'She's not in *our* league, is she, Mrs. Wingate?' And she smiled and put one of those diamond-studded claws on my arm. That—that harpy thinks she and I are two of a kind!"

"It's the money," Angela said, nodding sagely. "She thinks you're alike because you both have a lot of money. She's identifying with the pearls and the . . . you know . . . rings, and earrings . . ."

"But I'm not like she is!"

"Of course, you're not, Cal. And neither am I. Not now, anyhow," Angela added quickly. She had been perfectly well aware of her gradual change and the improved relations she was enjoying with the other residents. And although she would not admit it, she was glad of it.

"But wait," Caledonia said. "Then I said—you know, because I was so floored by all that rudeness and chumminess in one package—I said, 'Well, and were you in time to meet your friend?' or something close to that. Well, she jumped like I'd pinched her bottom—"

"Cal!"

"And she pulled her hand away, and she said, 'None of your damn business!' "

"Cal! She didn't!"

"Yes she did, too. Listen, I use quarterdeck language myself, sometimes, when I'm really riled. But I've always tried to watch it around here—and especially with strangers. She said, 'None of your damn business. You—you're just like the rest of them, aren't you? So damn nosy you can't wait to find out my private affairs!' And she turned around and headed for the building like she was going to a fire! I couldn't believe it. I mean, I just stood there with my jaw—''

"Why on earth do you suppose she ever came here then!'' Angela said tartly. "She doesn't seem to be fitting into group living, does she? She doesn't like us, and you can bet we're not going to like her.''

Angela couldn't know that Amy had since childhood suffered a recurring nightmare of dying alone and her body's not being found for days and days. When her husband suddenly left her a widow, Amy spent agonized weeks of sleepless nights, not because of grief but because of that haunting fear of being alone, of dying alone. And at last she had sought remedy in the communal living of Camden-sur-Mer and its attentive staff.

But a phobia is not a prediction of things to come, and she couldn't have been expected to see into her own future to realize that when she died it would be in a public place, so that her body would be found within a couple of hours. Nor, since she made no friends in her new home and shared no confidences, did she ever explain that highly personal motive for moving in to Camden.

And even if Angela had been able to guess part of all that, her speculations were destined to be cut short.

BLAMMMM!!!! Rattle-*BANG*!!! THUD-Rattle . . .

There was an appalling clatter outside near the front door of the apartment that brought all conversation to a standstill. "What on earth . . .'' Caledonia lunged upward, tangling herself in folds of aqua moire and lurching awkwardly toward the door.

"Were you ever *I-I-I-N* Killarney, in the spring . . .'' a hoarse voice bellowed.

"In the gentle hush of evening
You can hear the somethings *S-I-I-I-HING* . . .
Were you ever in Killarney *I-I-I-HIN* the spring!''

"Grogan! " both women said at once.

"Drunk again," Angela added. "Caledonia, I thought that once we said we were going to make that man a special project . . . try to do something about him. He is a fellow resident here, and he does need help. I never knew anyone who drank that much that often!"

"One of these days we should," Caledonia agreed, untangling her feet and surging forward. "Now, I suppose we'd just better go and see if that banging around means he fell and really hurt himself, or whether he's just bumping into things and maybe bruising his shins a little bit."

And they went outside to see to the cheerfully cross-eyed Grogan, who, having gathered himself into a heap after his fall, was sitting with his back to Caledonia's door, humming a happy tune and directing an invisible orchestra with his cane.

Chapter 2

AFTER THE disastrous bridge game, for yet another two weeks, nothing much happened to give the other residents of Camden a chance to see Amy Kinseth as anything less than the cool, slightly aloof, and rather wealthy lady she had first appeared to be. Only Caledonia and Angela watched her with suspicious eyes. Hazel Hanson—hostess of the disrupted bridge party—had the flu and couldn't come to meals for a while, so nobody learned how she felt about Amy. And true to her own insecurities, Tootsie Armstrong was sure "the new lady" had behaved in that extraordinary fashion because she, Tootsie, had done or said something unforgivable. So only Caledonia and Angela had what they felt was real insight into the character of the newest resident at Camden-sur-Mer.

Then one day, mid-morning strollers through the lobby were startled to hear Amy, her voice raised to a strident pitch, scolding someone in the main office. Tiny Mary Moffet, who was at the desk adding her name to a communal "Get Well Quick" card for Hazel Hanson, probably caught more of the actual words used than anyone else did, and she was happy to repeat the whole of what she had overheard to a group of residents waiting, an hour later, to go in for lunch.

"She was saying," Mary gasped, "that Patricia—you know, the secretary?—that she should see that Torgeson discharged Lola at once . . . *at once*! And she kept right on saying it, over and over."

"But why?" Mrs. Grant said in bewilderment.

20

"Because Lola had stolen something from her, she said. Some lipstick in a fancy case . . . quite an expensive one, I believe."

"That's a lot of nonsense," Caledonia Wingate snorted. "Lola has worked in my apartment all the years she's been here as a maid, and if there ever was temptation in someone's way, it would be all those little bits of jade and ivory I have sitting around on every tabletop."

The "little bits of ivory" were exquisite netsukes, currently very desirable and fast-selling items among Oriental art collectors, and the "little bits of jade" were clear, apple green jade figurines, daintily carved replicas of animals and birds. Caledonia had some pieces in glass and acrylic display cases, but some she just set around on tables—out in the open—as though they were any other ornament. Whenever Angela chided her about the careless way she treated her beautiful carvings, Caledonia merely shrugged: "They were meant to be handled. Those Oriental artists loved people to run their fingers over those cool, curved surfaces . . . it's supposed to be very soothing for the soul, or something. Well, you can't get soothed through the eyes alone; I'm on their side on that. So I set a few pieces out just so people *will* handle them. I don't want to put them away where they'll be 'safe.' If someone breaks something, that's just too bad."

Now Caledonia was defending Lola strenuously. "She could have taken any one of those ornaments and sold it for quite a bit of money—and she never did."

"Maybe," said Mrs. Grant cautiously, "she didn't know their value. But she might want a lipstick—I mean, well, that's something she'd use, you see?" Emma Grant had a new hearing aid that worked marvelously well. For several years she'd been unable to join in the before-meal conversation groups because she simply couldn't pick up half of what was being said. Now, despite her complaints that she could also hear the switchboard girl's phone conversations, the squeak of everyone's shoes, and the wind blowing outside the lobby doors, she wore her hearing aid constantly—

unwilling to give up, just because of a little background noise, the conversations she had been missing for so long.

Angela sided with Caledonia. "Lola won't even take a piece of candy from the box my lawyer sends me each Christmas—not without asking me, she won't. And at that, she often doesn't ask—she just dusts around it, eyeing it, kind of hoping with her eyes that I'll invite her to share. I simply don't believe she stole anything, much less a lipstick that wouldn't be at all her shade. I mean, she's so dark—and Mrs. Kinseth's coloring is fairly fair . . ." She glared as Caledonia grinned and started to say something. "I meant, she's *quite* fair," she said defensively.

Mary Moffet shook her head. "Mrs. Kinseth got the girls to promise to tell Torgeson. And to assign one of the new maids to her apartment. Lola will be moved to the cottage apartments till Torgeson decides."

"Well, everything has its good side," Caledonia said cheerfully. "I've got Lola back as a maid then . . . and she's a doggoned good one."

"I wonder if she's searched the apartment for the thing!" Angela said. "It could just have slipped down behind a cushion on the couch . . ."

"Oh, oh, oh . . . that's the part I forgot to tell you," Mary Moffet said excitedly. "I knew there was something. Lola does have the lipstick. It's just that she says Mrs. Kinseth gave it to her. She says as she was leaving this morning—it's a 'light cleaning' day and she just ran the vacuum once around the carpet, changed the bed linen, scrubbed down the bathroom, and started to leave—and as she was heading for the door with her mops and bucket, Mrs. Kinseth thanked her ever so sweetly and said she wanted Lola to have a present as a tip . . . and handed her the lipstick. Then half an hour later, she was out yelling her head off it was stolen and accusing Lola!"

"Can she be getting senile?" Emma Grant wondered. "We've seen it around here often enough to know all about it . . . they lose things and think they're stolen . . . they give things away and forget they've done it . . . they look for things that have been missing for years, and forget they've got things they bought yesterday . . .''

Angela shook her head with a sour smile. "Oh, not her! *She's* not senile, not one bit. I'd be surprised if she was even mistaken. No, either there was some misunderstanding when she and Lola were talking and Lola just thought she was getting a gift—and that's not what Kinseth meant her to think—or . . . or . . . or . . .''

Angela couldn't think of a single alternative that made sense. And she had to admit to Caledonia, as they sat over lunch, that even the one she'd dredged up wasn't very likely. "If Lola was one of the maids who didn't talk good English, that might work as an explanation—but she's not. I mean, she does. Talk good English, I mean. No, it has to be something else. Oh, Chita, could you bring us some more crackers?''

Conchita Cassidy was one of their best waitresses, a tiny girl who could carry a heavily loaded tray and still walk with a flirtatious wriggle, and whose never-failing good cheer was a real source of pleasure to the residents. "Sure thing, Mrs. Benbow, got some right here," she warbled, sliding a basket of assorted crackers neatly onto their table as she sailed past.

"Like Chita, now," Angela pointed to the girl disappearing through the kitchen doors at Mach One. "She understands every word we say and has no trouble communicating.''

Caledonia lifted her head from an excellent cream-of-broccoli soup that had been absorbing her entire attention. "You forget that Chita has an accent only because her mother is Mexican, born in Mexico. But her father's Irish and Chita was born here—talked English all her life—at home, in school, at play, everywhere. She's not a good example.''

Angela smiled as the pretty, dark-haired waitress appeared again, holding a huge tray up over her head like an umbrella and skittering between the tables as though she were running a race. Angela tolerated most of the help, disliked a few, and liked even fewer; Conchita was one of the latter, though

Angela would have considered it ill-mannered to show her favoritism.

"You're right, of course, Cal . . . Lola does talk good English. I wonder what the problem really was about?"

"Oh, I don't know, Angela—maybe it's just Kinseth being the ultimate witch again. Maybe she just enjoys being nasty and looks for ways to make trouble." Caledonia shrugged. "I'm not going to let it worry me."

But shortly, everyone in the place was speculating again on the newest resident's personality and motivations.

It started again about mid-morning. Jacques LaChaise had returned—nobody was quite sure why, but Mr. and Mrs. Jacobs, who had hired a decorator for their first home in Chicago, said that sometimes decorators came to call after you'd moved in, just to see if you were comfortable with all the new furnishings and the new room arrangements. La-Chaise was resplendent in fashionable white jeans with someone else's name embroidered in coral across one hip pocket, white suede jogging shoes, and a white cotton-knit sports shirt with the tiniest coral stripe rimming the edge of the collar. His outfit was topped off with a lemon yellow silk ascot tied jauntily around his neck.

The young decorator sailed through the lobby, nodding to the residents, trailing a cloud of sandalwood-and-cedar cologne after him, and asked Clara, the ever-cheerful, red-headed attendant on duty at the desk, to announce him. "Just tell the dear lady that Jacques is here," he said. "If it's convenient for her to see me now."

"Jock?" said Clara innocently.

"No, my dear," LaChaise said grandly. "*Dzhuh— dzhuh*—the continental pronunciation, please. Think of the sound in 'Zsa-Zsa Gabor.' It's *dzhuh*—" At that point he must have caught sight of a mischievous gleam in Clara's eye, for he cut his explanation short. "Just say it's her decorator, my dear," he finished.

Clara shrugged without losing her smile and rang Mrs. Kinseth's apartment. "Your decorator is here and wants to know if he can come up to see you," she said when the light on the old-fashioned switchboard went on. "Says his name is Jacques," Clara added, emphasizing the soft *J*.

There was a pause and her face assumed a strained look. "No, Mrs. Kinseth, I don't think I can tell him *that*. If you want to say something like that, you better say it yourself. But I'll tell him you're too busy this morning, shall I?" There was another pause. "All right, then." Clara broke the connection, and her smile was completely submerged.

"You go right ahead . . . she's in 175. Hall through the lobby, up four steps, to your left there, beyond the elevator. Oh, but you know that, don't you?" she murmured as he started cheerfully across the marble floor.

At lunchtime, Mrs. Kinseth emerged from her apartment followed by a dour, silent LaChaise, no longer confident and smiling. Mrs. Kinseth stopped briefly by the desk, LaChaise nearly treading on her heels when she quit walking so abruptly, and announced to Clara that she was bringing a guest in for lunch. "You'll have to sign for him," Clara started to say, handing across a billing slip. But Mrs. Kinseth had swept on, tossing over her shoulder a "Put it on my bill, my dear," the subdued Mr. LaChaise trotting sullenly along in her wake.

Mrs. Kinseth had been assigned a table on the far side of the room from Angela and Caledonia, and slightly removed from the tables of other diners—so that in Camden, where almost nobody had really good hearing, her conversation with LaChaise was well out of earshot of any of the other residents. Even Mrs. Grant's hearing aid wouldn't help at that distance, assuming the reserved Emma Grant would have tried to listen in.

It didn't look like a very pleasant conversation, as a matter of fact. Mrs. Kinseth spoke—a lot. And LaChaise listened—a lot. And as they talked, the other residents watched—a lot. The main course had just been served when LaChaise jumped to his feet and threw down his napkin. At last a portion of the conversation was loud enough to carry to the other diners.

"But if I take the furniture back," he was protesting, "do

you know what kind of loss that's going to mean? Besides, it's been nearly a month . . . I can't do it.''

"You can and you will." Mrs. Kinseth too stood up. She was not as tall as LaChaise, but she seemed to tower over him—or he seemed to shrink before her. "All of it. Or you'll never get another commission around here again. I can see to it. I'll call friends who know people in the trade. I'll take out a full-page ad in the local paper. When I finish with you, you'll be lucky to be hired as an apprentice swineherd! You'd certainly be through as a decorator! I'm sick to death of all that wicker and chintz. I want that entire apartment redone. Is that clear?'' He stood open-mouthed, unable to answer.

"Well, good. I take it we're agreed." She smiled pleasantly, seated herself gracefully, and took up her fork again. "Now do sit down, like a good boy, and eat your Cornish hen . . . it's lovely and tender and this is truly the most delicious orange sauce,'' and she picked at the chicken daintily, a small smile hovering around the corners of her mouth.

"I'd have walked out on her," Angela said later. "I wouldn't have sat down. But that—that decorator—he sat down and he put his napkin into his lap and picked up his own fork and he ate. I wonder he didn't choke!''

Caledonia shook her head. "What on earth do you suppose is wrong with her furniture? I had a look through the door into her apartment the other morning, and I thought her place was simply lovely . . . all white rattan with white and yellow cushions—all very tropical—very Florida—with just a touch of coral here and there . . . a vase, an ashtray. . . . So different from everyone else. We seem to run mainly to fake Chippendale around here!''

Angela giggled. "The color scheme sounds a little like Mr. LaChaise's outfit!''

"You're right. Well, maybe they're his favorite colors this season, or something.''

They may have been, but the white and yellow and coral went out—and some Swedish modern came in to replace the Florida look. Peering through the doorway whenever they could catch a glimpse, residents vowed they liked the new unconventional decor, with its blond birch and bright blues predominating. But everything in the room was certainly changed over, no doubt about it.

A week later, Amy Kinseth had another run-in—this time with Mr. Brighton, a man whom everyone liked, who moved slowly because of acute arthritis in his hips and knees. He was coming down the hallway past Mrs. Kinseth's apartment, shuffling painfully along, leaning heavily on his cane. Unfortunately for him, when he stopped to catch his breath and rest his aching legs, he was nearly opposite Mrs. Kinseth's apartment door.

Janice Felton, one of the youngest residents at age sixty-eight, had been coming along the hall behind him, and though he wouldn't tell the story himself, she was only too glad to share with the other residents what had happened next. The Kinseth door had opened suddenly and Mrs. Kinseth came darting out. "What are you doing here, spying on me!" she shrieked.

"My dear lady," Mr. Brighton gasped. "I wasn't . . ."

"Everybody here is just dying to know what I'm up to. I've never seen a bunch of people so determined to find out what's going on in here. So damn curious, you can't stand it unless you poke into things that don't concern you. Well, I want you to stay clear of me. Is that understood?"

Brighton was so stunned he couldn't answer. He simply stared at her. Just about that time Janice Felton caught up with him, and three other people appeared in the lobby end of the hall. "Are you having a problem, Mr. Brighton?" Janice asked, just to have something to say. She felt stupid making such an obvious comment, but she felt she had to say something. Mrs. Kinseth glared at her, looked down the hall at the others, and turned abruptly on her heel and went back into her own apartment. "Just stay away from me!" she shouted again as she slammed her apartment door shut.

"I helped Mr. Brighton into the lobby," Janice reported to the group sitting on the terrace in the late-afternoon sun. "In fact, one of the others had to help me help him. I mean, he wanted to get away from that crazy woman *fast*, and you know he just can't move fast at all . . . and he was trying to force his legs to move . . . and he was stumbling . . . it was awful. He had tears in his eyes—he was in pain and he was so awfully embarrassed.''

Caledonia Wingate shook her head. "What do you suppose is gnawing at that wild woman? Do you think she's having some kind of nervous breakdown?"

"He said she might be sick. Everybody feels cranky when they're sick. Of course, he puts a good face on everything. That's just his nature."

"Mr. Brighton *is* a dear," Mary Moffet agreed.

"Oh, I didn't mean Mr. Brighton," Janice said. "No. I meant Elroy Carmichael. You know—the *poet*." She said it with a kind of breathy reverence. You could tell that, had she written the sentence, the word "poet" would have appeared in oversized, illuminated capitals. "He was the man who helped me with Mr. Brighton."

Caledonia groaned. "Oh, lord, are we in for *another* program of his poetry this week? Hasn't that man read us every blessed thing he's ever written and half the stuff anybody else has ever created? What have we done to deserve him?"

Janice grinned in spite of her rather obvious pro-Carmichael prejudices—and in spite of her being one of the members of the program committee who had arranged Elroy's presentations. "Now, Caledonia . . . He *is* coming back officially in two weeks—to talk about Frost's 'The Road Not Taken,' if I recall. But he was just visiting today. He'd run into the twins in the lobby, and they'd asked him to come to their place for some mint tea."

The twins, Dora Lee and Donna Dee Jackson, were also on the program committee, and they had a special fondness for Elroy Carmichael because he had critiqued some of their verses at an earlier poetry afternoon and pronounced them "exquisite samples of the art of poesy," which set "the girls" twittering for a week.

Dora Lee and Donna Dee were identical twins, and they compounded the impression of their likeness by wearing identical clothing—usually in a shade of bright pink, their favorite color. Their car was even painted a shade of pink that was nearly fluorescent in its gaudy brilliance—"as vile a color as has been mixed by the brush of mortal man," Caledonia Wingate pronounced it the first time she saw it. The twins were of identical weight and height (about five feet three inches tall and nearly 160 pounds each); both had iron gray hair, done in an abbreviated page-boy bob; and they jiggled a little in the same places as they walked. In fact, the twins had only one major difference: one wore large round plastic-rimmed glasses, while the other wore rimless "aviator" glasses with a gold metal arch across the expanse of her face. But since nobody could remember which twin had the plastic rims and which the rimless, it didn't help people to tell them apart! "For all I know, they interchange glasses to confuse us," Caledonia groaned.

Dora Lee and Donna Dee lived together in a crowded, single-room apartment—neither being terribly affluent. They were both so sticky-sweet on all occasions—to each other, to everyone else, and about all things—that there was some feeling among the other residents that one of the girls—finally having OD'd on equal parts of treacle, sunshine, and banana oil—would probably go berserk one day and murder the other.

"No wonder you had to be the one who told us about it all," Angela snorted. "Mr. Brighton is too gentlemanly to say anything bad about anyone, even Mrs. Kinseth . . ."

"Tell the truth, I don't think he's recovered from it yet; I think he's still trying to catch his breath," Janice said.

". . . and the twins would wait to discuss it with us—wait until they could think of some positive interpretation to put on everything," Angela went on. Then she continued, mimicking wickedly in a lisping falsetto, "If you can't say something nice about somebody, dear, don't say anything at all . . ." She laughed. "I bet about this particular incident, the twins may be in their room working over a list of possible comments from now till Michaelmas . . . and they may never find a kind word, so they may *never* come out! And I'm not really sure I'd miss them!"

"How's the theory about murder working?" Caledonia said, laughing as well. "I mean, what are the odds now whether Donna strangles Dora or Dora poisons Donna first—or vice versa? About even, either way, the last I heard."

Janice grinned. "Oh, I'm not making book on the twins any more," she said. "I'm going to take bets on exactly when Mrs. Kinseth will get it in the neck instead. Any takers?" There were a series of smiles—a few negative waves of hand or head—and when the dinner chimes rang, the group dispersed, and the notion of any wager was simply forgotten.

Too bad. Because somebody could have made a bundle. The suggestion was not the only thing that died within the next twenty-four hour span. Sometime before dawn the next morning, Amy Kinseth died as well.

Chapter 3

"LISTEN, IT was just awful! You have no idea!"

Caledonia Wingate yawned mightily and stared at her empty coffee cup with uncomprehending eyes. "You're right. I have no idea. Not at this hour of the morning. What time is it anyhow?" She squinted at her wristwatch. "Oh, lord, it's only seven-thirty, Angela! Do you suppose I could have some coffee before you astound me with your news, whatever it is?"

"Cal," Angela scolded, "the pot's right there by your right hand!"

"Oh. I see." Caledonia looked at it blearily, thought the matter through carefully, and then lifted the pot and poured coffee into her cup. "Of course."

It was a time of the morning when no Wingate—not even one who had married into the name—admitted that decent people could be up and about. The late Admiral Wingate himself rose early only out of professional necessity, and Caledonia carried on the proud tradition of her husband's family by refusing to rise before nine o'clock on most mornings. But on this morning, Angela had phoned her excitedly and insisted—strongly enough to penetrate Caledonia's pre-breakfast mists—that Caledonia pull herself together and join her in the dining room. "I've got the most incredible . . . the most sensational . . . Cal, if you don't come, I'll never speak to you again! Truly. Now you get yourself out of bed, and you come!"

Fifteen minutes later, a bewildered-looking Caledonia—

her hair not quite combed, her spring-flowered sateen caftan hanging not quite straight, her eyes not quite focused—appeared in the dining room door. It was a mark of the haste with which she had dressed (and of the fog in her mind) that she had not worn her pearls. Angela scurried over and steered her friend to her accustomed chair and waited while Caledonia found her coffee cup, found the coffee, poured a cup, and at last drank enough that her eyes began to track. At that point, Angela could hold the news no longer.

"She's dead! She's dead . . . Caledonia, she's dead!!"

Caledonia was still not very cheerful about being waked at what she considered a heathen hour. "All right!" she growled. "I understand the word. Now tell me the rest. Who's dead?"

"Mrs. Kinseth. Amy Kinseth. She's dead!"

Caledonia's eyes finally pointed in the same direction and took on a livelier sheen. "Amy Kinseth? How on earth did she die? I'd have said she was the kind to invent immortality, if it could be done!"

"Well, somebody saw to it that she didn't. She was murdered! Clubbed to death, I think."

"My Gawd!" Caledonia was stunned, and for a moment seemed unable even to breathe. Then she blinked and shook her head. Her voice was husky. "That's—that's terrible! Tell me everything. And how on earth did you hear about this so early in the morning?"

"Well, I decided to join the exercise class, and this morning . . ."

"You *what*!"

"Cal, there's no need acting so surprised about it. After all, it was your suggestion!"

"Mine? I don't remember . . ."

"You said I might as well try it, because I was bored with everything else. So I did. At least, last week I talked to Carolyn Roberts . . ."

"To our activities director? Oh, lord, that woman makes me tired just to think about her, the way she gallops around. Now, there's a woman who'll never get old! To begin with, she's not going to let old age catch her. And for another thing, if she doesn't stop bouncing up and asking us if we wouldn't like to make beaded bags or stuff pin cushions or learn to rhumba . . .''

"Now, Cal, that's her job."

Caledonia took a sullen sip of her coffee. "Sure. But she doesn't have to be so—so lively about it all the time. And so cheerful! You'd think that woman invented shell collecting. And Ping-Pong. And canasta . . .''

"Cal, she's got to try to find something for everyone."

"I know. It's just—I hate to be organized. And she's organized with a capital *ORG*! Couldn't she be late just once in a while? Couldn't she just once be tired?''

Angela dismissed the whole matter with a wave of her hand. "Never mind about her," she said. "Do you want to hear the rest of this story or not?''

"Oh. Sure. Go ahead. Sorry." Caledonia lifted the pot and poured herself a second cup.

"Well, I asked Carolyn, you see, and she said there was room in the class and to come along, and she even brought me a stick . . .''

"Oh, now I remember when we talked about this. We were wondering what the sticks were for . . .''

"Yes. And you said you'd rather be horsewhipped than exercise. So I didn't mention it to you. But I got to thinking, why not? And Carolyn said they didn't really work hard in the class . . . just sort of got some muscle tone . . .''

"Hah!" Caledonia expressed her skepticism explosively.

"Well, you know, Cal," Angela said in a confidential whisper, "the underside of my upper arms has been a trifle loose lately . . .''

Caledonia at last broke into a grin. She tucked a stray wisp of hair behind one ear. "A trifle! Listen, with that much loose skin, you could gain another forty pounds, just in your arms, and ever get stretch marks."

Angela glared at her. "Never mind my arms . . . do you want to hear this story or don't you?''

Caledonia sipped at her second cup of coffee. "I sure do! Go ahead," she said, now completely amiable.

"Well, anyhow, I've been going over to the central meeting hall every morning about six-thirty . . ."

"Six-thirty! God in heaven . . ." Caledonia was appalled.

"Well, we're not all such late risers as you are," Angela said, a little on the defensive. "And besides, Carolyn gets us back in time to take a lovely morning bath before breakfast—at least, she usually does. I haven't even bathed this morning—but then I haven't exercised, either."

"I gather that's only because you're so excited about Amy Kinseth. You'd have been jumping around with all the other lunatics, otherwise. Well, go on with the story."

"We came straggling across the street to the hall, altogether maybe ten of us, spread out in twos and threes . . . all carrying our sticks . . ."

"What do you do with those sticks, Angela?"

"We swing them around and around . . . we reach the length of them . . . we roll them down from our elbow and catch them in our fingers . . . we step through them, holding both ends . . . all the exercises are built around our using those silly sticks. But—they're really very heavy, you see . . ." her voice trailed away.

"And—and somebody used one of those sticks on Amy Kinseth?"

Angela gulped. "Well, at least, Amy was all bloody—lying in the middle of that shiny hardwood floor, looking up at the ceiling—and there was one of the sticks beside her."

"Gosh!" Caledonia was listening, her whole attention on Angela, her mind reconstructing the scene as it must have looked to the prebreakfast exercisers arriving at the big double door. "I hope somebody sent for the police, by the way."

"That's the first thing we did," Angela said haughtily. But in that assertion, she was not strictly accurate. The first thing they all did, of course, was gape, gasp, and move cautiously forward to get a better look. There was, as they saw, no use in trying to revive the victim; the fatal nature of the wounds was all too obvious—so much so, that the second thing some of them did was go outside again to be actively sick.

Angela Benbow was made of sterner stuff, as she had proved often enough before, most notably on the sad occasion a few months earlier when another of Camden's residents had met death by violence. Angela and Caledonia had thrown themselves headlong into the hunt for the killer with an *élan* that dismayed their friends and horrified the officer in charge of the case, Lieutenant Martinez of the San Diego County Police. Convinced that they were better able than the police to understand their fellow Camdenites, Angela and Caledonia had hunted clues, talked to suspects, formulated theories, and interfered with every aspect of the official investigation. Besides, they had been bored with life at Camden, and rather than being frightened by the intrusion of a murder, they had been fascinated; rather than repulsed, they were stimulated.

It was not really her fault, considering her reckless enthusiasm for playing detective, that Angela had found the real answer to that puzzle. At least, that was the official police opinion. But Lieutenant Martinez thought otherwise. He genuinely liked the ladies, he appreciated their undiminished intelligence, and he admired Angela's rare intuitive abilities. Martinez would have said Angela and Caledonia were natural detectives.

At any rate, it was natural for Angela, when Amy Kinseth's body was found, to take command of the situation.

"I sent Mr. Sampson back to the lobby to ask the desk clerk to get the police, and I got the others into two teams—Carolyn took one group to the door to stand outside and see that nobody else came into the room. I took the other group and we stood inside and watched the body."

"Why? She wasn't going anywhere."

"Well, you remember last time? I mean, the last time something awful like this happened here? All sorts of people were messing around with things."

Caledonia grinned. "Mostly us, as I recall."

"Be that as it may," Angela said, standing on her dignity,

"I learned enough during that unfortunate episode to realize the police need things left the way they are. I wouldn't let anybody touch the stick that was there next to her . . . or touch her . . . we just closed the doors, and then we all sat down on those little folding chairs they have set around the edge of the room, and we waited."

"Well? What happened then? What did they find out? Who did they arrest?"

"That's all," Angela said, a bit deflated. "The police came and took our names and all, and they told us to go back home. They said they'd talk to us later. Well, anyway, it gave me a chance to go to my room and phone you. I don't think they've caught the murderer yet . . . but that's all I know about it."

"Oh, I doubt that, Mrs. Benbow. I really do." It was a man's voice, soft and deep, injected into the conversation from a point behind and above Angela's head.

Angela turned and glanced up to see who was speaking— and looked straight into the face of Gilbert Roland! At least, it was someone who looked very like the actor had in his heyday . . . black curly hair, a little black moustache, devastatingly romantic eyes, teeth that gleamed white against an olive skin, a slim, athletic build . . . "Lieutenant Martinez," Angela gasped with obvious delight. "It's you!"

"Oh yes, the bad penny, Mrs. Wingate." Martinez, still smiling, bowing across to Caledonia, who was beaming as widely as Angela.

"We're glad to see you, Lieutenant. Even at this incredible hour," Caledonia said, and she patted at her unruly hair and yanked her flowing garment into a semblance of order. "You're here about our latest murder, I suppose."

Martinez pulled a chair over to their table. "May I?"

"Oh, please do," Angela breathed, her eyes shining with pleasure. "Cal, pour him some coffee."

Caledonia got him a cup by simply swinging around in her chair and stealing one from the setup on the table behind them. "Let's see, Lieutenant, is it black? Or cream and sugar?"

"Cream and sugar both," Martinez said. "I shouldn't . . ." he patted his lean midsection. "But I can only suffer so much for the sake of my waistline, and drinking black coffee is not a penance I propose to pay. Thank you. Yes, ladies, I'm here for the investigation. Actually, I was on my way to work. The local police here in Camden called our main office, the office called me on the radio, and I simply turned the car around and headed back here instead of reporting down there. Or rather, Swanson turned the car around. He still drives for me, of course."

Angela nodded. "Where *is* Mr. Swanson?"

"Shorty is getting some preliminary notes from the men over at the crime scene. But he'll come here next. I promised him, when we knew we were coming here again, that he could have all his meals in the dining room."

Both women smiled. Their fond memories of the tall, skinny young detective who acted as aide to Martinez were almost exclusively of him at a table in the dining room, blissfully sampling the Camden cuisine with the expression of one who has at last found paradise. "We'll be glad to see him, too," Caledonia said heartily. And Angela nodded agreement.

"I've meant to come by here to check on you two," Martinez continued. "But something always got in the way. I got as close as the next block once last month, and the radio snapped on and I was sent off to a burglary in the hills— some householder had lost a TV, a VCR, a stereo, his wife's jewelry, and his dog in a break-in."

"His dog?"

"Well, it was a healthy young Shih Tzu male, registered and worth maybe five to eight hundred dollars retail, but worth a lot more as a stud. When I found Ping-Ping, the guy who stole him was charging nearly three hundred a time for Ping-Ping's services, and there were dozens of prospective takers—there are a lot of lonely female Shih Tzus in Southern California, apparently. Oh, he was taking wonderful care of the dog . . . he knew a good thing when he saw it. And Ping-Ping? He was in dog heaven, surrounded with a harem you wouldn't believe, all eagerly awaiting his attentions. Ping-Ping was living in a heated, double-sized room, eating fresh beef and raw eggs, lying on cushions filled with cedar shavings . . . He never had it that good at his owner's place. All the same, he was stolen property, and we returned him to his original master.''

"Poor Ping-Ping," Caledonia grinned.

"Oh, I don't know. The dumb dog was so happy to see his owner, he may not have stopped licking him and running in circles yet—and that was a month ago! There's no accounting for tastes. I thought his owner was a drip—and if I'd been that dog . . .''

"What about our Mrs. Kinseth?" Angela interrupted. "What can you tell us about our latest mystery here? I mean, I'm glad about the man getting his dog back and all, but that isn't really what I want to hear about. What do you know about all of *this*!''

"It's not what I know that's important, ladies. It's what *you* know. I just got here, anyway. So all I know so far is that some poor lady is lying . . .''

"Poor lady!" Angela snorted. "*Poor* is the *last* word you should every apply to Mrs. Kinseth, living or dead! And *lady* is probably the next-to-last!''

"Now, you see? That's exactly the kind of comment that's going to be most helpful to me. I was hoping you two would agree to talk to me before I discuss things with anyone else. I need an inside slant on the woman and her life here . . . her friends—''

"None," Caledonia snapped. "She had no friends.''

Martinez nodded. "Well, then, her enemies. That's exactly what I need to know about her. If she had no friends, why not? How about it, ladies? Are you going to help me out on this?''

Angela sighed with joy. "Oh, yes," she breathed, her little head cocked sideways, so that she looked up at him through the corners of her eyes, a pose more coquettish than practical. It amused Caledonia so much she had a hard time to keep from smiling as she added her agreement: "You know we'll tell you anything we can, Lieutenant."

Thus it was that the two ladies were the first to enter the second-floor sewing and meeting room that Torgeson reluctantly turned into an interrogation room for Martinez and Swanson.

When he saw them come in, Swanson jumped to his feet, dumping his notebook and pencil out of his lap onto the floor. Grinning widely, he walked up to them, holding both hands out in greeting. "Mrs. Wingate . . . Mrs. Benbow . . ." Suddenly he lurched forward, his large feet entangled in a cane-covered footstool he hadn't noticed. Automatically he flung his arms out, grabbing Caledonia's shoulders to steady himself against her huge frame.

The women beamed at him. "We're glad to see you, too, Detective Swanson," Caledonia said, "but it never occurred to me to give you a hug."

"Well, I didn't mean . . . that is, I wasn't trying . . ."

"Only kidding, young fellow," Caledonia laughed. "We are glad to see you again, even on such a sad occasion."

Martinez cleared his throat meaningfully, and Swanson ducked his head apologetically, picked up the fallen writing implements, and took his accustomed place in the shadowy corner, where his note-taking would be less obvious.

"Now," Martinez said, after the ladies were seated. "Start at the beginning . . ." And they did—with the very first day Mrs. Kinseth appeared at Camden, with the worried young decorator hovering about, the parade of moving men, the signs of her wealth. They told of her rudeness, her concern for privacy, and the insults she had showered on anyone she imagined to be unduly interested in her affairs. They snickered about her treatment of Torgeson, and they oozed sympathy as they told of her treatment of Lola, the maid, and of Mr. Brighton. They finished with a spirited account of her argument with LaChaise over lunch, reconstructing the dialogue between the two almost perfectly.

Martinez nodded from time to time but said very little till they'd finished. Then he rose. "You've given me a lot of possible starting points, ladies. She seems to have insulted everybody in the place and antagonized the help—I'd say the staff is as likely a group to question as the residents are. Then there's Jacques LaChaise . . . what a name!''

Caledonia snorted. ''And worse, he looks like his name! He's given to wearing pastels and dousing himself with perfume. You're going to have a time interviewing him, Lieutenant. He never seems to sit still for two minutes at a time, unless he's eating.''

''Ah, now, that gives me an idea,'' he said. ''What would you say to having your apartment redecorated, Mrs. Wingate?''

''Good lord, *no*!'' Caledonia said. ''Everybody knows I have some of the finest . . .''

''Well, then, maybe it should be Mrs. Benbow. But I think one of you should call on LaChaise at his shop and ask about plans and prices, get friendly and get him talking. Say that you admired the work he did for the late Mrs. Kinseth. Do you see?''

Caledonia nodded. ''In the course of conversation it would be perfectly natural to ask about that argument they had, and just maybe he'd explain it all to us.''

Martinez nodded. ''He might not tell me, but if you're really sympathetic and—I don't like to say it, but a little *motherly* to him—then maybe he'll open up to you.''

''Then,'' Angela bubbled excitedly, ''you could come and arrest him and it would be *us*! I mean, *we* . . . you know, Cal and me . . . who gave you the evidence you needed to solve the case!''

Martinez shook his head. ''Well, not exactly,'' he warned. ''It wouldn't be evidence we could use directly, because you can't even warn him of his rights officially, you know. But it'll give me information—or maybe a direction for sending out feelers for information. That's all I'm looking for—but it's important. So—how about it? Do you two want to operate as police undercover agents? Unofficially, now . . . Remember, nobody else is supposed to know about it.''

Angela jumped to her feet. ''Oh, this is wonderful. *Won-*

derful! To think I was telling Caledonia only the other day that I was bored. And now here's a chance to do something— to be really useful . . . Of course we'll do it, Lieutenant. Count on us.'' And she skittered off toward the door, where she paused and looked back at the other three, all sitting and grinning at her.

"Don't just sit there simpering, Cal,'' she said. "Come along. Maybe we can go this morning. I mean, his shop should be open at ten, shouldn't it? But I'll need to change clothes. I can't go looking like *this*!'' She waved a hand despairingly at her simple linen suit. "I have to look like a woman with money, don't I, if I'm going to play the part . . .''

Caledonia heaved herself to her feet. "Well, just so you don't disguise yourself with glasses and a funny nose and moustache, it's okay. And Lieutenant, for once I agree with Angela. You've had a good idea, and we'll be happy to carry it out. We'll check back with you as soon as we get back. Maybe this afternoon.'' And she rolled majestically toward the door.

"Ladies, wait a moment,'' Martinez called, going after them. "Please! Don't go today! I want to question him officially first, and you *must not* interfere with that. What I want you to do is to see him later, when I tell you it's all right. Is that clear? You may make plans today . . . but let me give you the word that the time is right before you go near that shop. All right?''

But Angela was halfway down the hall already. "Okay, Lieutenant,'' Caledonia said. "I'll sit on her for you.'' And she swept down the hall after her smaller friend.

Martinez returned to the sewing room, smiling to himself.

Shorty shook his head. "Nice ladies,'' he said. "Real nice. But Lieutenant, you sent them out to interview a murder suspect! I mean, that's not really—not really kosher! If the boss, Captain Smith, found out—I mean, well, I'm not trying to criticize, of course. But you shouldn't have . . . I mean, they couldn't . . .''

Martinez held a restraining hand aloft. "Of course I didn't

send them out to do my work! Or into a dangerous situation. Don't you think I know better than that? I met this fellow LaChaise once, some time ago, when he did up the apartment of my sister-in-law. Which doesn't mean he couldn't be a murderer, of course. But I have a hunch he'd be more likely to slap Mrs. Kinseth, if she made him angry, than beat her with a loaded stick.''

''But you can't be sure!''

''No, I can't be sure. So I'll investigate him first, of course. Then they can ask questions and putter around.'' He grinned. ''I don't want them breaking the law by impersonating police officers, either—or ruining our case by entrapping him into some damaging admission without his being read his rights. And I don't want them influencing what he says to me. Let's see—is there anything else?''

Shorty beamed. ''I should have known you'd thought of all that.''

''What I have in mind, Detective, is first to get any evidence there may be available from LaChaise. Second, I want to get a feeling for whether there'd be any harm in their talking to him. And if there doesn't seem to be, then third, I want to get two of the most inquisitive of the residents in this whole place out of the way and out of my hair while I work—without insulting two very dear people I consider my friends. You see why, don't you? You do remember what they did last time?''

Shorty nodded mutely, and Martinez went on: ''The list would take all day to recite, but it included breaking into a murder victim's apartment, not once but three times—once when it had a police seal on the door. It included burgling the main office here, concealing vital evidence, removing vital evidence from a crime scene, questioning suspects before we had a chance at them, and generally tainting the evidence.''

He shook his head dolefully. ''Of course, you know we couldn't have gotten a conviction on that case in a million years, and especially after they'd been playing ring-around-the-rosy with people and papers. We were just lucky it all worked out the way it did. So—they have to be gotten out of my way now, so they don't do the same thing. But—and this is very important to me—I don't want to hurt their feelings. I want them doing something that just might be useful . . . or at least something they'll think is useful. This LaChaise fellow sounds exactly right, to me."

"Oh, gosh, me too, sir," Shorty agreed, grinning from ear to ear. "Pretty clever, if you don't mind my saying so. You might be right too, you know . . . I mean, they might pick up something in the way of background for you."

Martinez beamed and stuck his thumbs into an imaginary vest. "And it came to me right while we were all talking here—on the spur of the moment. Pretty clever is right! I'm glad I thought of this. And after all, it's just possible they might pick up something we could use. Now, Shorty, let's call in the first resident and find out what we can. Let's start with the souse, what's his name?"

"Grogan," Shorty said. "His name is Grogan."

But Grogan, as the ladies could have forewarned Martinez, was having one of his melodic periods. He sang three spirited choruses of "Hut Sut Ralson on the Rillerah" and gave a soulful rendition of "Blue Moon." He was into "Buckle Down, Winsocki," complete with gestures, before they could get him out.

In fact, it wasn't until they talked to Torgeson that they got anything more than Angela and Caledonia had told them. It was from Torgeson they learned that on her entrance application, for next-of-kin, Mrs. Kinseth had written "None." And when the admissions office had questioned her further, she had added rather crossly, "I meant none that I wish to acknowledge." That, to a policeman's ears, sounded rather interesting.

The computers were set humming at headquarters, talking to other computers across the country, checking out possible family members. But for all the back-fence chatter of one electronic gossip to another, the police could find no Kinseths or Winfields who seemed related to Amy. The last of both families, except for Amy herself and her late husband, had been an uncle, Joseph Zachary Winfield, who had passed away at age ninety-three, according to official records, in Brainerd, Minnesota, in 1970, while shoveling a path to his garage during a massive blizzard.

Martinez shrugged. "Of course. It would have been too easy," he said regretfully. "It's usually a relative looking for an inheritance or settling some old family score . . . but that would have made it all too easy. Oh well . . . let's go on with the interviews of the residents and the staff."

And they did. For three whole days.

Chapter 4

FOR TWO of the next three days, during which they interviewed the residents and the staff and collated information (without much visible progress being made on the case), both Martinez and Swanson forgot about Angela and Caledonia.

Actually, they didn't completely forget the ladies. After all, they saw them at every one of the superb meals they took in the retirement center's dining room, and they spoke to the two women pleasantly as they passed in the hallways and in the lobby. It was just that neither man gave a thought to the women's growing impatience to be taken off the leash so they could go on their promised mission.

It was on the third day that the women marched into the sewing room, which everyone was now calling "the interview room," with such broad smiles on their faces that Martinez was instantly suspicious. He had just sent Lola away after an intensive questioning—her third. He still had been unable to shake her story that Mrs. Kinseth had given her the expensive lipstick in its gold case as a gift, a kind of tip.

Lola was a pudgy, fortyish woman who spoke English with only a slight Mexican accent, though it was really hard to tell, because she wept so copiously each time she talked about the lipstick and Mrs. Kinseth that both detectives had to strain to understand her words between the gasps and hiccups. The interview had been extremely painful for both men as well as for Lola, for they had come to believe that she was telling the truth—though neither had worked out why Mrs.

Kinseth would have reversed herself and claimed the maid had stolen the gift.

So Martinez was delighted to see his two friends come in, both radiating sunshine, after all the Latin rain he had experienced over the previous hour. Or rather, he was delighted for a moment. Then his knowledge of them and his policeman's sixth sense made the edges of his brain start to tingle.

"You two," he interrupted their exchange of pleasantries with Swanson, "you two have been up to something!"

Caledonia beamed at him. "You have a nasty, suspicious nature, Lieutenant." She turned back to Swanson. "Actually, I like it better when they put raspberry jam inside the buns . . . but if you really think they're better with just the cinnamon on the outside, you must have been pleased this morning."

Swanson nodded. "Chita gave me a couple to take back here. Haven't had a chance to eat 'em yet, because we've been talking to the maid."

"To Lola?" Mrs. Benbow asked. "About that lipstick?"

"That's right," Swanson nodded. "You know, we don't think she did steal it. We think—"

"Swanson!" Martinez used his best parade-ground bark.

"Oh. Oh, yessir." Swanson jumped to his feet, suddenly aware of the impropriety of his treating the two women like colleagues. "I—I think I'll go eat those two sweet rolls now, you know? Maybe get Chita to make me some coffee to go with them. Do I have time, sir? I mean, before we . . . whatever we're doing next . . . before we do it?"

"You have time," Martinez said, the frost crystals in his voice hanging in the air between them. Swanson nodded to the two women and headed down the hall for the elevator—fast.

"Now, ladies, I think we should talk," Martinez went on, closing the sewing room door and turning back to them.

Angela and Caledonia exchanged a glance that was heavy with meaning and bright with enjoyment. "Very well, Lieutenant," Angela said primly. "May we sit down first?"

"By all means." Martinez was exaggerated in his politeness. "Here by the table, perhaps?" He pulled a chair out for each—a large chair for Caledonia, whose royal blue sateen caftan belled out and completely hid the chair beneath her, so that she seemed to be perched on nothing at all.

"Where shall we begin? Cal? Well, maybe I will . . . that is, I was the one . . . or rather, Lieutenant, *you* were the one . . . it was your suggestion, you know. . . ."

Martinez closed his eyes a moment. "Well, just so somebody begins. Go ahead, Mrs. Benbow."

"We waited, you know, just like you said to. You said not to go near LaChaise's shop till you gave the word. So we waited."

"Very commendable. But that isn't what you came bubbling up here to tell me, is it?"

Caledonia laughed—a rumble like distant thunder. "Of course not. We have something much more important . . . at least, we hope you'll think it's important. . . . Oh, 'scuse me, Angela. Go on. It's your story, to start."

"Last evening, as you were leaving, we got your high sign."

"I beg your pardon?"

"Your signal. We caught it. Of course, we'd been looking for some more direct word . . . but I knew at once . . ."

"Just a minute. Am I to understand that you took something I did or said as a signal to go ahead and contact LaChaise?"

Angela looked surprised. "Of course. Wasn't that what it was? I mean, you sailed past us in the lobby on your way out . . . we were standing with the Jackson twins, talking, waiting to go in to dinner, and as you passed us, you said—Cal, help me to get the words right—"

Caledonia squeezed her eyes shut, remembering. "You pulled out your handkerchief, you see, and touched the corner of your mouth. And that white handkerchief was just like a flag to draw our attention. Or anyhow, that's what Angela thought."

"And then you said," Angela took it up eagerly, "you

said, 'All packed in for the night, ladies. Have a good supper. We'll see you again tomorrow.' "

"That is what you took for a signal? I don't see anything in that . . ."

"Oh, no," Angela said. "It was what you said afterwards. You said, 'I hope tomorrow will bring us more positive results. It's time!' And we knew that was the signal."

Caledonia nodded. "You said you'd tell us when it was time. And there you were, stopping to talk to us in the lobby, and saying 'It's time'—right in with other conversation. We thought it was very clever of you to give us a message like that."

Martinez bit his lips together—hard. After a moment, he apparently had control of himself, for he put a hand up and stroked his moustache and said in a soft, even voice, "All right . . . better tell me the whole thing. What exactly did you do, after you got my 'signal'?"

"I'd been planning for two whole days how to dress and what to say," Angela crowed, "so I was ready. This morning, Cal got on one of her inconspicuous outfits"—she pointed to the royal blue caftan—"because she was playing 'the good friend,' and I was going to be the 'lady who needs a decorator.' So I had to attract Mr. LaChaise's attention, you see. I wore this periwinkle silk . . ." she gestured at her own expensive suit, on the lapel of which was a magnificent antique brooch of pale green peridot alternating with small pearls and highlighted with tiny diamonds, the cluster centered around a single perfect cornflower blue sapphire.

"Mrs. Benbow," Martinez said, still gentle and patient, "can we skip the fashion commentary and get to the heart of the matter? I have to know exactly—*exactly*—what you two have done. And the sooner the better."

"I'm getting to it, Lieutenant Martinez," Angela said coolly. "Now, where was I?"

"Periwinkle," Martinez supplied wearily. "Silk."

"Oh yes. Well, as soon as we thought he would be open this morning, we walked down to the shop. It's only a little over a half block down the hill—after you get to the corner, of course." Martinez seemed about to spring to his feet, and she hurried on. "Well, it was. Open, I mean. And he was there. So we went in and he waited on us."

Actually, there had been a minor disagreement at the outset of the excursion about whether to walk or not. Caledonia resented having to walk anywhere, no matter how short a distance, and had suggested they call her limousine service. But it was too early. The service didn't open till ten o'clock (perhaps the wealthy don't have to travel early in the morning). Then they discussed and discarded the notion of asking Emma Grant to run them down. It wasn't that her driving wasn't careful; on the contrary, it was entirely too careful. On the highway, she drove at an overly cautious 35 mph in the extreme right-hand lane. But she also stuck to a hair-raising 35 mph through the heart of town! In addition, she never signaled until the moment before she intended to turn, and she turned either too short, so that she grazed the curb, or far too wide, so that she entered the oncoming lane at the widest point of her arc.

So, in a nutshell, neither Angela nor Caledonia was at all anxious to ride with her—even for a half block. Besides, as Angela said, "The walk will do us good," a premise with which Caledonia disagreed most heartily. However, for want of any reasonable alternative, she finally agreed to walk to the shop.

So Caledonia had started the adventure with a case of the sullens. But as she stumped majestically along, her caftan fluttering around her like a set of battle flags, she seemed to cheer up and to gather steam. She was walking at a brisk clip when she arrived at the LaChaise shop with Angela hard on her heels, and the ladies sailed in, like a royal blue battleship followed by a light blue tugboat.

It was slightly deflating to discover that there was no one in the front of the shop at the moment of their arrival, but it gave them a little time to look around. The decorator had set up "corners"—little scenes that showed off special pieces. In one "corner," a huge Imari vase of brilliant coloration held soft gray-green reeds that contrasted with a background of silver-pink wallpaper, and there was a single stainless steel abstraction in bas-relief hanging on the wall above it. Another "corner" was formed with a heavy blackened oak Mexican screen, elaborately carved, in front of which stood an art deco phone table of chrome and glass and a modish but forbidding Bauhaus chair. The firm of LaChaise, LaChaise et Cie was apparently devoted to scenes of violent contrast.

"Oh, boy, I *hate* that little table," Caledonia whispered. "It would collapse if I put one elbow on it while I was phoning. And besides, I like things that look warm and comfortable . . ."

"Ah, ladies . . . may I help you?"

They started, turned, and discovered that the man they'd come to see, Jacques LaChaise, had entered behind them. But he didn't quite look the same. He was again wearing jeans—but of plain blue denim. He was wearing a sports shirt—but of plaid cotton. He had battered sneakers on his feet instead of the white suede. And his whole demeanor was somehow . . . different.

"Mr. LaChaise?" Angela asked hesitantly. He nodded. "We've come to see about getting a small apartment done . . ." He said nothing. "Up at Camden, you see," Angela went on. "You know, the retirement center up the hill?"

LaChaise shook his head. "That was a nasty business up there. Nasty. I haven't gotten over the shock yet. The papers said Mrs. Kinseth was beaten . . ." He gulped and started over. "Mrs. Kinseth was . . . I mean, what I knew of her, she certainly seemed to be . . . that is, she was . . ." Whatever he'd intended to say somehow got caught in his throat, and Caledonia took pity on his stumbling attempt to find some way to avoid speaking ill of the dead.

"It's about her we came to see you, in a way. I mean, we saw what you did with her apartment. Really special . . . at least . . . well, we liked it, and when Angela wanted her own place redone, we thought of you."

He nodded silently. And suddenly Angela knew what was so different about him. The obsequious smile that had smeared itself across his face whenever he talked to Mrs. Kinseth on that first day and when he'd talked to Clara—that false smile was gone. On the other hand, so was the glower, the terrible scowl that he'd worn during the argument. He just looked . . . more ordinary, somehow.

"We . . . I . . . Are you . . . are you interested?" Angela was very unsure of herself now.

He nodded again and sighed. "Sure. I'd really like another commission. I need one. Your Mrs. Kinseth hadn't paid me for the first job, let alone for the furniture I changed over for her . . . Talk about a 'cash flow' problem! If I don't get a commission right away, my grocery store won't let me in the door . . . not to mention the business debts I owe!"

Caledonia was surprised and didn't mind saying so. "Listen, Mr. LaChaise, that's not very good salesmanship! I mean, you're supposed to act confident and successful—that's what makes people come to do business with you. . . . Or so they say."

He smiled at last, but he didn't show his teeth—it was a crooked smile that involved his eyes and one corner of his mouth. A sad smile. "Sure. I know that. But I don't feel like putting on the act today, that's all. Just for once I'd like to be myself, even with a customer." He gave a little bow. "A potential customer."

"Mr. LaChaise," Caledonia started, but he interrupted.

"And that's another thing! That's not my name. My name is Baird. Bobby Baird, if you want to know. I invented the business name."

"Why on earth did you need an alias in your business? Whatever is wrong with 'Baird'?" Caledonia asked.

"Too Irish. Customers expect something a little dramatic—like 'LaChaise.' French company names were all the rage back East. So I figured it would go good here in California. And it did . . ."

"Who's the other LaChaise?" Angela asked. "You're LaChaise, LaChaise et Cie."

"Nobody. I'm all there is. I'm both LaChaises and I'm 'et Cie' too. It's my company, to succeed or fail—and right now, it looks as though I just may fail. And if I'm going down in flames, I'm going down with my own name and my own . . .'' He gestured at his plain jeans and sneakers. ''What do you call it? Persona? I'm going to be Bobby Baird for a change. If clients don't like it . . .'' He shrugged.

''I suppose the police have been bothering you, too?'' Angela's voice oozed sympathy.

''Not yet. And why should they? I barely knew her. And I can't really blame my financial problems on her. Though she's got a lot to do with this mess I'm in.''

''But you've been in business like this for quite some time, I gather, Mr. LaCh—Mr. Baird,'' Caledonia protested. ''You've managed to juggle things just fine up to now, apparently, and to make a reasonable living. Surely this problem with Mrs. Kinseth not paying you—surely that won't mean bankruptcy.''

He ran a hand through his hair. ''It just all caught up with me this month, is all. I had a lot of outstanding billing to clients . . . and it just happened that none of them has paid me yet. And I had shelled out a bundle for Kinseth's things . . . I also had to pay cash to the painters, to do Kinseth's apartment—and my moving crew to get her set up *twice*! I argued—I pleaded—but she wanted all new stuff and that was it!''

''Why?'' Angela asked.

''Why what?''

''Why did she want all new things? We thought the first apartment you did for her was simply beautiful.''

''It was,'' he said fiercely. ''She specified she wanted it like something in Palm Beach . . . not a mansion full of gilded antiques on Millionaires' Row, you understand, but high-class 'Florida Modern.' So I had the walls painted that shark white and the drapes and carpets in the same shade. Then, when she all of a sudden changed her mind, I was kind of limited in what I could put in there in a hurry to replace the white rattan and the pastels . . . I didn't care as much for the Swedish modern. Maybe in a loft apartment with lots of skylights—but not in that little apartment . . .''

"I didn't care for it either, frankly," Caledonia agreed.

"But what can you do against that white-white background? And be within the 'modern' feel she said she wanted?" He shook his head. "But listen, do you mean it about your apartment? I thought maybe people up at Camden would—you know—feel funny . . . like having me do their apartments was a jinx or something . . ."

"No, no," Angela assured him. "Honestly—I would *love* to have you plan the decoration. It's a little crowded, now, and inconvenient . . ." Caledonia drew a sharp breath and glared at her, but Angela went on bravely. "I want you to take a good look at everything and decide what's needed to improve it."

He had brightened up a good deal as she spoke. "I don't like to do a decorating job till I know something about my client," he said. "Would you mind very much if I called on you this afternoon? I'd like to get started right away, and the first thing is to get to know you—to talk to you and get a feel for what you like and need—and to look at what you already own and at the 'traffic patterns' of your life in your apartment, if you see what I mean. How would one o'clock be?"

"Too early," Angela said. "We just get done with lunch close to one, and then I always take a short nap . . ."

"Unless she's out getting into trouble," Caledonia said in a silky-sweet voice.

Baird ignored the comment and went on: "Well, say about two-thirty then. And now, if I could have your name and your apartment number . . ." He fairly ran to the little office space at the back, where they could see a cluttered desk. He scooped up a couple of business cards, one for each of the ladies, and he wrote Angela's name and apartment number and the time (2:30 P.M.) prominently on a desk calendar—and as he gave them each a card, he began moving with them toward the door. "I'll look forward to this afternoon,' he said, with a trace of the old LaChaise jauntiness in his manner. And he closed the door behind them.

"Angela," Caledonia hissed, pulling at her friend's sleeve as they walked away, up the little hill toward Camden-sur-

Mer. "What are you trying to do, girl? What's possessed you? We were supposed to come here to pump him and ask him about Kinseth. . . . You were just going to *pretend* to have your place decorated. What do you think you're playing at?"

"Well," Angela said, "he was so sad. I felt so sorry for that nice boy. He's got a problem—and he had such a hard time with that Kinseth woman. . . . Cal, I'm not sure, but I think it might be nice to have the apartment all done over. I think."

Caledonia threw both arms up in despair . . . and she did it again when Angela finished a blow-by-blow account for Martinez. "Did you ever hear of anything like that, Lieutenant?" she asked. "All the same, we've made a good contact, I think, and we'll find out a lot for you."

Martinez shook his head. "Well," he said, "considering it was all a big mistake to start with, maybe no damage has actually been done."

"What do you mean 'mistake'?" Angela asked.

"I mean, I did not give you the high sign—The go-ahead—to visit LaChaise's shop. At least, not on purpose. I don't mind speaking directly to you when I want something. Trust me, I do not give secret signals and talk in code. Never. I haven't got around to questioning this fellow Baird yet. But I will now, believe me—before he sees you this afternoon. In fact, he may be a little late to his appointment with you, because I'm going to waylay him in the lobby and bring him up here for an interview. Or rather, Swanson will do it for me. So don't expect Baird to call on you till at least three or so."

Caledonia rose majestically. "I'm sorry if we jumped the gun a bit, Lieutenant. I guess, if I'd used good sense, I'd have realized . . ."

Angela was completely crestfallen. "I was so sure," she said. "So sure . . ."

"Well," Martinez assured them, "it's as I told you. No harm seems to be done—at least, if you told me everything that went on in the shop this morning."

"Scout's honor," Caledonia said, lifting a hand the size of a catcher's mitt. "You know everything we know, now."

The door creaked cautiously open and Swanson's head appeared around the edge of the jamb. "Is it okay to come in?" he asked almost timidly.

Martinez was relaxed again and beckoned easily. "Come on, Shorty. I've got a job for you to do after lunch, and I better be certain we understand each other completely. These two ladies have made it urgent that we talk to the decorator fellow today, and I want you to . . . Ladies, it's nearly lunchtime. Don't you think the two of you had better go on down to the dining room?"

Caledonia nodded and moved for the door. Angela seemed disposed to stay on and join the discussion, but Caledonia's hand was slipped beneath her elbow, and Angela was propelled, over her protests and will-she or nil-she, toward the hallway, the elevator, and the dining room in immediate succession.

Chapter 5

DESPITE THEIR chagrin over mistaking an innocent word for a signal, the two women left their interview with Martinez feeling rather pleased with themselves. They had accomplished, they privately agreed, a good day's work, and here it was not quite noon! Angela found her spirits lifting, once she was out of the Lieutenant's presence, and she chattered without pause all the way down the hall and in the elevator as it brought them to the main floor. Caledonia beamed down at her and agreed with everything Angela said, a sure sign of her own sense of satisfaction.

As the elevator door slid open at lobby level, the women started out, Angela peering up at Caledonia and twittering—"Yes, it's a job well done. A job well done!"—and Caledonia nodding agreement to her tiny companion. Just as they left the elevator, Mr. Grogan, his head sunk in misery, still limping slightly two weeks after his fall on Caledonia's porch, came cutting across the lobby from their right, headed for the dining room. They were none of them looking where they were going, and Caledonia came straight out of the elevator into Grogan, with a shocked "Ooof!" to mark the moment of impact.

"Watch where you're bloody well going, can't you?" Grogan snarled, his face contorted with rage. His eyes were scarlet-rimmed and a stubble of beard lay unshaven on his cheeks and chin. But as Grogan turned, he saw who it was he was scolding, and his face changed. He looked a trifle sheepish, more gloomy than angry. "Sorry about that, ladies. Didn't mean to bite your heads off. Most of the silly old cows around here, though, never look where they step. You're—'' He stopped, searched for an appropriate word, and came up short. ''You're different, of course. All the same, next time, look before you come blundering out and knock a man half off his feet!''

He stumped off, striking his cane heavily against the marble floor of the lobby as he went. They could hear him muttering in an undertone as well, but they could pick up no words.

''Sober,'' Angela said, shaking her head. ''He's sober today.''

''What a disagreeable man!'' Caledonia marveled.

''I really think it's a hangover talking, you know?'' Angela said apologetically. ''Because he was an absolute angel that time he was in the hospital for three weeks. Remember? After he fell down the back stairs head first? He wasn't the same man at all!''

''Yes, you were certainly impressed with him at the time, I remember. Of course, none of the rest of us ever saw him like that, so I'll have to take your word for it.''

''Cal, we really ought to see what we can do for him. I can't believe he enjoys being the way he is.'' Ahead they could see the lunch crowd moving apart to let Grogan through, then closing up behind him . . . a continuous ripple of movement like prairie grass on the Great Plains, bending to the passing of Dakota's incessant westerly winds. ''Why, he scares the living daylights out of people when he's like this. He's got no friends. . . . So I was thinking, why don't we—''

''—reform him? Of course. You would. Well, to be realistic, I doubt if we can, Angela, and I'm not really sure it's such a hot idea anyhow. Nobody should try to decide how someone else would be happiest living his life.''

''Cal, trust me . . . it would be a kindness. Please. I can't do it alone. . . . But if you helped . . .''

Caledonia grinned as Grogan's voice floated across the lobby to her ears, ''Damned silly rules anyway . . . Ought to open the dining room when they're ready, not wait for twelve o'clock as though there was some gawdamn magic in the time on the clock. . . . They've got the tables set up, so what are they waiting for? Open the door!'' The last words were accompanied by the drumbeat of Grogan's cane knocking against the stout oak panel of the dining room door.

Fortunately for both the door and the cane—and for Mr. Grogan's blood pressure—the Westminster chimes sounded and the doors swung open just as he was winding up for an all-out final assault.

"Oh, all right, Angela," Caledonia grinned. "We'll try to work on the old coot . . . for all the good it will do. I'd be willing to bet we wouldn't have any luck. But promise me you won't tell any of the others about the reclamation project, okay? I'm not sure Grogan would even notice, if he was drunk! But it would embarrass him, if he was sober at the time. And it surely might embarrass us! You know you have a tendency to blurt things out without thinking—"

"Cal! I do not!"

"Well, just promise me you'll keep it all a secret, okay?"

Angela beamed. "All right—all right—I promise." It's easy to agree to small conditions, when you're getting your way about the big items in the deal.

Baird arrived at Angela's apartment at three-thirty, and he, like Grogan, was looking the worse for wear. He was very pale, his eyes appeared slightly bloodshot, and his black, curly hair was hanging lank. "I'm so sorry to be late," he greeted Angela. "I suppose you know where I've been. . . . ''

She nodded. "I mentioned to the Lieutenant that you were coming to look at my place, and he said he'd like a talk with you first . . . not to expect you on time. Are you—are you all right?"

"Oh, fine. Fine." He straightened up a bit, ran a hand over his hair, and appeared to pull himself together. "Well—what do you say we get started at once?"

Angela would have liked to ask him more about his interview, but Baird pulled out a small notebook and pencil and began to walk the circumference of the room, taking in the furnishings, the colors, the bric-a-brac, even the way the chairs faced each other. He pulled the shades and turned on the lamps, noting where light fell and which parts of the room were in shadow. He opened the shades again and noted the patterns of light from the window. Then he pulled out a tape measure and noted the room's dimensions, and the size and placement of the doors and windows and of the major pieces of furniture.

"May I?" he said, gesturing toward the tiny bedroom. He strolled around there, noting and measuring and noting some more, went into the bathroom and out again, and came back to the living room.

At last he put tape and pencil away, put the notebook into a shirt pocket, and settled into a chair next to the one in which Angela had been perched, rather nervously watching him as he worked. "Well . . . I'm a little surprised you're thinking of doing the room over again, Mrs. Benbow. You've got perfectly lovely furnishings, you've integrated them well, the colors are blended beautifully, and it looks—it looks comfortable."

Angela waved her hands helplessly. "It—I thought I needed some change. It feels—it feels a little drab, I suppose. Crowded, too."

Baird nodded. "Let's talk about furniture styles. . . ." And for another half hour or so, they chatted their way through Spanish mission, French provincial, Early American, Eastlake, Bauhaus, and Louis the whichever. . . . Angela was on firm ground, for she knew her own preferences well. She showed him with pride the eighteenth-century fruitwood armoire that was the centerpiece of her living room decor, and she basked in his praise. The talk drifted to music, to books, to art. . . .

"Oh, it's five-fifteen already!" Angela was surprised when she glanced at her watch. It hardly seemed possible the afternoon was over. "Will you join me for a small sherry?" There was a time when Angela would have served tea in fine

Limoges, with a thin sliver of lemon and no sugar. But acquaintance with Caledonia—and having no kitchen of her own—had somewhat changed her habits.

Baird looked pleased. "That would be very nice," he said.

Angela went to the armoire and brought out a small silver tray, a half-sized decanter of her personal favorite—a cream sherry—and two sherry glasses and poured her guest some. "I hope you don't mind—it's a sweet sherry. Caledonia scolds me and says it's an old lady's drink. She always serves dry sherry. But—do you mind?"

Baird smiled and shook his head. "Not at all."

For a moment they sipped in silence. Then Angela simply had to talk about the murder. Truth to tell, she'd quite forgotten the real point in the afternoon's exercise, she had been so wrapped up in watching Baird work and in playing the part of a lady who wanted her apartment redone. But now, relaxed, sipping her sherry, she at last thought of the mission she was on to gather data. But she couldn't think of any tactful way to work Mrs. Kinseth's death into the conversation.

"What do you think about our murder, Mr. Baird?" she finally blurted out.

He looked faintly surprised. "Well, it's awful, of course. Nobody should die by violence."

"I mean, about who might have done it?" Angela said impatiently. "I think we can all agree it's wrong. That goes without saying."

For a moment, Baird looked amused. "Does it? Somebody obviously disagrees with that viewpoint. And there might be some who wonder if I would disagree, after the dressing-down Mrs. Kinseth gave me in public that day."

Angela dismissed that idea with an airy wave of the hand. "Oh, I thought about that, of course, but it doesn't make sense. . . . To begin with, you had the argument out in public. Right where all of us could see you and bear witness, later. You're not a fool, Mr. Baird, but you'd have to be, to murder her right after making it so obvious you were angry with her. A clever man would take pains to let people think he was friendly with someone he'd decided to murder. That's what you'd do, if you really decided to kill someone, I think.''

Baird gave a half smile. ''Thanks for the compliment—I guess.''

''Besides,'' Angela went on, ''I'd say you worked that anger out of your system anyhow—with the exertion of changing all the furniture, you know! It's hard to get up the energy to murder someone when all you want to do is sit down and rest!''

Baird seemed a little taken aback. ''I didn't think people noticed. I try not to look as though I'm working up a sweat. That just doesn't fit the usual notion of a decorator. People expect me to flounce around and wave my hands in the air. It's like the French name I chose for the company—and for me. It sells. Over the years, I've found you get more from people if you fulfill their expectations than if you refuse to play their game.''

He smiled and got to his feet. ''Well, look—I'll get right on a plan for this place. I'll go back to my shop and start work this evening. I draw sketches, make notes to myself, draw some more. . . . There's a lot of paperwork in a redecoration plan, though you might not think so, and the sooner I start the better.''

He had no more than closed the apartment door behind him, when Angela scurried from the apartment and headed upstairs to the interview room to tell Martinez everything. She didn't suppose she had any new information, but there might be something in it, something the detective could sort out.

When she was finished, Martinez smiled. ''Okay, very good . . . I agree with your reasoning. He doesn't sound like somebody who'd just knock off a former client in a rage. And he'd be too smart to kill her after a public scene.''

''I actually hope he isn't a murderer,'' Angela confessed, ''because I kind of like him. Besides, I'd hate him to start redoing my apartment and then be thrown in jail. I mean, who would finish the job? I don't think there's another interior decorator in all of Camden!'' She meant the town, of course, for which Camden-sur-Mer had been named.

Martinez was surprised. ''You're not actually getting your apartment redone, Mrs. Benbow, are you? That was just supposed to be a pose, so you could talk to him, learn from him—and evaluate him.''

It was Angela's turn to be embarrassed. ''Well, I liked him and he needs a commission so much just now. . . . Besides, I guess the place does look a little shabby—''

''Not at all!'' Martinez sounded appalled. ''I remember it as being perfectly beautiful!''

''Well, I mean, I've lived in that apartment now for more than ten years . . . it's time . . .''

Martinez held up his hand. ''All right. You don't need to apologize to me; I believe you. I guess I was just surprised, that's all. You have so many lovely things, and to have them all thrown out so you could start over . . .'' He shook his head.

''Oh, dear—everything? Throw everything out?''

''Mrs. Benbow, how do you suppose decorators make their money? Their fees aren't really all that high, so they make it up with a commission on the furnishings you buy.''

''So he'll want to—oh, dear! What will he do with all those nice things of mine? Those things I already have?''

''Sell them for you, I expect. I'm afraid you're in for a very expensive time, if you go through with this. And your apartment is so nice now . . .''

Angela's chin went up. ''I still have the right to refuse his plan, don't I? I mean, when he comes and tells me what he wants to do, I can still say no, can't I?''

''Sure you can, Mrs. Benbow. And I suggest you think about it, too. I'm really sorry, but it just never occurred to me you'd go through with the whole thing. I thought you'd stall him . . . find out anything you could and let the matter drop there. I never dreamed you'd keep the game going this way.''

And Martinez saw her out of the sewing room, shaking his head.

Angela headed straight for the Wingate apartment, which was located in the first of the small buildings called "the cottages" that ran down either side of the garden from the main building toward the sea-cliffs. She didn't even take time to wait for the creaking old elevator but dashed down the main stairs, keeping careful hold of the railing, of course—there's no point in being foolish, even if you're in a hurry. Out of the back lobby doors into the garden she scurried, puffing slightly as she chugged away. The exercise class had not yet done much to improve her wind.

"Oh, Caledonia," she sighed as she finished her story. "Martinez says that young man will throw out my beautiful furniture and replace it all!"

"Well," Caledonia suggested unsympathetically, "it's not as though you can't afford it. You've always had plenty of money."

"It's not the money! It's—my beautiful—all my—oh *dear*!"

"Then I suggest you start practicing charming ways to say no. Because the ball will be in your court when he comes in with a scheme to turn your place into the Taj Mahal," Caledonia went on with a malicious leer. "Incense burners, gilded Buddhas, paper lanterns, and satin cushions . . ." She had muddled her Oriental decors, but Angela didn't even notice.

"Actually, Cal," she said, cocking her head to one side and gazing up slantways at her taller friend with that winsome, three-cornered smile that reminded everyone so strongly of Vivien Leigh about to say "Why, fiddle-dee-dee, Cap'n Butler . . ."

But what Angela really said was, "Actually, Cal, I was wondering if you wouldn't do it for me? You're so—assertive. And you do things like that so well."

"Oh, no you don't! You don't soft-soap me into pulling your chestnuts out of the fire, Angela Benbow. And I want to be there to watch you when you have to do this! Be sure to call me for a ringside seat when the fun starts. Now, let's go in to dinner. It's lamb shanks tonight, done in a new sauce with wine and mushrooms. . . . I hear Mrs. Schmitt has outdone herself on the green-bean-and-almond casserole, too.''

"Oh, Cal . . ." But Caledonia had started out her apartment door, headed full steam for the main building and the dining room, and Angela found herself trotting along behind, like a rowboat swept along in the wash of a giant freighter.

But halfway up the walk, they came upon Grogan. A happy smile lit his face. He was still unshaven, still red-eyed, but completely transformed from the snarling monster of midday. He was sitting on one of the little wooden benches placed at strategic intervals beside the garden walk to give an intermission to residents whose weakened legs or aching joints would not take them more than a few yards before requiring a rest. But Grogan bestrode the little bench with his skinny legs as though it were a horse, and he was crooning, "As I walked out in the streets of Laredo . . . as I walked out in Laredo one day . . . I saw a cowpuncher all dressed in white linen . . . Dressed in white linen as cold as the clay-*HAY*!'' As the women came parallel with him, he doffed an imaginary hat and smiled with unfocused pleasure at them. "Ah, good evening, ladies! A pleasant night, isn't it?'' and he threw his head back for a few more spirited bars: ''. . . to ri-*hide* after cattle till da-*hay*'s work is done . . . Oh would that I were there, in the fragrance of spri-*hing*, to hear in the moonlight the mockingbird si-*hing*!''

"Mr. Grogan,'' Angela tried to make herself heard. ''Mr. Grogan . . . will you stop singing a moment? We have something to say to you, Mr. Grogan . . . Mr. Grogan, *please* . . .''

Angela shot a glance at Caledonia, who looked startled, then shrugged and nodded. "Oh, all right, Angela,'' she said. Then she too lent her voice to the stilling of Grogan. "Yes, Mr. Grogan, please . . . just one moment . . .''

Grogan looked at them sideways, a mischievous smile on his face. "Why, certainly ladies. If you'll just wait while I let my horse cool down—I've been riding quite a—''

"Mr. Grogan!" Caledonia reached out, put a massive hand on his shoulder, and swung him around. He had already started to lift one leg up to throw it over the bench and resume a normal sitting position, but with Caledonia's pressure on his shoulder, Grogan—a slender man—fairly spun around to face forward.

"Mr. Grogan," Caledonia said coldly, "have you enough wits to pay attention? Or do you want to sober up before you listen?"

He sagged forward and might have slid off the bench if Caledonia had not kept his shirt clutched in her hand. He hung from that one shoulder, as though he were a marionette with all strings cut but one, and peered upward at her. "Dear me, you're quite serious, aren't you, good lady?"

"Quite," Caledonia said. "We have been talking about you . . ."

"We?"

"Us. Me and she! *Her!* Caledonia and me, that's who's 'we,' " Angela said, dancing around Caledonia's shoulder so that she came again into Grogan's uncertain line of vision. "And we have decided it's time you took stock of yourself. And of your life—or of what's left of it."

Grogan shook his head and immediately seemed to regret it, for he cupped a hand against his temple, as though to hold loose brains from spilling out, and groaned. "Oooogg . . . Me head . . . Ma'am, have pity. I'm in no condition . . ."

"That's just the point," Angela interjected. "You're not in condition, now or ever, to listen, or to anything! And you're such a nice person, Mr. Grogan. Hardly anybody here has ever seen you the way I have . . . when you were in the hospital . . ."

Grogan beamed blearily at her. "Hospital . . . Did I come to visit you there, my poor dear lady?"

"No!" Angela stamped her foot in exasperation. "I came to visit you! Oh, Cal, this is hopeless when he's—like this."

Caledonia shook her head. "True. But this is still going to give us our best shot at him . . . if you're still keen. What do you say, Angela? Shall we try your little scheme?"

"Right now? With him like that? But—but—dinner—"

"Dinner can wait, if you're really serious about this," Caledonia said. And when she said that, Angela knew Caledonia had decided firmly to support her in the Grogan project, for nothing short of the sudden departure seaward of all land west of the San Andreas Fault would normally have come between Caledonia and lamb shanks.

Angela sighed. "Very well. I'm game if you are. But I don't know what we should do. I thought we could talk to him, you know—reason with him. Like this, he's—oh, I don't know—"

"Well, I do," Caledonia said stoutly. "Angela, can you take his other arm? I can almost manage him by myself, but it's the steering that's difficult. When Herman—you know, the Admiral?—when Herman used to tie one on with the boys—not that it happened often, but once in a while—he could stay on his feet all evening."

She panted with exertion as they hoisted the limp and unprotesting Grogan to his feet. "He'd never show in public how much he'd absorbed, and he'd make it home, just inside the door, where nobody could see him. Then he'd collapse. Well, that was when I took over. And I'll take charge now—but it'll be easier if you'll help me. I'm not forty anymore—or even fifty for that matter."

"Or sixty, if you'll pardon my saying so," Grogan interjected cheerfully.

"Just relax, Mr. Grogan. You're in good hands," Caledonia said, pulling one of his arms across her shoulders. "Angela, you slip in on the other side and sort of guide him . . . I'll manage most of his weight, but you kind of push or pull so we miss the shrubbery."

And they started out, tacking left, then right, in great parabolic arcs along the walkway, to reach Grogan's cottage door. His was the second building on the right, second door from the near end—and Grogan appeared to enjoy the erratic trip, despite the wear and tear it put on the toes of his shoes to have his feet dragging behind him on the concrete, as he rested all of his weight on their shoulders.

"A Spa-*hanish* cavalier stood in his retreat, and on his guitar played a tu-*hune*, de-*hear* . . ." He had begun another song. "The music so swee-*heet*, did something repeat, the something of my country and you-*hooooo*, de-*hear* . . ."

They reached the shelter of his front porch without having run into another resident, literally or figuratively. Perhaps the others were already inside the lobby, waiting for the dinner chimes to sound and the doors to swing open, welcoming them to lamb shanks.

"Here, Angela, get his keys out of his pocket."

"Door's not locked, dear lady," Grogan smirked.

Caledonia shoved the door open, elbowed through first, dragged Grogan in behind her, and half-released, half-pushed his arm away from her neck. His remaining arm slid limply off Angela's shoulders, and he sank toward the floor like a deflated gas balloon . . . and with a sigh that sounded as though he indeed had sustained a puncture.

"Oh Cal . . ." Angela wailed, "I never bargained for anything like this!"

"Shut your noise and the door in that order. And let's get busy." Herman Wingate must have smiled down from the bar of heaven at the excellent imitation his widow was giving of the Admiral himself, at his most imperious. "Hop to it, girl . . . we don't want this to take all night."

"Well, what . . . what do we do?"

"First, we undress him. What did you say?" Angela had given a nervous squeak, and Caledonia glared her to silence. "Honestly, Angela, you act as though you'd never seen a man without his clothes! Leave his skivvies on, of course. I wouldn't want you shocked into an early heart attack! We'll get him under a shower, undies and all. Cold, then hot, then cold . . ."

And the ladies, puffing and red-faced with exertion, went to work.

Two hours, three showers, a lot of walking back and forth, and generous portions of fruit juice, coffee, aspirin, vitamin tablets, and soda crackers (the only food that Grogan seemed to stock plenty of in his cupboards) went into turning Grogan into at least the shadow of a human being. But at last a reasonably aware and relatively coherent Grogan emerged from the travail.

His hair soaking and plastered against his scalp, rivulets running down his face and neck, Grogan huddled in a chair clutching his umpteenth cup of coffee, wrapped from his scrawny neck to his bare toes in a blanket to guard his shivering body against California's evening chill, which was invading the apartment through the open windows. ("Must we, Cal? If someone should hear—" . . . "Just open the windows, Angela; the air will be good for him, and lord knows we could stand a little fresh air!")

"Ladies," he was saying sadly, gazing at them with woeful spaniel eyes, "you should have left me lying wherever you found me. You should have let me die in some seawater cave, covered in algae and slime . . . drowned in a tidal pool . . . chilled by the rocks . . . nibbled by the little sea creatures. . . ."

"Oh, shut up!" Caledonia was in no mood for Celtic fantasy. She'd had about all of Grogan she could take for one evening. Her splendid brocade caftan was a sodden ruin, soaked with equal parts of water and spilled coffee, speckled with orange juice and cracker crumbs.

Angela's hair had come adrift from her neat chignon. It was the first time Caledonia could remember seeing the Benbow coiffure less than perfect, and Angela's little face was pink and puckered with a mixture of fatigue and annoyance. "Yes, shut up!" she chimed in. "Just listen, for a change." Crossly, she wrung water from the sleeve of the cashmere sweater that had looked so smart through the afternoon hours.

"We've heard your entire repertoire," Caledonia scolded. "You've yodeled your way through Sigmund Romberg and Jerome Kern and Cole Porter and Tom Lehrer . . . You've done Appalachian ballads and German lieder . . . And it's time you kept that Irish mouth firmly closed and used your ears for a little while. Why do you think we've been doing all this?"

"I—I don't know, really. And it did occur to me, once,

about an hour ago, to ask you why,'' Grogan said rather humbly. Then he ruined the effect by adding, ''But you had me head under a cold shower, and when I opened me mouth, the water ran in. A shocking experience for a man of my tastes . . . so I simply closed the porthole and suffered in silence.''

''We're trying to save your miserable life, Grogan,'' Caledonia said.

Angela nodded. ''You're killing yourself slowly.''

''Not so damned slowly, either,''. Caledonia growled.

Angela nodded. ''So we decided, because you're much too nice to waste yourself this way—''

''Well, I don't know about that,'' Caledonia said. ''But the point is, you have to be reasonably sober to talk about it at all. So we sobered you up.''

''It's high time to look to the future and do something for yourself,'' Angela said, ''and we want to help.''

Grogan sighed pathetically. ''Oh, ladies, I feel bad. I am shivering with the cold, sick to my stomach, and none too steady on my feet. . . . I really think I could do with a drink!''

''Absolutely not,'' Caledonia said firmly. ''That was the whole point of this evening's exertions! You've had enough for any two men your size—and any four men your age. It's time to dry out for a while. Now, we're going to put you in your bed, and then we're going to talk to you about all this tomorrow.''

He tried to stand and swayed dizzily. ''Oooo—that wasn't too good. My head feels a little light . . .''

Caledonia nodded. ''I tell you, you should go to bed and get a good night's sleep, and start out tomorrow morning with a walk and a big breakfast.''

Grogan nodded cautiously. ''If I can,'' he said doubtfully. He reached up and touched his temples and seemed pleased that the top of his head did not come off into his hands. ''Well, then, I'll go to bed . . .'' His knees buckled under him.

''Uh-huh,'' Caledonia said. ''Okay, Angela . . . once more . . .'' and she grasped Grogan as he was heading, slack-kneed, toward the floor. "Get the other side, there . . . and let's lift together. One, two, three . . . upsy-daisy . . ."

Together they maneuvered Grogan into the other room and eased him down, unprotesting, onto his bed. He whimpered "Oh, my head," once, and then seemed beyond further sound or motion.

"Oh, Mr. Grogan, I'm so pleased with you," Angela bubbled joyfully, tucking him carefully under a blanket, her damp cardigan forgotten. "I just know you're going to make it and be a happier person for the effort. . . . "

"Come on," Caledonia growled, moving toward the door and pushing Angela along with her. "He's already sound asleep—didn't hear a word you were saying."

As they headed back up the garden toward Caledonia's apartment, Angela was smiling, very pleased with herself and with Caledonia and with Grogan and with life in general. For a moment, she quite forgot murder and redecoration and everything else in the warm glow of having helped a fellow human being.

"Thank you for everything you did, Cal," she breathed. "I just know we've made a start at a new life for that poor, poor man."

Caledonia merely answered, "Umph."

"Aren't you delighted with the way the evening turned out?" Angela asked.

Caledonia said, "Good lord, Angela. Do you think we've accomplished anything?"

"Why, certainly," Angela said. "He's sober, and recovering . . . he seemed genuinely touched . . . I'm sure that tomorrow he'll see . . ."

In spite of her own fatigue, Caledonia grinned and shook her head. "You are one of the most naive women . . . Sometimes, you can be as simple as Mary Moffet! All we did was get him to go to bed. He's not really sober yet—and he hasn't promised us one single thing, except he did say he'd try to get up and eat breakfast tomorrow. We still have our whole job ahead of us, if we're going to get him to straighten up and swear off the booze."

"Oh, you'll see," Angela said smugly. "You'll see, Cal. He'll be a changed man. Well, I think I'll turn in myself now," she yawned. "And you'd better, too. You look," she said with a touch of her usual acid candor, "like a pile of wet laundry."

Caledonia didn't dignify the remark with a reply. She was bone-weary, and the idea of bed sounded like the most intelligent thought that had been expressed all evening. It was a mark of her extreme fatigue, in fact, that she never once remembered, till she woke up ravenous the next morning, that she had not eaten a bite of supper!

Chapter 6

At breakfast the next morning, Angela was a bit apprehensive that she might run into a rejuvenated Grogan—sober, healthy, full of life, and anxious to talk about his future. She didn't quite feel up to it without Caledonia's support.

But Grogan did not show up. Neither, of course, did Caledonia. Grogan was sleeping off an incredibly painful, record-breaking hangover, and Caledonia never came to breakfast if she could possibly avoid it. So Angela dined alone in the relative peace of her own thoughts.

After eating lightly—a nibble of toast and jam and a few sips of coffee—Angela felt restless. Instead of heading for her room and the rest of the "Today Show," she turned her steps toward the outdoors. First she did a circuit of the whole block on which the main building stood. It was a walk long enough that, on an ordinary day, she would have felt tired by her exertions. But today she still felt what she called "needley"—unsatisfied, on the gad, poised for an unknown action. So she walked around in the gardens for a while, up and down between the rows of cottages.

The walking, unaccustomed exertion though it was, did not have the desired effects. The mental prickling still went on—the sense of ideas nagging to be realized, of problems swirling, unresolved, of memories pushing and shoving to be released from their crowded storage places in the brain. . . .

At last she crossed Beach Lane, the little city street that cut between the bottom of the hotel grounds and the edge of the sea-cliff. The company managing Camden-sur-Mer had sold off most of its incredibly valuable beachfront property early in the process of building the retirement community— as a way to finance the renovations the old building had required and to build the rows of cottage-apartments that extended toward the sea from either arm of the U-shaped main building. Cheap rental bungalows and ugly but expensive motels had crowded in on the shore, leaving only a small stretch of open cliff-top, exactly as wide as the hotel gardens and directly opposite them, through which the residents still had an uninterrupted view of the beach.

It was a gray morning; the sea-mists had not yet burned off in the June sunshine, and Angela's face and hands felt damp. The dolphins that fed in the kelp beds just offshore had not yet arrived; perhaps they, like Caledonia, had chosen to sleep in today. Even the pelican population, plentiful though still recovering from the depredations of DDT, had gone to hunt for food somewhere else this morning. And the little fishing and excursion boats that usually dotted the water, having come up from San Diego and down from Oceanside, were missing; advised by radio that fishing was off around the area, they had anchored at some other spot. There was nothing to look at but gray water, gray sky, a rockstrewn strip of sand, swollen green ice plant clinging to the hillside to keep at least one small part of California from departing toward Hawaii, and a few beer cans flung toward the beach by weekend surfers in passing cars.

The lack of excitement didn't bother Angela; she was occupied with thoughts, rather than with sights. She was reviewing what she knew about Amy Kinseth—which was very little—and what she knew about the residents and staff whose lives had touched those of the dead woman—which was a great deal.

"I wonder," she muttered aloud to herself, "I wonder if it's something from her past . . . We don't know much about her before she got here. Of course, we know entirely too much about the way she carried on after."

She stopped and looked guiltily around her, but there was

nobody nearby who could have heard her soliloquy—or close enough who could have seen that her lips moved. "I must pull myself together," she scolded herself—this time silently. "Talking to myself . . . Only those silly old people whose brains are falling out do that!"

So as Angela started back from the sea-cliff, across Beach Lane toward Camden's peaceful gardens, she strode along with her head down, apparently examining the sidewalk with great care but actually making a determined effort not to move her mouth as she discussed matters with herself.

As her steps brought her opposite the ends of the U that was the main building, her eyes were attracted to an open basement door in the north wing. (It was not, strictly speaking, a basement, for it was only partially below ground. At the entrance, the area was at surface level; but the ground sloped upward toward the front of the old building, and by the time one got into the basement as far as the furnace room, one was completely underground.)

Under the south wing of the building there had been a spa—a whirlpool bath, massage tables, and the remains of what had been a fairly extensive but very small exercise room when the hotel was a luxury hotel catering to the wealthy. But old people's knees will not accommodate exercise bicycles, their muscles are not up to weight-lifting, and they seldom swing from rings or balance on parallel bars. The whirlpool baths had been maintained, but other than that, the south wing lay empty.

Across the gardens under the north wing, there had been a nursery and playroom for keeping children of the old hotel's guests occupied and out of mischief while their parents vacationed. Now that space housed only a furnace room, janitors' closets, a workroom, and supply and luggage storage, including a warehouse area of "dead storage" for residents' furnishings—things that they were reluctant to part with but that would not fit in their tiny new apartments, such as Christmas decorations, out-of-season clothing, luggage, old tax forms, and gilt-framed paintings of long-dead relatives.

Spaces in the storage area were marked with chain-link fencing fitted into stout metal frames; each frame had a nameplate affixed to it so you could tell which space was which without difficulty, and each frame contained a steel-mesh door with a giant padlock. It was unlikely that anyone would want to steal what the storage areas contained, but age does odd things to the mind, and petty pilfering was not unheard-of in Camden. So as a rule, residents closed and locked their apartment doors, lest one of the more absent-minded residents wander in to watch TV or to pick up an ornament or a sweater they caught sight of through an open door—some item that in their confusion they assumed was theirs.

Angela had come back after supper during her first week of residence to find Claude Pearson, a spindly little man with pebble-thick glasses, two hearing aids, and a walker, using her bathroom. He had meant to stop off, on his way down the hall to his own rooms, at the men's room—maintained for staff and visitors off the same hallway and clearly marked to the right of the lobby. Pearson, gradually failing in body and wits alike, had trouble remembering left from right, and he turned left instead, walking into Angela's unlocked suite.

Asked about it afterwards, he remarked that it had seemed strange that they would put such a fancy outer lounge in the men's room—and a bedroom as well! But then, as he told the nurse who came to lead him away, people decorated bathrooms oddly these days—why, he remembered when the only decorations were the fancy-cut window shaped like a crescent moon and the Sears catalogue hanging from a nail beside the seat!

Angela had been forgiving about the lapse, but she had learned to lock her doors. And so did all the residents and the staff. Thus a padlock hung from each storage-compartment door, for which each resident owned his or her own key—with the only duplicate kept by the main office.

It was the door to the north wing that now stood ajar. Angela almost paid no attention to it and kept walking toward the main building. It was early, and she simply assumed some staff member had left the door open purposely. But a thought struck her; she wondered if Amy Kinseth had stored anything of interest in that marked storage area.

It didn't take Angela but a moment to decide to investigate. It never occurred to her for a second to ask anyone's permission. While she and her Admiral had lived in Washington, Angela had walked into the offices of senators and lobbyists alike, unannounced (and often unwelcome). She had gone into the workrooms of haute couturiers and behind the scenes at theaters with never a thought that she might not be wanted. So it never crossed her mind that she should check with the office before she entered the usually locked north basement, or before she tried to investigate Amy Kinseth's belongings.

Once inside the basement, she hesitated for the first time. It was unpleasantly chilly and slightly damp-feeling. The scent was familiar—"Old, wet laundry!" she thought. "Laundry that got washed and couldn't be hung out to dry because it rained for a week." (Angela's only personal experience with wet laundry dated back to her youth—before her affluent life with Douglas Benbow, and before the days of automatic dryers.)

It was also very dark. Her eyes became accustomed to the dim light quickly, but because the only windows were at the head of the passageway, on either side of the door—or were shut away from the hallway she stood in—it was still hard to pick out details. Angela could not recall ever having been in this part of the building; she had left the storage of her own odds and ends to the handymen.

She moved slowly down the dank, blank hallway, opening every door as she went, looking for the storage compartments she'd heard described. First, to the right, she found a carpentry workroom; Angela knew there would be one somewhere, when she thought about it, because residents of the north wing complained constantly about the disruption to the TV reception caused by power tools. On the left she found a room apparently belonging to the janitorial staff.

Mops and buckets and sponges and rubber gloves were stacked on the shelves and hung along one wall.

Neither room seemed to Angela to hold any chance of being remotely interesting. So she moved along. The hallway became gloomier as she moved farther into the building and away from the outside door and the little windows. The dank smell increased as well.

It was the storeroom that Angela came to next. There was a partition that closed off the end of the hallway, and it gave slightly as Angela pushed against it—"Wallboard, plywood, and poly-foam," she said scornfully, "not like they *used* to make walls and doors!" The wall was no deterrent to a determined person with strength, nor was it intended to be: it merely furnished a screen from prying eyes and a barrier to casual curiosity.

The door was not locked, though there was a hasp fastened to it and to its frame, with a padlock hanging from the hasp. It was odd, as she commented to Caledonia long afterward, that it did not occur to her that the padlock was normally kept shut, and that it must be open for a reason.

She pulled the door open wide and stepped inside, but even opened at its widest, the door admitted very little light. Angela wrapped her arms around herself to stop the involuntary shiver that shook her.

"There must be a light somewhere," she said aloud. "Where are you, light switch?" She ran one hand over the wall to the right, the logical place for a switch. "Nothing. Well, maybe behind the door . . ." And she stepped further inside, holding the door's edge as though for security, and then stepping around it and groping along the wall behind it. "Nothing. Mmmmm . . . Oh! Of course!" She remembered the basement in her uncle's home—and the overhead light, a naked bulb hanging at the end of its cord, just over head-height, with a little pull-chain. She put both hands over her head and moved her arms back and forth . . . back and forth . . . "Ah-*HA*!" Her fingertips touched the bulb and pull-chain, and she yanked gratefully.

Torgeson's economies had extended even to the storage

rooms. The bulb was only a forty-watter and shed barely
enough light to let one see one's way. But at least Angela
could make out the nameplates on the storage-compartment
doors nearest the exit, though as she got farther into the
storeroom, she had to peer closer and closer to make out the
letters. Fortunately, Amy Kinseth's storage compartment was
only halfway along the room, just at a point where Angela
might have had to give up the search for want of a flashlight.

"Next time," she growled, "you bring a flashlight before
you start out hunting for a name in a dark room, you id-
iot. . . . Oh, Caledonia will be so . . . Why, it's unlocked!"

The padlock to Amy Kinseth's compartment, like the padlock on the storeroom door, hung free, dangling from the
wire mesh of the door.

"That is so careless!" Angela said in a cross little
voice. "I hope mine isn't open like this. I really must
speak to Torgeson about all this. . . . Open doors, open
padlocks . . ." and she pulled the door wide and stepped
into the enclosure.

Then everything seemed to happen at once, and she could
only register the next events in sensations of sound and scent
and feel. First there was a rushing noise—kind of a whoosh—
that she felt as much as heard. Air moved, dust stirred, and
something or somebody dashed at her out of a dark corner
of the compartment from behind some boxes. She had no
chance to see who it was, for a big cloth was thrown over
her head—a slipcover or an old bedspread, she couldn't tell—
something big and made of heavy material like upholstery.
It smelled like old garden soil after a rain.

Angela staggered under the attack, and her first thought
was to get free of the heavy folds of fabric that encumbered
her arms and legs, weighed on her head and shoulders, and
felt as though they might stifle her. As she thrashed about in
the smothering embrace of the cloth, she heard metallic
sounds, footsteps, and the slam of a door . . . and then suddenly she was free of the cloth, which dropped to the floor.

Her attacker had left the little light on, and after she worked
free from the darkness of the cover over her head, she seemed

able to see details somewhat better than she had when she first entered the storeroom. "I'm locked in a wire cage!" she blurted out, outraged. "I'm in a *cage!*"

And she was right. The attacker had closed the steel-mesh door, snapped the padlock, and closed the storeroom door as well. "I suppose *that's* locked, too!" Angela raged. "Let me out!" she shouted. *"Let me out of here!!!!"* She paused. There was no answer. *"O-o-o-o-oooooOUT!"* she shouted, as loudly as she could—but her voice seemed muffled, the sound absorbed by cloth and leather packed into all the storage bins around her. Angela knew at once that her shouting was doing no good.

"Unless someone comes down here," she said hopefully. "To get something from their storage area . . ." But tears sprang into her eyes almost as soon as she said that, for she knew that the other residents came to the area about as often as she did.

She put both hands against the door and shook it in its frame. It made a tinny, rattling noise, but it was firmly locked and soundly set. She reached one little hand through the wire mesh and twisted the padlock. "Hmp! That's no use," she told herself.

Looking around, she spotted a flat-topped trunk. "Well, it isn't pretty, but at least I can sit down while I think." She tugged the trunk around till it was parallel with and right against a pile of cardboard cartons—being careful to push using the muscles in her legs and not her back, since it's no use throwing your back out if you can help it. Then she took the crumpled cloth that had so recently been dumped on her head, mounded part of it into a kind of lumpy cushion, and seated herself on the trunk-top. "Now what?" she asked. But there was nothing but silence. And it seemed so chilly . . . She pulled one edge of the upholstery fabric up around her shoulders the way Grogan had pulled the blanket around him last evening, leaned her back against the closest stack of boxes, tucked her feet up under her, and huddled down to wait. And wait, And wait . . .

Even in adversity, old people fall asleep easily. Angela had not eaten heavily, but she often nodded off after even a light meal—and before she knew it, she had dozed, curled into her makeshift blanket, with her feet comfortably pulled away from the concrete floor.

It could have been hours later that she woke. Her wristwatch said ten-thirty. "In the morning, I presume," she said aloud, though she had a sudden sinking sensation in the pit of her stomach. It might, after all, be ten-thirty at night. Hers was a conventional watch without A.M. and P.M. marked on it. "Douglas asked me once if I wanted a digital, twenty-four-hour watch," she mourned. "I said no. Dumb!"

"Douglas, I'm sorry," she muttered. "I wish I'd listened to you." Then, because she had no alternative, she simply made the assumption that it was still morning, partly because she seldom napped more than a few minutes during the day, and she thought she would have felt differently, somehow, if she'd slept twelve hours or more.

She sighed. She didn't feel better that it was still morning. That only meant that it would be a longer time before she was missed. "They'll come looking for me," she said in a confident little voice. "Yes. They'll see I'm missing at lunch, and Caledonia will want to know where I am. But they won't have a checkout note for me at the desk, so they'll know something's wrong and . . ."

She paused and remembered the number of times she had violated the strict rule about notifying the front desk if you were going to miss a meal. "For anybody who's especially feeble or who's sick," she had always told Caledonia, "the rule makes sense. But not for me!" Now she groaned at her own improvidence.

"When I don't come to lunch, they'll just assume I'm out shopping at the mall, like I was last week, or taking lunch downtown at a restaurant, or something! Oh, dear. . . . " She sighed, then she cheered up a little. "Well, anyhow, at supper they'll realize something's wrong and start to hunt for me."

That, at any rate, was true. No resident could go missing indefinitely without someone on the staff going to the apartment to check. And when they found that her purse was right there, sitting on her little table across from the TV in the living room—sitting athwart the remote control, as she recalled—they'd realize she didn't just go shopping! She sighed again, more with relief than with anxiety this time. Yes, she might have to wait, but probably only till suppertime or a little after. Caledonia would make it hot for the office till they located her. . . .

And as long as she was right there in the storage compartment with all Mrs. Kinseth's things . . . "Well, why not?" Angela said aloud, a bit more cheerfully. "That's what I came here to do, after all. To see if I could find anything." And she pushed the slipcover-bedspread off onto the floor and set to work on the trunk she had used as a settee.

Chapter 7

THREE HOURS later, a dusty, cross, tired, and very hungry Angela Benbow was sitting in the midst of a circle of odds and ends taken out of boxes and trunks, none of which seemed to say "This is something that might cause a murder," or "I am a *clue*!" but all of which looked—at least to Angela's eyes—like possibilities to be investigated further.

There was, for instance, a stack of old letters. Angela had not bothered to read them yet, and with the light so dim she might have had trouble making the words out anyway. She had simply put them aside—one never knew what indiscretions the writers might have let slip.

There were two files of canceled checks and several bank passbooks, an envelope holding old tax returns, and a cardboard file-box full of what looked like receipts and business letters. Angela was quite capable of simple accounting herself, but she always denied it. "Anything with numbers on it makes my head ache," was the way she used to say it whenever, for example, she had been asked to serve as treasurer of some women's club or charitable organization.

Now, faced with a mountain of business and money-related facts to sort through, she pushed them aside more through habit than anything else. Besides, she told herself righteously, Lieutenant Martinez would enlist someone—a professional accountant, for instance—who would be able to tell much more quickly and reliably if there was anything suspicious in the mound of miscellaneous papers.

After the cache of papers and a few snapshots, Angela

found lean pickings through several boxes. These contained items best suited to the table at a garage sale that's marked "Any Item Here 50¢." Angela found a matched set of kitchen implements with clear plastic handles—into which were embedded what looked like real fresh vegetables. There were at least a dozen calendars and unused address books, some with brightly colored illustrations—of the presidents of the United States at their inaugurations, of lurid sunsets being gazed at reverentially by groups of horseback riders, of monkeys dressed as businessmen with smart sayings in the speech balloons over their heads. There were three boxes of matched toilet water and dusting powder sets—odd items in a climate as dry as that of Southern California.

In fact, much of the contents of the last box she judged to have been gifts, the type laid out in department stores at Christmas and Valentine's Day for impulse buyers to give to nobody in particular—more elaborate than a card, less troublesome than a personal visit. These gifts are, of course, not only impractical and unwanted; they are also too good to merely throw away, and they are kept with the idea that "well, maybe I'll give that as a gift myself someday." One almost never does, of course.

"I wish she'd lived long enough for us to ask her for a contribution to the White Elephant Sale at the bazaar," Angela thought—and then was a bit ashamed of herself.

The next box into which Angela looked held an assortment of items that could only be discards from the cleaning-out of old purses—nearly-used-up lipsticks, stray bobby pins, a half bottle of aspirin, a nail file, two pencils without points, a plastic fork, a couple of dog-eared shopping lists, a folding scissors with one broken tip—the kinds of things women always carry, and when they change purses, do not want to transfer. But they generally also hate to throw these things away—"You never know," runs the argument of the natural-born jackdaw, "when you might want just this size of rubber band, a spare paper clip, a container of artificial sweetener tablets . . ."

Nothing seemed of consequence, and it was all replaced.

And that was the last unopened box. Angela's "Let's Keep This" pile now contained all the old letters, the financial materials, and a few snapshots, including one of Mrs. Kinseth's late husband, Gordon, rabbit-teeth protruding through a happy grin as he accepted the "Insurance Man of the District for 1962" award, a couple of pocket notebooks with pages of scribbled entries, a filled-up address book, and two fully used pocket appointment calendars from recent years.

When Angela replaced the lid on that last cardboard carton, her back was screaming for relief. She had bent and lifted and shoved and tugged, then she had sat on the floor to avoid bending over any longer and found the leaning and stretching in that position to be eventually more painful than bending over had been.

"If this is detective work, I just wasn't built to be a detective," she groaned, as more carefully and slowly than when she was starting her search, she maneuvered the last box into line on one side of the enclosure. The final things to be examined were the suitcases—that magnificent set of matched leather luggage she remembered from the time, six short weeks before, when Amy had moved in. She pulled a handsome Pullman case forward, snapped up the latch, and was delighted that it opened easily. As she lifted the cover, however, she was surprised to see that the fine taffeta lining had been ripped free from the inner surface. "Good heavens," she gasped, "but the woman was hard on her things!" But the next case—a larger version of the Pullman—was in the same condition. So was the makeup case—so was the attaché case. And in the two largest suitcases—wardrobes to hold several dresses and suits on built-in folding hangers—the linings had been slit by something sharp, rather than merely pulled loose.

"Why, I do believe someone did that on purpose!" Angela said. "Someone looking for something? That's all it could be . . . but what? A paper? A picture?" There was really no telling. Anything flattish, without much depth, could have been laid between the case and its lining, perhaps with a sheet of cardboard over it, and the lining glued back in place. "It could be almost anything! Weapons . . . uncut diamonds . . . cocaine . . . or secret papers! Maybe she was a spy," Angela said, her assumptions leaping, as they customarily did, well ahead of her proof and her logic. "That's what that man was doing here . . . the one who nearly knocked me over and tried to smother me in that . . . that . . ." she kicked at her onetime blanket with a foot. "That piece of *cloth*!" she finished, with an emphasis that suggested that wrapping the Benbow body in less than gold foil was a desecration. "I've got to tell the Lieutenant! I've got to get out of here! *Help!!! HE-E-e-e-ELP!!!!*"

The yelling appeared to be as useless as it had been when she first tried it. She went over to the steel-mesh gate and shook it so that it clattered noisily against the uprights. "Let me *out*!" she raged, kicking futilely against the door.

A glance at her wristwatch showed her that it was nearly three in the afternoon. "It'll be at least three more hours till they realize something's wrong and come looking," she told herself aloud. Talking aloud was more soothing than yelling had been, and the sound of her own voice made it seem less lonely and dark. She began to feel a little better, and she busied herself for another couple of minutes making neat stacks of her findings so they would be easy to pick up and carry along to show to the Lieutenant after she was rescued.

Then, with a sigh, she sat down on the little trunk again and reluctantly pulled up her erstwhile blanket, which seemed to smell even more damp and musty than it had before. With another, deeper sigh, she wrapped it around her and leaned back against the boxes stacked behind her. Her impromptu easy chair wasn't really at all comfortable, but she felt warmer and cozier, all curled up and covered from the basement air. And in a moment, despite the hunger pains that she felt—stomach contractions that made her remark, "It's so uncomfortable being hungry! I won't be able to rest properly" —she fell asleep once more.

Sometime later she woke. She remembered to check her watch: it was four-fifteen. During her nap, her head had been tipped backward against the stack of boxes at a most uncomfortable angle, and she rolled it back and forth as she rubbed the aching muscles of her neck. "Oooh, I don't know if I'll ever be able to look straight ahead again! Gosh, why didn't I try to lie on the floor!" she was saying, rubbing her shoulders and neck with both hands . . . when suddenly, she saw her means of escape!

The steel-mesh partitions had been built using standard steel frames measuring eight feet by four feet, so that they might hold uncut sheets of plywood, foam insulation, wallboard, or what-have-you. Each preconstructed frame had been bolted into the concrete floor across its bottom brace, and the next frame bolted to the first, till a three-sided pen was completed, its last vertical brace bolted as well to the concrete block wall of the basement, which formed the fourth side of the compartment.

Across the top of each enclosure, steel braces had been welded from corner to corner to help steady the structure. Then the steel-mesh "walls" had been affixed to the metal framing, already standing rigidly in place. Lastly, the door panel had been set in, closing a gap left for that purpose in the center front of the fencing. But unlike the panels making up the walls, the door panels were not eight feet tall. The door panels were just about six and a half feet tall. So Angela was gazing with delight at a space above the top of her confining door—a space perhaps three feet wide by about one and a half feet high—a space in which there was no steel mesh at all, no barrier between her and freedom. "Except," she said, standing up, "I don't have a ladder!"

"On the other hand," she said, brightening, "I have my bed here . . . my sofa . . . Amy's trunk . . ." and she tugged and pushed and with great difficulty slid the trunk across the floor so that it was tight against the door. By climbing carefully up on the trunk, Angela found that—short as she was—she could reach the space over the door with both hands and forearms, and she thought, "*Bingo!* I'm as good as out. Caledonia will laugh at me for not seeing it sooner." Then she stopped. "But what do I do to get down on the other side?"

For an athletic young person, the drop would have been of

small consequence—less than a foot and a half, when one was finally hanging with both hands from the crossbar that formed the top of the door frame. For a woman in her seventies, with small strength and brittle bones, the drop might mean a turned ankle or even a broken leg. The climb would be difficult and would require all her stamina—but when it came to hanging full-length down the outer side of the door and letting go . . . Her heart thumped unpleasantly, and her throat felt tight and full. "But I'm going to try, anyhow," she said aloud with a forced cheerfulness she did not feel.

Balancing carefully on the trunk, she gradually took her weight onto her arms and began to pull herself upward, at the same time wedging her toes into the steel-mesh diamonds that made up the fence, so she could help lift her weight using her legs as well. "I wish I'd gone on that diet last year," she panted . . . and then let herself back down onto the trunk-top.

"If I'm going to be an acrobat, I might as well have a gym mat," she said more cheerfully, and gathered up the wads of musty upholstery under which she'd been sleeping. The material was very heavy, and it was more of a struggle to lift it overhead than she'd anticipated, but she managed to hoist a healthy corner of it up over her head and push it through the opening. Then, with the greater part of its weight off her, she was able to feed the rest over, letting it slither down on the other side and fall in a heap in front of the door. "Maybe that'll be enough to cushion me, if I let go too soon and fall," she said hopefully. "Okay . . . here goes."

Straining and pulling and clawing and scrambling, Angela worked her way slowly up the mesh door to balance aloft with her waistline athwart the thin steel beam, which cut uncomfortably into the soft tissue. "I bet I'll have a bruise you wouldn't believe," she groaned, and she continued to ease her way through.

Of course, she had to go through the gap headfirst to begin with, and for a moment she was frightened. If she fell that way, headfirst onto the concrete, she might never live long enough to explain to anyone why she'd been climbing around

in the storeroom. But she eased and squirmed and wriggled
. . . first one leg doubled beneath her, then eased onto the
other side, then her torso and head swung back the way she'd
come and the other leg doubled under and eased through—
"Oh, gosh, that hurt more than the time I learned to do the
splits when I was seven," she gasped in genuine pain at the
unaccustomed stretching and bending—and then she had both
legs outside, her head and shoulders inside, and she began
wriggling downward, as slowly as she could manage, her
feet braced against and seeking purchase on the metal mesh,
her arms taking more and more of the strain as she got closer
to the floor.

At last the moment could be delayed no longer, and she
released her hold. Actually, it's doubtful if her aching arms
and hands would have sustained her weight for one more
moment, despite her being able to brace her feet against the
door. She fell heavily, her legs collapsing under her weight,
the greatest share of the shock being taken by her hip and
thigh, and she let out a huge sob—half with the jolt and the
way it hurt, half with relief. She was out!

She picked herself up off the heap of musty fabric. She
seemed able to function, and both legs seemed to work all
right. She limped off as rapidly as she could toward the door.
One knee had been wrenched, her shin seemed numb, and
the hip where she'd landed was throbbing, but she was free.

No, she wasn't! The storeroom door did not open to her
touch. It appeared to be locked—and this time, there was no
open space overhead.

She banged against the door and called, "Yoo-hoo . . . is
anybody there? Is there somebody out there in the basement?
Hello! *Hello! Help!!!!*" But there was no sound from outside.
Either there was nobody in the area, or her voice was not
carrying through the partition. She tried a few more kicks
against the door, a few more rattles of the knob. The flimsy
door gave slightly in its frame, and the ill-constructed wall
seemed to waver under her assault—but both stood, faithful
to their designated task of keeping people out—and now, of
course, keeping Angela in.

More slowly than she had come, she limped back to the heap of cloth and sat down on it. It shielded her from the damp of the floor, but she hurt in several places, and tears started to leak down her face. "I can't wait till they come for me. I *can't*!" And then "I can't" changed to "I won't," and Angela gritted her teeth and tightened her face, pursing her lips into a tiny circle—the stubborn look that Douglas Benbow had learned to dread and to call her "mule look."

"There *has* to be a way out of here," she said, and with some difficulty, she got to her feet and returned to the door, her limp more pronounced as her aching muscles began to assert themselves, to demand attention. This time, she examined the entire wall in which the partition stood, from one concrete-block outer wall to the other. Nothing. "Oh, why didn't I think to bring a flashlight," she sighed. And with some reluctance, but with an air of defiance, she set out, back down the line of steel-mesh cages, beyond the point where she had spent so many hours, toward the other end of the long room.

It was so dark at the far end that she could barely make out another temporary partition wall and a door. "Of course," she said aloud. "Of course! The furnace room. It has to be here somewhere." To her pleasure, the knob turned and the door opened easily. She raised her hands above her head, groping till she found another hanging bulb and pull-chain to switch on the light.

The furnace room was much smaller than the storeroom, so the forty-watt bulb cast some dim light even into the farthest corners. Its floor was a continuation of the concrete slab that floored the storeroom, its walls more of the concrete block. But the permanent walls formed three sides here, rather than just two—for the furnace room was at the end of the excavation beneath the north wing. In the center of the room stood the old gas furnace, ducts and pipes and tubes running out of it at crazy angles. It was dirty and scuffed. "An antique," Angela muttered. "It's a wonder it works at all!"

She circled the squat, evil-looking box, ducking her head as she passed under a low duct. To her eyes, the back looked

the same as the front, and the cinder-block walls were un-
broken by anything that could be an exit to a creature larger
than a rat. That thought gave Angela no pleasure at all.
Throughout her ordeal she had steadfastly closed out images
of rats and mice and snakes and spiders. Now, by sheer will,
she closed her mind to the pictures again and completed her
circle of the furnace.

"Nothing! Nothing at all. I'm still stuck! I might as well
have stayed in that cage, for all the good it did me!" One hip
throbbed, her shin had stopped being numb and now
burned—a sure sign she'd scraped it going over the top of the
metal partition (she hadn't dared to look)—and her knees and
shoulders and wrists ached. In a fury of frustration, she
grabbed up a small, rusty wrench lying near the furnace, the
only thing in the room that was not bolted to the furnace or
the walls, and began to strike out erratically, tears squirting
from her eyes.

When she was a little girl, Angela had dropped and broken
a favorite doll. Flossie was shabby from being toted everywhere that Angela went, but Flossie was—well, she was just
Flossie! As she stared in despair at poor Flossie lying there
on the sidewalk with her head split beyond repair, little Angela's frustration had burst forth in a fit of temper. The little
girl had picked up a stick and started flailing away at shrubbery and trees, at leaves and at flowers, at the house and at
the sidewalk . . . Weeping and whipping with her stick, the
little girl had moved around her parents' garden, attacking
inanimate objects and sobbing, "Dirty tree . . . dirty bushes
. . . mean sidewalk . . . bad, bad, bad . . ."

Now it was Flossie all over again. "Rotten pipes . . .
dirty, dirty old furnace," Angela raged, turning her anger at
circumstance into anger against things, flailing away at anything she could reach and sobbing out her helplessness. "It's
so mean, mean, unfair . . ." She bashed her wrench against
the pipes and the side of the furnace. Dents appeared in the
ductwork, and still she worked out her fury and her inabilities
on the inanimate metal. "Not fair . . . rotten . . ." *BANG—
BANG—BANG—*

Above on the main floor, in the library, Tootsie Armstrong was reading the evening paper before the dinnertime chimes summoned her to the meal, and Emma Grant was checking on the location of her grandson's new job in Ketchikan, Alaska, using the big atlas located on the "Reference" shelf. Grogan, his head still aching, was sitting glumly in a large chair trying to bury himself in a biography of Custer.

BANG—BANG—BANG—

"Aaach, me head . . ." Grogan clutched his temples. "What is that banging away down in the basement?"

"Emma, they can't be fixing the hot water pipes, can they?" Tootsie said hopefully. "I complained yesterday that the hot water ran out before I finished my shower, and Mr. Torgeson promised me they'd so something, but it usually takes so long. . . ."

"Yes, very likely that's what it is," Emma Grant soothed, and surreptitiously reached up to remove her hearing aid. Background noise like the wind or the rustling of Tootsie's newspaper was one thing—metallic clanging, even far away and underfoot, was quite another.

BANG—BANG—BANG—

"They're not stopping," Tootsie said, rather pleased. "Perhaps there'll be plenty of hot water tonight. Do you think so?"

"Mmmmm," Emma responded with an agreeable smile. For the many years she'd been deaf, she had defended herself against questions she couldn't hear and conversations she couldn't enter by nodding and smiling and seeming to agree. She had gained a reputation for being amiable, charming, and a bit dense. After she got her hearing aid, people were surprised at what seemed to be a jump in her IQ. But now, without it for the moment (to avoid the noise of what she too assumed was the workmen), her automatic defense sprang once more into action. She beamed widely at the conversation she could no longer hear—and went serenely on with her reading.

Only Grogan seemed disposed to take action against the racket. "I can't hear myself think with that infernal clanging,'' he growled. ''You'd think they wouldn't start a job this close to quitting time. It's—why, it's five-fifteen now!''

''Why, so it is,'' Tootsie agreed brightly. ''How unusual. I've never known the men to stay after hours. Now, that's rather fine of Mr. Torgeson to pay them overtime to work on the hot water . . .''

BANG—BANG—BANG—

Grogan hauled himself to his feet and threw Custer onto the ''Return All Books Here'' table. ''Damn if I'm going to be able to eat with that going on. I think I'll go and ask the fellows when they think they'll be through. Better than sitting here and vibrating in time to the hammers.''

Thus it was that Grogan, of all people, was Angela's rescuer. He stumped angrily to the basement, rehearsing his conversational gambits in his mind. ''I'll just ask them politely what the hell is going on and how flaming long they intend . . .''

He found the north-wing basement door shut but not locked, and the hallway light turned off (quite properly, for Torgeson would have skinned alive any maid or handyman who left an unnecessary light burning). ''Bloody hell . . .'' Grogan blundered around till he found a switch and turned it on. ''Ha! Tiniest light the skinflint could afford, of course.'' And he stumped toward the first barrier, the storeroom door.

''No, maybe I'll tell 'em the truth—that I have the biggest headache of the decade, industrial strength pain—and I'll ask 'em politely if they can't let the damned hot water go till the morning. Or no, because if they start up at nine o'clock tomorrow morning . . . Hello, the lock is snapped!'' Grogan had reached the storeroom and found the padlock closed. But a key protruded from the lock.

Actually, the key had also been in the padlock when Angela found it hanging free on its hasp that morning, but in the dim light, she simply hadn't noticed. She would have been horrified to realize that the staff habitually left the key there, for their convenience. They ordinarily snapped the padlock shut, however, and now the lock had been pushed into the closed position, the key still in place.

"Damn strange," Grogan said, turning the key and letting the padlock spring open. "Locked themselves in! How did those fellows manage that one?"

He entered the storeroom, leaving the door wide open behind him, and strode its length to the furnace room door that stood ajar. There he stopped abruptly, his jaw sagging. Limping around the decrepit old furnace, a wrench in her hand, was the usually elegant Angela Benbow. *Elegance* was not, however, the word that sprang to Grogan's mind this evening, as he took in her condition. Her stockings were torn and hung in tattered rolls around her ankles. Her shins were bloody, her print crepe dress was ripped in three places, her sweater was pulled off one shoulder and smeared with dirt. Her hair, tidy to a fault day in and day out—Grogan had once speculated to Mr. Brighton that she must smooth glue over it each morning!—was wisping free around her face. And her face . . . her face was red with exertion and contorted with emotion. Tears streamed down her cheeks, and she was shouting as she beat on the pipes: "Dirty, rotten, it isn't fair . . . Oh, my God, Mr. Grogan!"

She rushed at him, and for a moment, he thought that he, like the ductwork, was in for an assault. But she discarded the wrench as she ran and began to gasp and cry, "Oh, Mr. Grogan. Thank God!" And she threw her tiny self upon his scrawny chest and wept.

"There, there, dear lady," said the bewildered man automatically. "There, there . . ."

"Don't you 'there-there' at me, Grogan," Angela snuffled with a touch of her spirit returning. "Just help me out of here. What time is it? Where's Caledonia? How did you find me? Is that policeman, Lieutenant—Lieutenant—Damn! Whatsisname . . . Lieutenant . . ."

"Martinez," Grogan supplied blankly. "He's gone home, I think."

"Oh, I can't think of names when I . . . get me to my room, please. No, get me to Caledonia's—it's closer."

And with stumbling gait, many pauses, and a chorus of moans and sighs, an appalled and embarrassed Grogan and a hiccuping, chattering, and sobbing Angela came staggering out into the fresh air of evening and across the garden toward Caledonia Wingate's apartment.

To Grogan's everlasting gratitude, Caledonia answered to his first frantic knocking, and with her shock and surprise firmly under control—for the sake both of the wailing Angela and of the pale and trembling Grogan—Caledonia took charge.

An hour later, Angela was snuggled onto Caledonia's couch, tucked under a lush green and white satin quilt. Her head was propped against a fluffy pillow, her face and hands were clean again, and the torn and dirty clothing was discarded for a robe (too big, but she didn't complain). Her scraped shin was bandaged, and having eaten a pimento-cheese sandwich from Caledonia's none-too-well-stocked larder and having drunk a small whiskey from Caledonia's very well stocked bar, Angela was feeling a bit more like herself again.

Grogan sat, glum and silent, in one corner; Caledonia bustled about the room getting drinks, plumping pillows, and patting Angela's hand; and Lieutenant Martinez sat on a small chair drawn up beside Angela, so that he faced her. He was, to Angela's obvious joy, flatteringly attentive. Behind him, near the foot of the couch, sat Swanson, notebook in hand as always, his long legs wrapped awkwardly around the rungs of his chair, as though he thought that if he let go, he would perhaps float off toward the ceiling. His tongue was sticking slightly out as he earnestly took his notes.

Martinez had asked Angela to repeat her story three times, and three times she had obliged, dwelling longer and longer each time on her own outraged reactions, on her own cleverness in finding a way out, on her own strains and scrapes and bruises. "So then"—she was finishing the second repetition—"I banged on the pipes until someone heard and came to unlock the door and let me out. Mr. Grogan." She gestured at the scowling Grogan.

Grogan had been in a state of bewilderment when he

brought Angela to Caledonia's apartment. And he had been very concerned about her; it showed in the solicitous way he helped to ease her onto the couch, and it was evident in his silent, watchful attitude as he stood nearby while Caledonia washed Angela's face and hands, dressed her scraped shin, and helped her smooth down her hair. At length, Angela had to limp out of the room to exchange her ruined dress and sweater for the embrace of Caledonia's gigantic robe, because Grogan seemed rooted to the spot, and she found herself too embarrassed to ask him to turn his back or to step out onto the porch while she changed clothes.

When she came back to the room, barefooted and swaddled in terrycloth, Grogan had apparently decided that Angela was safe and that she was going to settle down and stay put, for he backed away from the couch and seated himself on the edge of one of the gilt chairs near the entrance. Since that moment, he had seemed to grow increasingly more gloomy. Now he said nothing—only listened.

"Well, if there's anything useful in that pile of papers and pictures you so kindly sorted out for us," Martinez was saying, "you can be sure we'll find it. They'll be gone over by experts, I promise. Swanson got a key from the office immediately, after you told us about your find, and went over and picked up the whole pile of—of—things." That sounded a bit lame; he had decided against the word "junk" as insulting, and then against the word "stuff," and finally against the belittling "bits and pieces." The word "things" was nothing if not feeble. He shook his head and went on without apology.

"You know, it's a wonder nobody would think to mention the storeroom before. And we never thought to ask. She had a couple of pieces of soft-sided luggage in a closet in her room, and a lot of odds and ends in drawers and on shelves—we just assumed that was all there was. 'Assumption is the mother of screwups'—my favorite motto, if you'll pardon me. I really do know better than to jump to conclusions, but I still keep doing it!"

"We all do it, Lieutenant," Caledonia reassured him.

Angela beamed fondly at him. Despite her aching joints and her fatigue, she still felt a kind of glow being there with this handsome young man paying her every attention. He was such a dear person! "I know *I* do—leap to conclusions, I mean," she said. "For instance, I assumed that the door to the basement had been left open innocently, didn't I? I mean, I'd never go in there if I knew somebody else was searching the storeroom, would I?"

Caledonia grinned. "You might! You've done sillier things."

Angela turned up her little nose, not deigning to respond, and looked away toward Martinez, who went back to a question he'd asked before. "Do you have any idea at all who it was?"

"None whatsoever. I'd have told you immediately—you wouldn't have to pump me. I wish I could help you, Lieutenant. I truly do. But all I know is, he moved very fast."

"You keep saying 'he,' Mrs. Benbow. Stop and think . . . what makes you believe it was a man?" Angela looked puzzled. "I mean," he went on, "was the person very tall?"

Angela shrugged. "Everybody's tall, compared to me. Grogan over there is not a big man"—she pointed and he glowered back—"but to me he's big. I'm four eleven."

Caledonia grinned. "Didn't you notice what a shrimp she is?"

Martinez smiled back in spite of himself. "Did this person touch you? Brush against you? Did you feel the material of the clothing? Leather—or something like tweed? Or maybe soft and silky? Did you feel a bare arm—hairy or smooth? Or a hand? A big hand, maybe with calluses? Fingernails—long or short . . ." She shook her head regretfully.

"Well," Martinez went on, "how about a scent? Perfume? After-shave? Shoe polish? Motor oil?"

She shook her head after each suggestion. "All I remember smelling is the musty odor of that awful cloth . . . some kind of upholstery material."

Swanson nodded from his corner and spoke for the first time. "I saw it when I went down there. It was a kind of woven material like tapestry, with a cording edge. I think it was the kind of cover you put over a bed . . . a king-sized bed, probably, judging by the size of it.''

She agreed. ''Yes, and it was rough to the touch. . . . It smelled a little damp, too . . . mildew maybe. But I was glad to have it when I crawled out over that wall.'' She smiled ruefully. ''It was supposed to be a cushion for me, too. To break my fall when I dropped, you know. But it wasn't thick enough for that, and it kind of spread out too much when I dropped it over.''

Martinez looked interested. ''Why didn't you guide it over gradually, so it piled up in one spot?''

''Oh, it was much too heavy for me to handle easily. I could barely lift part of it, when I used it as a blanket. I just used one end around me—most of it still dragged on the floor. And when I had to lift it up over my head, over that gate, I could only lift a corner. I sort of snaked the rest up, once part was resting on the crossbar so my arms didn't have to take the weight.''

Martinez stood up. ''Well then. That's how you decided your attacker was a man.''

''What?''

''His strength. Didn't you tell me he rushed at you with that bedcover thing held up in the air so that he brought it down over your head and covered you completely?''

Angela was amazed. ''Yes. He did.''

''Well, do you think a woman could have lifted that whole coverlet that way?''

''No! Oh no! Not one of us women here at Camden! Of course, most of the men here couldn't either. I don't think Grogan could—'' Angela gestured across at him, but he still glared and said nothing. ''Caledonia might. But I'd have known someone that big—she'd have bumped against me—I mean, I don't think she could have got past me in that little space without bumping—I mean—''

''Don't apologize, Angela,'' Caledonia said cheerfully. ''I know I have to turn sideways to get past people. My bulk is certainly no secret.''

Martinez nodded. "So you're eliminated as a suspect, Mrs. Wingate."

"Oh, I was a suspect?"

"Everyone is. Always. You know that." Martinez was moving toward the door. "Now, we must see that you get a full night's rest, Mrs. Benbow."

Angela sat up higher in her makeshift bed. "Lieutenant, wait . . . you will tell us if you find anything, won't you? I mean, about the man in the storeroom—or anything in those papers I found?"

Swanson joined Martinez and eased ahead of him to hold the door open for his superior. "Mrs. Benbow, Mrs. Wingate . . . and Mr. Grogan . . ." Martinez bowed briefly toward each in turn. "It's been a long day and I suggest everyone get some sleep. In the morning, ma'am, I'd see your doctor. That shin should get treatment, and you may have some bruises."

"Wait. You *will* tell us . . ."

He turned, half out the door. "Oh, I'll be back. Never fear. And I'll tell you first about any announcements I make. Believe me." And he was gone.

Grogan stood up and moved toward the door himself. "Goodnight," he muttered, looking at his shoes.

"Wait," Angela called after him. "I still haven't thanked you properly for helping me."

"No thanks needed." He moved a bit faster.

"Not so fast, Grogan," Caledonia said. "We have you here now, and goodness knows if we'll get the chance to talk to you in private again. We wanted to say something . . ."

"Oh, yes," Angela seconded her. "We want to tell you . . . no, to *implore* you . . . to mend your life while you still can." Grogan cleared his throat nervously.

"Well, I wouldn't exactly put it that way," Caledonia corrected her. "But you've got to do something, Grogan. You go on these binges . . . you're probably ruining your liver—at least, I'd hate to see a picture of it in its present condition . . ."

"Nobody wants to see a picture of anybody's liver," Gro-

gan growled, his head hung lower than ever, his shoulders
hunched in a posture that spoke of self-defense. "Damn ugly
thing. And you two can leave *my* liver alone, thank you. An
occasional lush is what I am, that's all, and perhaps I'm the
better for it."

"Well, it's true that when you're not drunk, you're almost
always grumpy and bad-tempered," Caledonia agreed.
"Admit it, Grogan, you're a mess!"

"Cal!" Angela reproved her. "Mr. Grogan can be very
sweet . . ."

"So you say," Caledonia said doubtfully.

"Jesus-Mary-and-Joseph! Not sweet! *Never* sweet!" Grogan groaned.

"Well, you can too be sweet! Sometimes. That's why we
want you to stop drinking, Mr. Grogan," Angela said in her
most wheedling voice. "Then you'll stop having these awful
hangovers! I think—I've thought all along—you wouldn't be
so ferocious if you didn't feel so terrible most of the time!"

Grogan looked pained. "I only booze it up once a week
or so," he protested.

"And then you're hung over for two days," Angela said.
"That's three or four days wasted out of every week!"

"Well, that's true . . . but it's my foul temper that's really
at fault for the way I act, you know. I can't control it. It's
these stupid people! Little old ladies always give me a pain
in the—present company excepted," he interrupted himself
hastily. "Still, this place suits me as a place to live, if these
stupid old cows would just leave me alone in my misery.
And, with all due respect to you two—though I've always
said you're different from them, and I mean it—with all respect, why don't you two leave me alone, too? I'm miserable
half the time, but didn't you ever stop to think that I might
like being miserable?"

"That can't be true!" Angela protested. Caledonia just
grinned.

Grogan's expression grew sourer than ever, but his voice
was sad. "Of course, I admit that, feeling like I feel today,
I'd give my soul not to feel like this again—if you follow me.

The problem is, you see, that sober, I'm not a happy man. But when I've been drinking—''

"Please, Mr. Grogan. You're killing yourself, and I think you owe it to us to try to straighten out," Angela went on smugly, with the air of one producing a trump that the declarer has obviously forgotten to count. "Don't the Chinese believe that if you save someone's life, you have to look after them ever after? Well, you saved my life tonight, didn't you? And how can you fulfill your obligation to me, look after me, if you don't stop drinking?" She spread her hands in triumph.

Grogan looked a bit dazed at the spate of logical argument. "Perhaps I do owe you something . . .''

"Try it, Mr. Grogan," Angela urged. "Please . . . for us . . .''

"We'll see," was all he conceded, as—with one more ferocious glower at the rug, a shuffle of the feet, an attempt to say something, and finally, the discovery that he really had nothing to say—he stumped out into the night.

"There," Angela glowed. "He's going to reform! He promised us he wouldn't drink.''

"Nothing of the sort, Angela. You're jumping to conclusions again, just the way you did with Martinez. *He* made no promises, despite what you may think. And Grogan made no promises—none at all! If he didn't feel so awful today, he'd probably have another snootful this very minute. The man's a habitual souse.''

"Cal, you can't mean that!''

"Can and do—and now it's time for you to go to bed. Little girl, you've had a busy day.''

Angela sighed. "I'm not sure I'm up to going home . . .''

"Of course not! You're going to stay right here on this guest bed—this couch folds out. You can stay right where you are.''

Angela had grown up believing you must protest an invitation with genteel refusals like "Oh, but I couldn't . . . ,'' but tonight, she was without polite protests, and within a half hour, she was sound asleep on the folding couch. It was a beautiful couch—with clean lines and elegant upholstery—and Caledonia had paid an enormous amount for it. So she would have been distressed to hear that, folded outward as a bed, it was hideously uncomfortable. Had Angela stayed awake long enough to become conscious of the sags and lumps, she would certainly have reported the bad news in the morning, but she slept soundly the whole night through. And nothing disturbed her sleep; courtiers waiting anxiously to see if the true princess felt the pea beneath the mattress would have been doomed to disappointment that night.

Chapter 8

THE NEXT morning, Angela awoke automatically at her usual hour—close to six-thirty. Considering what she had been through, she didn't feel at all bad, although her leg gave her some pain and one shoulder ached. Moving quietly so as not to wake her hostess, Angela dressed herself in the tattered clothing she had removed the evening before, leaving the borrowed robe behind on the hook on the bathroom door; then she limped home to her own apartment, cleaned herself up, and breakfasted alone—Caledonia, of course, was not likely to stir until nine o'clock.

After breakfast, Angela made her way to the nurses' station—a small room near the dining area, where the old hotel's gift shop used to stand. Nurses and a doctor were available in the health facility across the street, of course, but for routine matters (daily blood pressure readings for some residents, medication administered to the forgetful, treatment for minor injuries, and the dispensing of aspirin and Band-Aids) there was always one nurse on duty right in the main building.

To Angela's dismay, today it was Connie Maddox, the brisk woman with the chilly manner. Angela much preferred dealing with almost any other of the nurses.

"Something?" Connie asked, not looking around from the cabinet before which she stood, apparently taking inventory. She held a clipboard in one hand, a pen in another.

"I need treatment for this abrasion on my leg."

Connie half turned and spoke over her shoulder, her mind

still on her supply cabinet. "The doctor's on duty across the street," she suggested.

"I said it was my leg that was hurt. I walk on my leg, not on my hands. If I felt like walking that far, I'd have gone there!" Angela snapped. Her patience, never very long, had reached its limit quickly this morning.

"Well, there's no need to be that way about it," Connie said, without warmth, but at last turning fully around and laying down the clipboard she'd carried. "Of course I'll take care of you. Sit down here. Now, what seems to be . . . oh, boy!" She was lifting the dressing Caledonia had applied and looking at the torn skin underneath. "That's a bad scrape! Fell, did you? On the sidewalk maybe?"

She cleaned the wounded area, quickly removing dead skin and dabbing on antiseptic. To her credit—though Angela would not have admitted it—she worked efficiently, causing Angela only a minimum of discomfort. But when she applied a clean new dressing, she found a way to infuriate Angela once more. "You old people sure do have your problems walking, don't you? Maybe you'd better carry a cane when you go out of the building."

Angela could not leave the nurses' station fast enough. Back home, she put stockings on, making her bandage a bit less conspicuous, and sat down to think through the events of the day before. It seemed to her that she was missing something—some idea that teased at the corner of her mind. But nothing came clear, and after a while she turned on the television and dozed through a couple of the quiz shows that offered big money for facile knowledge. When a quarter to ten came, she phoned Caledonia.

"How're you feeling now?" Caledonia boomed.

"Much better," Angela said, a little surprised that the social response, so easily given, was quite accurate. One didn't expect to bounce back from the kind of experience she had undergone—not at her age. She was rather pleased with her own resilience. "My shin tingles a bit, but it's mending; I had a nurse look at it and dress it. That's all that seems wrong. Why, I ate," she added in a confidential tone, "like a *horse* at breakfast!"

"You always do," Caledonia mourned. "I eat a teaspoonful of shredded wheat and gain a pound. You eat a ton and never gain an ounce. It isn't fair. And even if I skip breakfast, it doesn't help."

In truth, of course, Angela did no such thing. Old people simply do not eat the volume of food they did when they were younger, and Mrs. Schmitt in the kitchen served the residents only small helpings of her incredible meals. But Angela, like so many others at Camden, did indeed clean her plate.

"What's on the agenda today?" Caledonia went on, with a lazy yawn.

"Are you up yet?" Angela asked. Caledonia's answering the phone was no guarantee she had gotten herself vertical for the day. She had a bedside phone extension, which meant she might well be lounging around, still undressed.

"Oh, sure. Even combed my hair and put something on the body. What did you have in mind?"

"Exploring in Kinseth's apartment," Angela answered instantly.

"Of course," Caledonia sighed resignedly. "I knew you'd suggest our breaking and entering sooner or later. That's your style. You were doing it on your own yesterday—no reason we shouldn't go right on today."

"Well, are you going to come with me or not?"

"Of course I am! I'm every bit as curious as you are—it's just that I don't quite get up the nerve to do some of the things you do."

And that was certainly true. Caledonia had often said that she couldn't understand where Angela packed away her self-confidence in that tiny body. "Now, you'd think I'd be the brave one. I have plenty of room for a lot of guts," she said. Angela had made a face and responded that she didn't care for coarse words like "guts," which made Caledonia roar with laughter. Caledonia, usually the leader in any group, had gotten used to sailing along ahead of any companion.

But when Angela was around, Caledonia had also gotten used to being pushed from behind, made to travel at a pace faster than she might have taken for herself.

About a half hour later, Caledonia knocked at Angela's door and together—making sure nobody was watching along the length of the hallway—they walked quietly on down to the halfway point, where Amy Kinseth's apartment stood. The police had put an extra lock on the door earlier, but now the lock had been removed.

"Keep lookout and let me know if anybody turns the corner from the lobby, or if one of these doors on the hall starts to open," Caledonia warned, and she set to work testing the knob to see if, by any chance, she could make the door open by simply working on the latch. But she could not. It wouldn't budge.

"Some of these keys in this old building fit other locks than their own," Angela whispered. "Remember? We got into the main office one time with an apartment key." Simultaneously, they fished out their keys—but neither would slip into the lock.

"Now what?" Caledonia wondered.

"Well, there's always the window," Angela said. "Of course, we wouldn't want to try going in through a window in broad daylight. And it's not as private as down at the cottages, either—so we'd have to be very careful, even at night." The windows of the main building apartments on Amy's side faced outward to the street. Anybody walking past the building would have seen an attempted entry through a window.

Angela and Caledonia walked down the hall and out the back entrance into the garden, trying to look like two women out to admire the flowers and smell the sea air. Once outside and around the corner, they quickened their steps—but long before they reached Amy's part of the building, they realized they were on a futile expedition. The apartments on the ground floor had all been fitted with ornamental and protective wrought-iron grillwork.

"Well, I knew that," Angela said in a disappointed voice.

"I mean, I have it on my apartment windows, and I should have guessed everybody on the first floor would too. I just thought maybe they'd missed hers, or something."

Caledonia looked left and right. There was nobody within a hundred or more yards of them, and those people who were out seemed to be minding their own business in a very satisfactory way. So she lunged between the bushes planted along the foundations of the building, till she stood directly beneath the window they had been eyeing. Her caftan was of a light material rather like percale—brightly figured in abstract swirls of color—and as she moved between the shrubs, which had grown in California's perpetual summer to be over ten feet high and very full-bodied, the branches caught the caftan and held it. Her body moved forward, but her body covering did not.

Anyone walking past would have seen what appeared to be a queen-sized bed-sheet spread out to dry, as peasant women traditionally dry their laundry in the sun. And behind it, they would have seen a woman with only her head, feet, and arms visible, apparently swinging energetically from the iron bars of the window overhead. Not that the sight would have caused any comment in Southern California, where men go for strolls in puce knickers and lavender golf caps, and the proper tennis court attire can be a designer-created white satin body stocking.

"It's no use," Caledonia reported. "Those bars are set firm as a rock. We can forget about getting into the room this way."

Above her, framed in the window, two heads suddenly appeared—topped by iron gray page-boy bobs and terminating in frothy pink angora sweaters. It rather looked as though two elderly women were standing there wearing giant cones of cotton candy. Before a startled and guilty-looking Caledonia could gracefully withdraw from the shrubbery, the window was flung open, and the Jackson twins chorused, "Good morning, Caledonia," as with a single voice.

"Dora Dee . . . Donna Lee . . ." Caledonia acknowledged, trying to carry the moment off with aplomb.

"Dora Lee . . ." one twin rebuked gently.

"Donna Dee . . ." the other corrected her. "I swear, I don't know why y'all don't remember that . . ."

"What *are* you doing in the bushes, Caledonia?" Dora Lee asked pertly, the smile never wavering on her face.

"We heard you sort of knocking on our window," Donna Dee added, beaming. "Rattlin' at those ol' bars . . . We never used to have bars on windows."

"Not home in Anniston we didn't," her twin affirmed. "Nicest little ol' town . . ."

"Well, not so little any more, of course," the other amended. Then they both stood smiling brightly down at Caledonia, waiting for her to say something.

Angela felt she had to rescue the situation. Caledonia, struggling to free herself and her flowing garment from the embrace of the natal plum on the left and the giant hibiscus on the right, was growing flushed and disarrayed, and the mental rigors of thinking up some excuse—added to the physical labor of extricating herself from the shrubbery—seemed beyond her for the moment.

"We heard there'd been a prowler," Angela lied valiantly, stepping forward into the line of the twins' vision. "We were checking bars . . . My window looks out this way too, you know. But Cal couldn't reach my window because of the Mexican gardenia bush there. So we just moved on down here till she could get between two—"

"*AAaaghhHHAA!*" Caledonia roared, giving an excellent imitation of a karate fighter attacking as she ripped her caftan, in a fury of frustration, free from the clinging thorns of the plum bush.

Both twins, startled by Caledonia's cry, started back from the window for a moment. Then they pressed forward again, their smiles still firmly in place. "Why don't you just go around and test the bars from inside the room?" one asked. The other nodded. "That seems so much easier than doing it from the outside."

There was a moment of silence as Angela and Caledonia looked at each other, invention failing them. Then Angela was inspired. "But it doesn't matter if they're firm from the inside," she said. "A burglar would be trying to come in from the *out*side. You see?"

"Ah! Of course!" Both twins nodded in satisfaction. "Now we see."

"Dora Lee and I were just going to have some mint tea," Donna Dee twittered cheerfully. "I do hope the two of you will come in and join us?"

Caledonia and Angela exchanged a glance, then both shrugged as though to say "Oh well . . ."

"Be right there," Caledonia said, waving with feigned good cheer. She watched as the window slid shut and the twins stepped back into the shadows inside their room. "I guess we're stuck," she said to Angela, as they circled the building. "Fast thinking there, girl. I'm proud of you. But that was by all odds the dumbest story . . ."

"They believed it, didn't they?" Angela said.

Caledonia nodded. "I guess you tailor the level of your lies to the level of your audience." She sighed. "I hate mint tea, you know. But it seemed as though we'd be less conspicuous if we came in and joined them."

Angela smirked. "I *thought* you had the wrong window, by the way."

Caledonia stopped in mid-stride. "For Pete's sake, why didn't you say something?"

"Well," Angela apologized, "you always get so cross when I correct you. And you're usually right. And if you're right and I'm wrong, you—you crow!"

"I never crow."

"Yes you do!" Angela responded tartly. "And you say I'm silly. You make me feel foolish. I've told you about it before."

"Well, pay no attention to me!" Caledonia said. "*You* know you're not stupid! You shouldn't believe me when I say things like that. And in heaven's name, when I'm walking into the men's room by accident, or stepping off the edge of a cliff because I'm not looking where I'm going—*say something*!" And she strode off again, her spirits restored by the exchange. Even the prospect of mint tea (which she did indeed despise) with the twins (whose company bored her) did nothing to make her feel less cheerful. The truth was that Caledonia was at last opening her eyes fully and getting up to full speed, a condition that took a long time in the mornings.

Of course, once inside the Jackson apartment—the apartment that was one closer to the garden end of the hall than Amy Kinseth's—Caledonia did not feel quite so exuberant. She found the unremitting sweetness of the Jackson twins to be cloying, their tendency to slow thinking to be depressing, their predilection for anything colored pink to be next to nauseating.

The tiny apartment was cluttered with little tables and whatnot shelves that overflowed with ornaments of the kind that Caledonia most despised: china shepherdesses (with suspiciously almond-shaped eyes) stamped "Made in Korea"; a blown-glass swan filled with colored liquid; an Elvis Presley "commemorative" plate; plastic roses in a plastic imitation of a Wedgewood vase; a velvet pincushion shaped like a heart and stamped "Souvenir of Montgomery"; a collection of Avon perfume bottles shaped like comic strip characters (Daisy Duck, Minnie Mouse, Betty Boop) . . . and everything was pink or had pink in it or on it. Caledonia felt as though her eyes hurt in their sockets.

On a white and gilt coffee table the twins laid out their tea set: a pink pot shaped like a large cabbage rose, cups painted with pink petals, and green saucers shaped like leaves. The creamer and sugar bowl were rose glass with lavender bubbles in it; the spoons had handles of pink plastic; the plate that held the Fig Newtons was shaped (and tinted) in the image of an anemic strawberry; even the sugar was pastel-dyed "coffee sugar" from which all the colored crystals but the pink had been removed.

Caledonia closed her eyes as she accepted her cup. Angela did not even wince, for she was a woman with a mission. It had occurred to her that these two might have useful gossip about their late next-door neighbor.

"Such a pity about Mrs. Kinseth," she said, starting the conversational ball rolling.

The twins looked at each other for a moment in silence. "Mmmmm," one said, "Well . . ."

"Yes, of course," the other interrupted. "A shame." She nudged her sister with a surreptitious elbow. "Any violent death is a shame, isn't it?"

"All I meant was," the other one explained, "she wasn't awfully nice, you know. That's all I meant."

Caledonia opened her eyes to join Angela's fishing expedition. "Did you visit in her apartment? I understand it was beautifully decorated, but I was never invited inside."

The twins simpered. "Oh, she did ask us in the first day after she arrived," Dora Lee said.

"She said," volunteered Donna Dee, "that since we were living right next door, she knew we'd be curious about her place."

And, Angela guessed silently, she wanted to get it over with—get you in there early and then, with your curiosity satisfied, you wouldn't be so likely to snoop later! But of course she didn't say it aloud.

"Did she have many visitors?" was what she actually said.

Dora Lee looked faintly puzzled. "I'm not sure she knew too many people around this area. She came down from . . ."

". . . from Anaheim," Donna Dee supplied. "Lots of people from here called on her . . . most of the—you know, the important staff—and quite a few of the residents . . . But not people from outside. And I don't remember most people coming to call more than once. She wasn't very . . . well, very cordial."

"Well, Carolyn, the activities director, came twice," Dora Lee said. "First she wanted to sign her up for a sewing group—to help with a quilting project . . ."

"And then she wanted her to go to morning exercises."

"How did you know that?" Angela—seldom tactful—could not be expected to hold back every comment. This one simply tumbled out like a challenge, and for a wonder, the twins caught the note of disbelief.

"Oh, you can hear a lot through the wall," Dora Lee said defensively. "It wasn't that we were listening, of course . . ."

"Of course not," Caledonia soothed. "Whoever would say you were?"

"She would!" Donna Dee blurted out. "That Kinseth woman as good as said so one day. We were coming out of our door to go to breakfast, and she came popping out of hers as we passed . . ."

" . . . like a jack-in-the-box," Dora Lee finished the thought, as the twins so often did for each other. "And she said, 'You can hear everything that goes on in here, can't you?' and she meant in her own living room, because . . ."

" . . . because she has two rooms, you see, and that's the one next to ours, you know," said Donna Dee. "I asked her whatever made her think that . . ."

" . . . we didn't want her to think we spent our time listening to her, you know . . ."

" . . . and she said, 'Because I heard you this morning talking about what kind of toothpaste to buy!' You see, our bathroom wall was especially thin, or it seemed to be. We could hear . . ."

" . . . her faucets running, and hear her flush the toilet . . ."

" . . . plain as though it was in our bathroom. It wasn't quite as easy to hear what went on in the main part of her living room. But when somebody walked by her bathroom door . . ."

" . . . not that we stood and tried to listen, you understand . . ."

Angela felt faintly dizzy from turning her head from one twin to the other, and her confusion of the two was becoming pronounced. She understood their point, however. Because the building had been originally a hotel, each room had a bathroom. The wealthiest residents, who rented two-room suites, as Mrs. Kinseth had, therefore got two closets, two entrances, and two bathrooms—one off the living room and the other off the bedroom. Bathrooms in adjoining rooms backed against each other—and apparently one of the Kinseth bathrooms was set against the Jackson bathroom, sharing a common wall.

"You mean," Angela asked, just to be sure she did understand, "that you could hear through the wall? So you pretty well knew who called on her and who didn't?"

The twins nodded solemnly. "Yes indeed," Dora Lee said. "And a lot of the residents came at least once—or tried to. Most of them she just stopped right at the door—didn't invite them in at all. Some she did ask in, of course . . ."

". . . no rhyme nor reason to it that we could see," Donna Dee chimed in. "We didn't think she was awfully nice even to those she did ask in for a while."

Dora Lee was saying, "Not that we could make you a list, understand, but I think there may have been fifty or so visitors in all . . ."

". . . and she only let maybe ten of those inside the apartment. Let's see," Donna Dee went on, to Angela's delight, without a bit of prompting. "There was Hazel Hanson, of course, who asked her to play in a bridge game. And Tootsie Armstrong. Torgeson came once about something or other— she probably complained about her bill; we heard her say over and over she thought they were charging too much here. The nurse came to take her blood pressure, I think; she came more than once—about twice a week, I'd say. And Mrs. Schmitt stopped by to see about her diet—and our activities director, Carolyn Ro—oh, I told you that. And Janice—uh— uh—you know, Janice—uh . . ." she stalled on the name, and so did her sister.

"Janice uh . . . uh . . ."

"Felton," Caledonia supplied.

"Felton!" they cried together. "Oh, don't you *hate* it when you can't remember a name!" Donna Dee amended.

"She wanted," Dora Lee said, "to get Mrs. K. to join the program committee. No luck," she beamed. It was obvious she hadn't wanted Amy as part of the committee she served on herself.

Caledonia gazed earnestly at a picture on the wall—a pink kitten painted on black velvet by a Mexican artist who drew his inspiration from a greeting card—and the sight was enough to help Caledonia control her impulse to grin widely. So the sisters claimed they didn't hear much? Didn't stand with their ear to the wall? Only knew a few of the visitors? In a pink kitten's ear!

"Of course there were the two of us," Donna Dee went on. "More than once."

"Oh, really?" Angela tried not to sound too skeptical.

"Truly," Donna Dee said. "We brought Elroy Carmichael with us that second time. He'd been to call on us, and she came out into the hall and said, real friendly, I thought, why didn't we all come in for coffee. So I think you might say we're the ones who brought them together."

"Brought them together?" Caledonia asked incredulously.

"Oh, not a romance . . ." Dora Lee laughed airily. "I mean creatively. He read us a few of his poems that day, and she simply loved them. Said she'd never heard anything like them. Elroy writes with such . . . such *heart*!" Caledonia cocked an unbelieving eyebrow over to Angela, who turned her face away to discourage Cal from commenting; this was no time for her to interrupt the twins with some bit of sarcastic literary criticism.

"I know she had him back at least once for a private poetry afternoon," Donna Dee said, her mouth tightened down like a rubber band, hard against her teeth. "And he didn't even tell us. Didn't even stop by to say hello on his way . . ."

". . . or when he left, either!" Obviously both twins had felt the slight most keenly. "Of course, she had plenty of money and Elroy was looking for someone to help him publish a slim volume . . ."

". . . of some of his best. He mentioned it to us—I think he hoped we might make a suggestion about where he could find money. We couldn't, of course, and we felt really bad about that, because he's such a dear young man. . . ."

"So talented!" Dora Lee assured them. But she sounded

a bit pleased, all the same, when she added, "Of course, now that Mrs. Kinseth has passed away, I'm afraid Elroy will still need help publishing his poems. Whatever *she* may have promised him!" she added smugly.

"Well, now," Donna Dee corrected her, "she didn't actually say she'd pay for the book."

"Well, she as good as did," Dora Lee protested. "You stood right there with me . . . she said to sit down, she'd get him a soft drink. And she said, 'Why not amuse me while I work? Read me some of your things.' "

"He said could he help—he's such a polite boy," Donna Dee smiled fondly. "Well, she just about bit his head off and said to sit still and she'd get it. He should read to her and stay out of her way. So he did. Read to her, I mean."

Dora Lee nodded morosely. "All those poems that he'd read to us! Of course," she brightened a little, "they didn't sound nearly as good when he had to say them so loud. I mean, she must have been in the next room, and he was almost shouting." She sounded very smug when she added, "It sort of spoils the mood to yell!"

Donna Dee beamed at the memory. "Oh, my yes. Indeed it does. They had no atmosphere at all . . . no tenderness, shouted like that. But, all the same," she sighed, "when he told her about the book, she agreed to put up the money. He said something like, 'The book is my first priority, of course. I have to take care of that before I give my attention to anything else. Don't you agree?' "

"And she said," Dora Lee took up the story, "of course she agreed, and then she said she'd give him a lot. . . . She said something like, 'You'll get plenty. I'll see to it—don't worry.' Enough to publish his poems, you see."

"Well," Donna Dee sighed again, "of course we're sorry she didn't live long enough to help him and all, but there's a bright side to everything. Maybe now he'll come and read to us again."

Dora Lee nodded vigorously. "We so enjoyed our little poetry afternoons. I was thinking we might ask him to come next week. What would you say to that, dear?'' she asked her twin.

Donna Dee nodded. ''That would be lovely; just lovely.''

Dora Lee reached for the pink pot. ''Another cup of mint tea?'' she asked. ''Another Fig Newton?''

''I really couldn't,'' Angela said, and Caledonia joined in with a hasty ''No, no, no thank you . . .'' as they both rose quickly and moved toward the door.

''It's been lovely of you,'' Angela said. ''You really must come down to my place next time.''

''Oh?'' Dora Lee looked interested. ''When?''

''Well, you know . . . sometime. Right now I'm terribly busy, but we'll get together real soon.'' Angela was backing up so rapidly, she trod on Caledonia's toe and got a sharp nudge in the back because of it. But they both managed to get out, leaving the twins smiling over their own Fig Newtons.

''Oh, dear, I never . . . Listening through the walls . . .'' Angela began, but Caledonia put a restraining hand on her arm.

''They have ears like police dogs, those two,'' she whispered, bending over to bring her mouth very close to Angela's ear. ''Don't say a thing till we're way down the hall.''

Angela started to move rapidly in the direction of her own rooms, anxious to make some of the comments she had bottled up while she was inside the Jacksons' quarters, but suddenly she became aware that she was alone. Caledonia had stopped, dead in the water as it were, outside Amy Kinseth's bedroom door, the second one away from the Jacksons. Caledonia was on her knees, bending over almost double. Angela came back just as quickly as she had gone.

''What are you doing?'' she hissed. ''Peeking through the keyhole?''

Caledonia held up one large hand. ''Ssshhh . . .'' She stayed bent over, and Angela realized she was running the other hand under the edge of the hall carpet. After a moment she rose, put a finger to her lips, and then ran her hand over the framing of the bedroom door. Suddenly, a smile lit her face, and she brought the hand down—holding a key. Again she put a silencing finger up before her mouth, and she carefully slid the key into the lock, cautiously exerted pressure on it, and watched with huge satisfaction as the key turned easily and silently, with only a small click as the tumblers fell, and the door came open before her.

"Come on," Caledonia whispered, stepping through the door and beckoning with her whole forearm. Glancing once more up, then down the hall to be sure they were not observed, Angela followed her friend into the late Amy Kinseth's apartment.

When she had closed the bedroom door behind them, Caledonia whispered, "Now, not too loud, no matter what you find. Those Jacksons would hear a pin drop, even if they're one room away. But here we are—and we can look everything over."

"How did you know where to find a key?" Angela marveled.

Caledonia looked terribly smug. "Well, I remembered when I first moved in, before my cottage apartment was ready, I stayed for a while in a double suite upstairs in the other wing. I carried my main door key—the one to the living room door—everywhere. But I was so scared I was going to lose it—and look like a damn fool going to the desk to ask for help getting into my own room—that I hid the key to the other door—the bedroom door—the one I almost never used. I put mine under the edge of the hall carpet."

"Oh, Cal, how clever of you!" Angela marveled, and Caledonia blushed like a teenager. "Well," Angela continued in a whisper, "what do we do first?"

"Desk, I suppose," Caledonia said, gesturing toward the living room.

"And the book shelves," Angela said, remembering the people she'd known who'd used old letters as bookmarks, then left them in the books when they were finished reading.

So they went into the living room and wordlessly began to work. There were not many papers stored in the little bleached-wood desk with its wide-open pigeonholes. The police might have taken some away, Caledonia thought, but it made her job easier—and less interesting, for she found nothing beyond a bill for a new coat from an expensive women's shop (she grimaced reflexively at the price); a few desultory letters from old acquaintances that sounded faintly unfriendly and contained no secrets; insurance policies on a car, on household goods, on jewelry, and on Amy's life (The North Shore Animal League in Port Washington, New York, was in for a pleasant surprise); and an 800-calorie diet scribbled on a doctor's prescription blank and clipped, incongruously, to another handwritten slip headed "Henri Louis's Carrot Cake" and containing a recipe so sinfully rich, Caledonia felt fatter just for reading the ingredients.

There was an invitation to an art show in Laguna Beach; the announcement of a chamber music concert; another recipe—this one for a beauty mask featuring egg whites and mayonnaise ("I'd look like a plate of salad and smell worse," Caledonia muttered); and, stapled together, some typewritten verses, to which was attached a pale blue Post-it note with the handwritten message "You asked to sample my verses. Enjoy, dear lady. . . ." It was signed "Elroy."

Idly, Caledonia glanced at the first.

Oh woeful, woeful, woeful day!
Most lamentable day that ever I did yet behold.
Oh day, oh day, oh hateful day!
Never was day so black as this.
Oh woeful day, oh woeful day . . .

"Oh woeful day? Oh Gawd!" Caledonia breathed in genuine distress. "That's perfectly *terrible*!"

"What is, Cal?" Angela whispered, looking up from the last books on the bottom shelf. So far she had found nothing—not a turned-down page corner, let alone a piece of paper. And the books were mostly paperbacks—all of them novels of romance. Angela recognized Barbara Cartland, but most of the other authors meant nothing to her. There weren't even any of the mystery stories Angela favored in her own quiet moments.

"Elroy's poetry." Caledonia waved the sheets at her. Angela shook her head and made a face. "You don't know the half of it," Caledonia said, putting the material back onto the desk. "Oooghh . . . This must be the stuff he read to her and it's awful! Prime-time first-class top-of-the-line awful!"

She levered herself up from the desk chair and came over to Angela. "Anything?" Angela shook her head. They made a circuit of the living room, but the style of the decor discouraged the leaving of letters or photographs around the place. They opened the closet door and looked through pockets in the garments . . . no success. They opened hat boxes, ran their fingers down into shoes . . . nothing.

The bedroom furniture was as spare and sterile in style as that in the living room. "It's a little like hospital rooms in here, isn't it?" Angela whispered, shaking her head. "I don't think I could have lived here."

They stood before a large dresser, opened its drawers, and gazed at elegant and expensive things, at a rainbow of cashmere sweaters, coiled snakeskin belts, satin evening bags, real silk blouses, and a dozen Liberty scarves. But nowhere amid the evidences of wealth were evidences of murder—not a loose paper or a concealed love letter or a stolen diamond bracelet . . . assuming one could have told by looking at it whether or not a bracelet was stolen.

"Where is her jewelry?" Angela asked, struck by the thought.

"Maybe the police took it," Caledonia guessed. "Or it's resting in Torgeson's safe, waiting for her lawyer to claim it. Or whoever."

"No papers," Angela said dolefully.

Caledonia shook her head. "Nope."

They went to the bathroom and looked into the medicine chest, where prescription tubes and jars lay helter-skelter in no apparent order—then into the cabinet immediately below the sink, where extra toothpaste, combs and brushes, manicure implements, rolls of toilet tissue, towels, partly used makeup, and bobby pins lay in total disarray. However clean and uncluttered the decor of the rooms themselves, the medicine chest and cabinet drawers looked like someone had inserted a Mix-Master at full power.

"I think the police . . ." Angela began.

"Shhhhh—the wall," Caledonia said, gesturing toward the bathroom wall that adjoined the neighbors'. "Who lives there—on that side?" Caledonia asked.

"Oh, Sadie's deaf as a stone," Angela reassured her, but she whispered all the same. "Still, no use taking chances . . ." She pulled Caledonia along and shut the bathroom door behind them.

"The police left an unholy mess in there," Angela said, once they were clear. "I wonder if Lieutenant Martinez knows about that? Do you suppose—could someone—someone besides the police—have been searching in there, maybe?"

"For what?" Caledonia snorted. "An eyebrow tweezer? Half a lipstick?"

Angela shrugged. "Well, that's surely all there seems to be, all right."

Only one thing remained to be examined—the odd little lingerie chest that stood just outside the bathroom. And to Angela's surprise, when she slid the first drawer open, it was completely empty. So was the next . . . and the next.

She nudged Caledonia. "What did she keep in here, do you suppose?"

Caledonia stepped one place backward to look over the *semanier* as a whole. She shook her head. "It really is a lingerie chest . . ." Angela opened each of the seven drawers in turn—and found nothing in any drawer. Then she stepped back one pace and looked at the *semanier* with a puzzled expression. "You know, Cal, something's wrong with that thing."

"What do you mean?" Caledonia took another pace backward herself, though with her longer stride, she ended up a foot and a half farther away from the chest than Angela was. "Oh . . . Oh, gosh! I see what you mean. For one thing, it certainly doesn't suit the decor." She looked around her at the spare, clean lines of the Swedish modern—at the satiny bleached wood, at the curves and edges without ornamentation beyond their own pleasing, gentle arches. The narrow chest stood out like a waterfall in the Sahara. It was of a vaguely formal design, what the hardware catalogues call "American federal."

"Style: 'Grand Rapids Accidental,' circa 1960, I'd say," Caledonia said. "Except that it's been painted white. Unusual—and not very attractive."

Angela moved close to it again. "The wood ought to be, oh maybe cherry. Yes, I think maybe it is—but it's been painted over. You know, stripped and painted . . ."

"By an amateur, apparently," Caledonia said, frowning at the streaks and runs in the paint. "How did she get hold of a thing like that? That Baird kid certainly messed up when he bought this!"

"Wait! She brought that with her, Cal. Didn't he—the decorator—say something about a chest that didn't fit where he'd planned to put it? The day she was moving in. You were in the lobby with me, waiting for lunch, and we both heard . . ."

"That's right!" Caledonia smacked her forehead with an open palm. "Of course. This is the same chest she brought with her when she first came . . ."

"Hhsssshhh . . ." Angela realized that in their enthusiasm of investigation, they had forgotten to speak softly. They were talking in normal tones now, and the slap of Caledonia's palm against her forehead had sounded like a .22 in the silence of the bedroom.

"Oh. Oh, sorry," Caledonia whispered sheepishly. "What exactly did Baird say, now? Let me see. . . ."

"He said it didn't fit against the wall where she wanted it, and it would have to stand near the bathroom door . . . right where it is now, I imagine. And it would make the entryway a little tight . . ."

"It does," Caledonia agreed. "Well, that solves that little mystery."

"Not really," Angela said. "I'd say it didn't fit with this stuff she has now any better than it would have with her 'Palm Beach' decor. Well, except for the colors, of course."

"You've got a point," Caledonia marveled. "I wonder why she was so hot to hang on to it? She moved it in from her house in the first place, I guess, and then when she didn't like her furniture and had the whole place changed, everything went out except this chest . . . and she kept it again!"

Angela shrugged. "Well, maybe her husband made it for her and it had sentimental value."

Caledonia shook her head. "Not her style to be sentimental, I'd imagine. Besides, it looks like factory-made, to me."

"I know," Angela said. "But somebody's certainly made it worse than the original with that awful paint."

Caledonia shrugged. "Well, come on," she whispered. "We're not going to be able to learn anything by looking at a few wooden boards and some drawer pulls. Except that somebody didn't know how to put paint on smoothly—and that she felt sentimental about a cheap piece of furniture! Come on—let's go."

Cautiously, Caledonia cracked the door open. One elephantine eye rolled left, then right, but there was nobody in the hallway—not so odd for mid-morning, when most residents watched the TV quiz shows, changed their most casual breakfast-going togs for decent daytime dress, caught up on correspondence before the mail went out at noon, or rode with the daily van to the bank and to the shopping mall to do their errands. The two were able to slip out, ease the door gently shut behind them, and head innocently off toward Angela's apartment before they could be discovered.

Chapter 9

Within an hour, Angela and Caledonia had delivered to Martinez a written list of Amy's callers and an oral report on everything the Jackson sisters had said. They were careful, of course, not to add anything about their own trip into the Kinseth apartment. They were more than a little disappointed that Martinez seemed only slightly interested in their information.

After that, for another two days, nothing much happened, and Angela, at least, fretted with impatience. She saw Lieutenant Martinez come and go—he always bowed a little as he passed and smiled at her, but he seemed to have no inclination to chat. Once he did stop by her table in the dining room, as he and Shorty Swanson moved through on their way to their own lunch, to ask if she had "fully recovered from the ordeal in the basement."

She assured him she felt like herself again and took the chance to ask him about Amy Kinseth's jewelry. Caledonia shot her a warning glance across the table, so she didn't say—as might have been her impulse—that they knew for a fact that the jewelry was gone. She said instead, "Lieutenant, Cal and I were thinking—Mrs. Kinseth had so much jewelry, most of it real, by the look of it. We were wondering if . . ."

"If that was the motive for the killing?"

"Well, sort of. Being as how it's missing—I mean, *if* it's missing—I mean, well, there's a lot of pilfering around a place like this—everybody loses small items all the time. Of course, a lot of it isn't really stolen at all—just mislaid. But

we thought maybe—'' Martinez seemed to Angela to be staring at her with a question in his eyes and she blundered
onward, eager to obscure any hint that she and Caledonia
had been in the Kinseth apartment themselves. ''Not that it's
missing. I mean, not that we know whether it is or not. But
it needn't be connected with the murder, even if it is missing.
I mean, Emma Grant missed a ring last month and she never
has found it . . . and there was that nice gold locket Tootsie
Armstrong had . . . I mean,'' she finished a bit lamely,
''Mrs. Kinseth's things weren't taken from her, were they?''

''No they weren't—or at least, we don't think she was
robbed. We took two handsome jewelry boxes full of very
fine pieces down to the station that first day and checked
them against her insurance company's inventory. Everything
of importance seems to be there—plus a few pieces she hadn't
listed. You're right, she had some very expensive jewelry.
But we have it safe. Don't you worry.''

Angela, relieved that Martinez hadn't seemed to notice
anything unusual in her utterance, pressed forward. ''Well,
how about the man who attacked me in the basement? Have
you any ideas yet about who that might be?''

Martinez shook his head. ''Believe me,'' he said, ''I'd let
you know if we'd found out about that. Sorry.'' And he
moved on to join Swanson at their luncheon table.

Swanson had also stopped to talk to them a few times by
himself, usually as he went through the lobby with a cup of
coffee in one hand and a dessert plate heaped with sweet
rolls in the other, on his way to the elevator, headed for the
second-floor sewing room where he sorted papers and filed
notes and generally ''minded the office'' for the Lieutenant.
But for all the information Swanson passed along, he might
as well not have bothered—except that he was able to find
out by mid-morning what the main dish would be for lunch,
which was a great feat of detective work since Mrs. Schmitt
liked to surprise the residents and swore the dining room
staff to silence.

The secret of Shorty's success was, of course, Conchita
Cassidy, who had taken a special liking to him. When he ate

in the dining room and she was not assigned to his station, she swapped places with one of the others, so that it was she who brought his meal. The head waitress just pretended not to see. When Swanson stopped by for a snack in mid-morning, he was not turned away as a resident might have been; Chita would make a fresh pot of coffee and heat up some of the breakfast rolls, or find some of Mrs. Schmitt's homemade cherry marmalade to put on toast.

Martinez found the extra attention they got at meals to be to his liking, though he wouldn't usually allow himself to taste the snacks Swanson carried up to their room. "Chita's going to have you as fat as a piglet, Shorty," he warned. "And I'd hate to have an inside view of your arteries! You had three helpings of bacon at breakfast. Yesterday you packed down extra sausages. You always have butter, real butter, all over those rolls and that toast . . ."

Shorty shrugged. "Doesn't seem to do me any harm, though."

Martinez leaned over and patted his assistant's shirt, just above his navel. "Ah, I thought so . . . a little roll of fat starting up there . . ."

Shorty was without an extra ounce anywhere, but he looked faintly alarmed, and that morning when he went down to get his caffeine fix in the dining room, he told Chita, "No cream and sugar today, thanks, Chee. Oh, the Lieutenant wants some coffee today, too—with the trimmings—but I'll take it black."

"I have for you some excellent hot cinnamon-raisin bread," Chita beamed. "Fresh from the oven."

"Well, maybe just one slice," Shorty compromised. When she came bustling out of the kitchen with four slices, already swimming with melting butter, he said not a word in protest but smiled down at the top of her head. "Gee, thanks, Chee. And I decided . . . well, how about just a little sugar . . ."

"Sure, Swans-sohn," Chita said happily. "I've got it here for you. Now today, maybe you take a tray to carry all this? You got two cups of coffee and that plate of hot bread. Listen," she said, as she loaded everything on a small tray.

"You be sure you come for dinner tonight. It's beef stroganoff, and Mrs. Schmitt puts it over crunchy chow mein noodles instead of those soft egg noodles. You gonna *love* that." She beamed up at him. "I give you double."

"Great! I love stroganoff. Wouldn't miss it," and he beamed back as he made his way out into the lobby through the door she held open for him.

When he got to the elevator, Shorty had another problem—how to push the button to get the door open, still holding the little tray carefully in two hands but trying not to spill the brim-full coffee cups that sloshed dangerously every time he tried to raise a finger up from its grip on the tray's edge. He tried using an elbow to push, but he couldn't depress the button deeply enough into its brass casing to make contact.

The entire elevator rig, including the call-buttons, dated back to the 1920s, when things were built to last—and when ladies didn't push their own elevator buttons. Age had eased the stiffness of the spring somewhat, but it still took a firm push, and the button needed to go into its socket nearly an inch to effectively complete a circuit.

Swanson had just turned to put the tray down on the table while he rang for his elevator, when Angela appeared. She had been for a morning walk and beamed upon him almost as widely as Chita had done. "Detective Swanson!" she chirped.

"Oh, am I glad to see you," Swanson said. "Push that up button for me, will you?" She obliged.

"Oh! You have snacks for yourself and the Lieutenant, I see," she said, hoping to start a conversation while behind the oak sliding door, the elevator's cables and pulleys set up a doleful creaking and groaning that meant the machinery had begun to function.

"Yes ma'am," he agreed, glancing upward at the indicator light over the door.

Angela cocked her head up at him with amusement. "Detective Swanson," she said, "have you ever watched people waiting for an elevator? It is not really as though they think the elevator will arrive sooner if they fix their eyes on the indicator needle. I think it's probably just because people are comforted to know things are working as they should—for once.''

Swanson, a little startled, glanced down at her for a moment, then automatically returned his eyes to the indicator above the elevator door.

"I like to think, Detective Swanson, that we are in the age of the machine—of the plotting, wicked, malicious machine that amuses itself at our expense. I really believe machines lie in ambush for us. I think they stay awake at night scheming how to frustrate us! Machines were supposed to free us— but we have become slaves to machines! It's machines that run the world!''

"Ma'am?" he said, puzzled, with another quick glance at her.

"Well, watch the faces of people waiting for the elevator. Don't you think they look—oh, almost worshipful? As though they were imploring favor from the gods of Mount Otis! And somewhere up there''—she pointed at the groaning elevator behind the oak doors—"there's the spirit of the elevator— chuckling as it arranges to stop the car two inches below floor level, so you'll trip as you walk in.''

Swanson broke his stance again to look at her, stepping backward slightly as he did so—just as the oak doors slid open. He entered the cab rather hastily, tripping slightly because the elevator floor stood a modest half inch above the lobby level, steadied the tray, and grinned uncertainly. "Thanks again, Mrs. Benbow, for the help. I'm not sure about all that other . . .'' Then as the doors slid shut, he called out, "Oh, Mrs. B., it's beef stroganoff on chow mein noodles tonight for dinner!''

Angela watched the great doors close and heard the wheels and pulleys go to work. "How does he *do* that?" she marveled. "They won't tell *me* what's for dinner. Anyhow, a fat lot of good it was to try to get him talking about the case!'' She sighed. It was annoying how little like a "Perry Mason" rerun real life could be! "He wouldn't tell me a blessed thing—and me gabbling on like a fool. He probably just thinks I'm getting senile,'' she muttered, and she turned back toward her apartment—and as she turned, she caught sight of Bobby Baird coming out of her hallway carrying a lamp, followed by two men in work clothes, each of the pair supporting one end of a couch, and a third carrying two slim birchwood chairs, one in each hand. ''Oh, Mr. Baird,'' Angela called.

He nodded to the men. ''Put it all into the truck and keep on—I'll be with you in a minute.'' And he came over to Angela.

''I've got a report ready for you, Mrs. Benbow,'' he smiled pleasantly. ''On redecorating your place. Remember? You're going to be surprised, I think, and very pleased.''

Angela kept a brave smile on her face. She really had less confidence in the redecoration of her place than she liked to pretend. ''I was going to ask how you were coming, of course. But it hasn't really been long. And I'm not really in any hurry, you know. It's just—when you get time. I see you're moving out Mrs. Kinseth's things?''

He nodded. ''The police said it was all right. And her lawyer. He said to go ahead. They packed up the clothes and private things—linens, cosmetics, her papers, all that stuff— yesterday. She hadn't paid me for any of the furniture, so it still belongs to me, unfortunately.'' He gestured over his shoulder behind him, as his men came back through with another load. The two men had the funny little *semanier*, and the one who seemed to work by himself had an armchair he balanced upside down on his head and back.

''What will you do with all of it?'' Angela asked.

''Oh, most of the furniture can go back to the furniture store, I think. The area rug I bought to tie the living room together—that's secondhand, so it's not a great loss. Besides, it's a really nice shade of blue—I think I can sell it to someone else. The paintings I'm not sure about. Listen, I'd love to stay and talk, but I pay the men by the hour, and if I don't help, the move will take longer. I'll be in touch tomorrow or the next day, I promise. Okay?'' And he backed away, ''rapidly, but not rudely" (as Angela later described it to Caledonia) and carried his lamp out to the truck.

Angela went into the garden, straight to Caledonia's apartment, to report. But Caledonia was out—tending to some banking, as she explained later to Angela. "I got these checks yesterday from my trust fund officer. I don't like to have them sitting around, of course, so I went with the van."

"Cal, you *never* ride in the van if you can help it!"

Caledonia nodded. "You bet. The step up to get in is too high for me, the seats are too narrow, and the drivers aren't at all careful. But I thought this time . . . oh, well. Now, what is your news."

Angela told her. "They'll rent Kinseth's apartment again, of course, and as soon as they decently can. I'm glad we thought to go in before it was all cleaned out."

Caledonia shrugged. "It didn't make a bit of difference. We didn't find a thing, did we? And now—well, now I think we've done all the investigating we're going to be able to do. You looked in the basement . . . we both looked through her apartment . . . what else would there be to look over? No, Angela, I think this time we're going to have to ask the Lieutenant what *he* finds out. This will be his case—without our help."

Privately, Angela hoped that was not so, but she only nodded. "I guess you're right."

Caledonia, as it happened, was wrong. Dead wrong.

The next morning, a customer, arriving at Baird's shop to ask about the redecoration of her husband's den—a birthday surprise she'd planned for him that would have created a terrible family argument—found the shop door open and Baird lying dead on the floor of the back office. He had been hit on the head, as the police subsequently discovered, and stabbed three times—all the injuries, the blow and the stab wounds that killed him, probably inflicted by the gold-headed sword-cane that lay beside him, the blood from its blade staining the handsome Oriental carpet.

Angela heard about it first at lunch. She strolled out to the lobby to join the others, gathered in various small groups waiting for the silvery sound of the Westminster chimes that meant the door was open and they could go to their table. She joined Tootsie Armstrong, Mary Moffet, and Mr. Brighton, who were talking over Torgeson's latest outrage. The Wart Hog had decreed that bed linens would go unchanged for ten days, instead of being changed every week, as the maids had always done before. Dropping from fifty-two laundry days a year to only thirty-seven would result in a considerable saving of money.

It wasn't that they minded his saving money. It wasn't even that they thought the sheets would get too grungy between changes. It was just, as little Mary Moffet was complaining, that it was hard enough to remember which day the maid was coming when it was only once a week! "I confess I get muddled sometimes on whether it's Tuesday or Thursday for me . . ."

"You don't know what day of the week it is anyway," Angela agreed rather sharply.

Mary just shrugged and sighed. "That's true enough, I'm afraid. It usually doesn't matter, of course. Unless it's Sunday and we are supposed to go to chapel. Or unless it's the maid's day . . . I do like to have my bathrobe hung up and my slippers out of her way when she comes, you know."

Tootsie nodded. "Oh, I do too. I like to get my crewelwork picked up and put into the basket and all. If she does it, she mixes the colors and tangles the yarn. And I'm like you, Mary. I can't ever remember . . ."

Grogan strolled by the group, his head down, his shoulders hunched. Angela called, "Good morning, Mr. Grogan," in a cheery voice, but he just looked at her, barely moving his head, the picture of dejection and misery, and kept walking without a word.

Mr. Brighton was saying, "There are those here, you know, who will never remember which is maid's day at all. Failing memory hits us all, as we get along . . . but some more than others. Greta Sanderson, for example . . ."

They all shook their heads. Greta Sanderson, in the early stages of Alzheimer's disease, spent a lot of time in the lobby, sitting and staring hopefully at the main desk. She could never remember when meals were served nor when the mail was put into the residents' boxes. The mail delivery was actually made from the downtown post office by about noon on most days, and the mail was put into the boxes by the day clerk, Clara, before the residents had finished lunch. But whether she got mail after lunch or not, by one-thirty Greta Sanderson was back, sitting in a high-backed chair across from the desk, positioned so that she could observe the other residents and judge from their actions whether she should go to the desk or to the dining room.

One thing was certain: If after the five years she'd been a resident, if after five years of going to meals at exactly the same time every day and getting the mail at exactly the same time every day, if after 1,847 days of invariable routine, Greta Sanderson could not remember the meal and mail times, how could she be expected to remember which day was "every tenth day" when the maids would come? Torgeson might not understand the problem, but the other residents all did.

While one group tut-tutted and fretted about the new regulations, other residents were gathering in twos and threes throughout the lobby. And over at the desk Emma Grant was standing, her hearing aid cocked toward Clara, the red-headed desk clerk, who had paused with her hands full of mail to be sorted and was talking gleefully and steadily. Emma Grant would listen and shake her head, listen and shake her head—repeatedly. And when at last Clara finished her story, Emma fairly flew across the lobby to Mary and Angela and Tootsie and Mr. Brighton.

"Did you hear about our latest murder?" she gasped.

"No!"

"No!"

"Great heavens no!"

Only Tootsie did not respond, but her eyes were round and her mouth was open.

"Who? Tell us who!" Angela begged.

"Oh, not another resident . . . Camden will be getting such a bad name," Tootsie twittered unhappily.

"No, not a resident, but someone we all knew . . . more or less. That decorator fellow . . ."

"Goodness me!" That was Mary Moffet's strongest exclamation, and it showed her intense surprise. "Jacques LaChaise has been murdered?"

"Baird," Angela corrected automatically.

"Say what? Beg pardon?" Mr. Brighton asked.

"Baird. His name was really Bobby Baird. The shop name—his French name—they were fake—a kind of fancy advertising gimmick, I guess. What do you mean he's been murdered? That can't be true. I saw him yesterday. Here."

"No, no, it's so. Clara says. They found him this morning—at his shop. Stabbed."

Angela caught her breath and sat down on the nearest chair, an uncomfortable leather imitation of Renaissance Spanish furniture. "That nice young man," she said. "That *nice* young man."

"Who's a nice young man?" Caledonia said, flowing up to the group in a caftan of such startling yellow that it seemed to bring sunshine directly into the shadowy lobby.

"H-h-he's d-d-dead," Tootsie Armstrong stammered.

"Who? Who's dead?"

Emma Grant was happy to answer. "That decorator fellow, LaChaise. Except Angela says his name was really Baird."

"It was," Caledonia said. "But you better tell me the whole thing. Start at the beginning. You say he's dead? Tootsie . . . go ahead, you first . . ."

"Oh, dear—my sakes!—it's your story, Emma, you tell her." Tootsie Armstrong flapped her hands about limply in a good if unconscious imitation of the late Zasu Pitts.

Emma was all too delighted. "Got this from Clara," she said in a confidential tone that forced the others to lean forward into a tight circle, each head canted at a conspiratorial angle. "She says somebody came to the shop this morning about opening time—and there he was, spread out on the floor of his office, blood everywhere . . ."

"Oh, *my*," Tootsie said. Mary Moffet stepped closer to the circle, as though the warmth of the others could protect her from the chill news.

"Clara says," Emma went on, her eyes gleaming, "that he'd been knocked down—maybe knocked out—and then stabbed. Stabbed—more than once—with"—she paused to give her announcement more dramatic emphasis—"with a sword-cane!"

"A what?" squeaked Mary Moffet.

"You know—one of those things you always saw in the movies—a cane, but it comes apart in the middle. The top is the handle and the bottom is hollow, and there's a sword inside it."

"I had a cane that came apart in the middle, once," Mr. Brighton said, reminiscing. "It didn't have a sword, of course. It had a brandy bottle—a long, thin one. You took the top of the cane off, and there was this silver screw-top. . . . The flask only held one good swallow, of course. It was supposed to be for emergencies, you see . . ."

"Men used to carry them a long time ago," Caledonia said. "For protection, I suppose. I remember seeing one in an antique show once."

"I think they're against the law," Mr. Brighton added.

"Of course," Caledonia said. "Concealed weapons, and all that."

"Well, this one was probably in the shop—you know, for sale," Emma Grant said. "At least, that's what Clara says the police are saying."

Tootsie was trying to follow it all—not the easiest thing in the world for her, since her brains were as curly and fuzzy as her frizzy halo of graying red-gold hair. "So someone just killed him in a fit of temper? Just took the weapon closest to hand? Then it wasn't a murder somebody planned, I guess, was it? It was something that just—that just happened?"

Caledonia said, "You know, I seem to remember from the time we went to the shop—I think there was an umbrella stand near the office door. It had a lot of canes and things—Angela, don't you recall—it was one of those awful things that look like an elephant's foot."

"They *are* elephants' feet, dear lady," Mr. Brighton supplied. "Hollowed out and the hide put over something stiff, like a metal cylinder. The hide is cured first, of course . . . but it's a real elephant's foot and leg, all right."

Caledonia rolled her eyes to the ceiling. "Oh boy! Talk about bad taste . . ."

Angela woke up enough to get in a dig. "I wouldn't talk, Cal. Anybody with a Garfield telephone in her bedroom, right in the middle of the most beautiful antiques . . ."

Caledonia laughed. "It's cute . . . I like it . . . and it annoys you. Three good reasons to hang on to it."

"Ladies, ladies," Mr. Brighton interrupted. "I'm sure Emma has more of this unfortunate story to tell us. . . . Or rather, it isn't the story that's unfortunate, dear Mrs. Grant . . . just that it's about something so woeful . . ."

"Oh woeful day . . ." Caledonia breathed.

"What?"

"Oh, just quoting Elroy Carmichael's latest. I'm sorry. Emma, go ahead . . . I promise I won't interrupt."

"Well, there really isn't much more to tell," Emma said. "I mean, Lieutenant Martinez and his young helper . . ."

"Swanson," Caledonia prompted.

"Swanson . . ." Emma Grant nodded. "They came back up here about fifteen minutes ago and they were talking about it in the dining room—they had coffee and some of the tuna salad—"

"Emma! Nobody cares what they ate!" Caledonia said.

"Now, Cal, you said you'd let her talk," Mary Moffet chided boldly. She seldom interrupted Caledonia, but she was hanging on every word of the story, and Caledonia was being a nuisance.

Emma Grant continued as though Caledonia and Mary had not spoken. "And Chita Cassidy got to talking with them and they told her that much. Then she told Dolores, the head waitress, and Dolores told Trish in the office, when she went in with the guest bills from yesterday—you remember Mrs. Haywood had her nephew with her and the dining room brings those bills for guests to the office to put in with our bills for rent . . ." There was some audible shifting and a sigh or two, and Emma hurried her story. "Anyhow, she told Trish—Trish in the office, you know—and Trish told Clara. And Clara told me, of course."

Just then the chimes sounded, and the scattered groups of residents sprinkled around the lobby began to coalesce into a single body, rolling forward toward the big double doors. Conversation wasn't really possible, with everyone crowded around—and besides, Angela moved quickly and Caledonia moved slowly, so that Angela skittered ahead of the other residents and was at her table by the time Caledonia got through the door. But once they were at the table . . .

"You okay?" Caledonia asked as she got to her chair.

"Oh yes," Angela said. "It was just—you know, the shock."

Caledonia spread her napkin with a huge flourish, snapped it out like a banner, then tucked it into her lap in a kind of triangular tent, so that one large point stood up directly between her great bosoms. "You were full of excitement when Amy Kinseth died, girl. Like it was gossip or scandal. You didn't turn all pale and fainting!"

"Well, I didn't know her well. And I didn't like what little I did know of her. You were the one who played bridge with her and got invited to her apartment . . . she hardly talked to me. But young Baird . . . well, Cal, I liked that young man. I really did. And I saw him just yesterday, you know . . . so it's a bit of a shock."

Caledonia reached across and patted her hand soothingly. "There, there . . . It's been very unpleasant for you, of course. You just settle down and try this homemade tomato aspic . . . food is always good for you at a time like this. I ought to know. I was relatively thin before Herman died, and it was the shock of his death that finished off my last attempt to diet.''

"You've always been heavy, Caledonia," Angela said tartly, but with some of her old vigor. "Don't you try to pretend you just gained weight because you were feeling sad!"

"I know," Caledonia grinned. "But saying so made you sit up and take notice, now didn't it? Now eat something."

Angela sighed. "I'll try. Oh, Cal . . . he told me he had the plan done for my apartment, too. And he said that he'd see me soon. Oh, that poor young man. Mmmmm . . .'' She had just tried a forkful of the aspic, and her eyes lit up. She dipped the fork again. "Of course, shock or not, I must keep my strength up.''

Caledonia grinned. "You betcha," she said, piling into her own appetizer.

"Why do you suppose someone would want to kill that nice young man, Cal?" Angela mused. She reached out for a hot crescent roll.

"Atta girl—have some butter to go with it, and show that you're really being brave. I wonder if the shop was robbed . . .''

"We must ask . . . Oh! There he is!" Angela's chair was turned toward the dining room entrance, and she saw that Lieutenant Martinez had come hastily into the room. He walked directly to their table.

"Mrs. Benbow . . . Mrs. Wingate . . . I wonder if you'd spare me a moment after lunch? I'll be upstairs in your sewing room on the second floor. I don't know if you've heard the news . . .''

"About Bobby Baird? Oh yes we have. Sad, so sad . . .'' Angela shook her head dolefully.

Martinez did not smile as he said, "I should have realized that the jungle telegraph would operate at top speed. Well, if you'll just stop by to see us . . . we're working up there.''

It was not a question, but he raised his voice at the end of the sentence all the same.

"Of course we will, Lieutenant," Caledonia agreed, and Angela nodded. "Of course." And the Lieutenant walked as briskly out of the room as he had when he entered.

Chapter 10

WHEN ANGELA and Caledonia got to the second-floor sewing room, a woman neither of them knew was just coming out—an attractive woman in her late thirties or early forties, nicely dressed. She carried her head erect—"nose in the air," as Angela expressed it later—and looked neither left nor right as she walked off and took the main stairway to the lobby.

"She's not one of us," Caledonia commented as they entered the sewing room. "Not just because she didn't take the elevator like one of us would . . . but she's too young. Rules say you have to be sixty."

"Who was that?" Angela asked Martinez. She was nothing if not direct, when she wanted to be.

Martinez shrugged. Why try to keep this particular secret, after all, his expression said. "That was Mrs. Kaplan, the woman who found the late Bobby Baird this morning."

"Oh, of course. I see. But why hold your interviews here?"

"Mrs. Benbow, it's a very convenient location. Everybody in town knows this place by sight, and even a newcomer could find it with no trouble. So it's handy for us to ask people to call on us here."

"Speaking of which . . . You asked me here, but I don't think you really want me, Lieutenant," Caledonia put in. "It was Angela who had all the dealings with Baird, even the one time we went down to his shop together. I was just window dressing, so to speak. They did most of the talking."

"Oh, but I do want you here, Mrs. Wingate. You're a shrewd observer, and you might have seen something . . ."

"Like the umbrella stand," Angela said.

"What?"

"The umbrella stand, Lieutenant. We were all in the lobby talking about the murder. And Cal said she'd noticed an elephant's-foot umbrella stand, next to the office door, when she and I were down there at the shop. The walking stick was probably in the stand . . . or anyway, we thought so."

Martinez nodded. "That's right. We think it was. And that's the kind of thing . . . Mrs. Wingate, where exactly did it sit in relation to the door?"

Caledonia closed her eyes. "Let me think . . . the door opened inward toward the office, with the knob on my right as I stood in the shop looking toward the office. That means the umbrella stand was on my left . . . on the left of the door, Lieutenant."

Angela nodded emphatically. "Mr. Baird was right-handed, Lieutenant. I noticed it when he was taking notes around my place. Naturally, if he was placing an umbrella stand, and if he had a choice, he'd put it where his right hand would reach out to it easiest. So he put his umbrella stand to the right of his office door—so he could reach into it easily as he came out of his office."

Martinez smiled. "Very good, Mrs. Benbow. Of course, most of the things in that umbrella stand were rather obviously for sale. They weren't things he'd be reaching for every day. I mean, he didn't have his own umbrella in there. There were three or four silk parasols with carved ivory handles—very dainty, and quite old I'd say—maybe a dozen canes of different descriptions with different ornamentation . . . some with curlicue handles, some very plain, like . . . Well, you didn't either of you notice this one, I suppose?"

He pointed to the big table that ran the length of one end of the room, usually as a cutting table for patterns when the ladies sewed, now used as a worktable for the two detectives. On it, besides a couple of empty coffee cups, a supply of pencils, and Shorty's notes, there lay half a cane. Of beautifully worn and polished mahogany, it tapered gracefully to an irregularly scuffed brass tip, worn as well but polished so that it shone. In the wider end, there was a hole, a tunnel running down into the body of the stick.

"Oh." Angela shivered. "Is that—you know—*it*?"

Martinez nodded. "The murder weapon. Yes. At least, the bottom part."

"Where's the top?" Angela asked. "The part with the sword?"

"Oh, that's at the lab. They took fingerprints off this part, and I brought it along to see if it jogged anyone's memory."

"I'm sorry, Lieutenant, but I don't think I remember seeing it at the shop," Caledonia said. "Of course, the handle of a cane is the distinctive part. The bottom—well, it's just a cane."

"I agree," Angela said. "If it was in the umbrella stand, I certainly didn't notice."

"Well," he sighed, "it was just a thought. At least, Mrs. Wingate, you remembered where the umbrella stand was, and we do suppose that the stick was in it."

"Why do you need to know where it stood?" Caledonia was curious. "Had the stand been moved?"

"Knocked over. And it rolled some. We couldn't be sure . . . And it was to the left of the door as you face it, so perhaps that means the person who grabbed it and used it is left-handed. That's why I wanted to know."

Angela's imagination constructed the scene. In her mind's eye, a shadowy hand grabbed for the sword-cane—anger and haste made the hand clumsy—the hand pulled at the cane to free it from the tangle of sticks and parasols . . . the stand tottered . . . the hand yanked and jerked at the . . .

"Lieutenant," she said, "do you suppose whoever killed Bobby Baird didn't even know that was a sword-cane? I mean . . . there were all these canes and umbrella-handles all tangled up together, weren't there? Well, I was thinking, he might have just reached and grabbed hold of some weapon—*any* one, you see—and might have taken the first one that came out in his hand. And if that's so, then it was just luck—Baird's bad luck—that it was a sword-cane!''

''Hmmmm . . .'' Martinez walked over and picked up the stick. His own mind's eye seemed to be busy now. ''You may have something, ma'am. This stick is smooth, and the top, the part we still have, ends in a rounded knob, not like the rough carved canes and the ones with curved handles—they would all be tangled up with each other. The only one that would kind of pop into his hand easily, so to speak, would be a smooth, straight-line stick . . . like this one.''

''Yes, that's exactly what I was getting at,'' Angela said eagerly. ''I was thinking that the murderer might just have wanted to get Baird out of the way, you see. But then by accident, he got hold of a weapon he hadn't counted on—a sword. And he lashed out . . . a killing on impulse, you see?''

Martinez started to smile, then quickly hid his reactions by rubbing his silky moustache and looking earnestly at the ground, his head bobbing in what could be taken as agreement.

''Oh, I know you'll be able to tell more about it when you've looked at . . . when you've completed . . .'' Angela couldn't bring herself to refer directly to the autopsy, so she hedged: ''When you've looked into things a bit more. But I'd bet you anything you like that you'll agree it was just what I say—an impulse.''

The Lieutenant's head bowed cautiously again. ''I will tell you this much. We do know Baird was unconscious, or at least stunned, when he was stabbed.''

Angela nodded. ''I see. That's what you meant when you said he was stabbed after he was hit by the cane. That the blow came first.''

''I said that?''

Caledonia grinned in spite of their grisly topic. ''You spoke of our jungle telegraph, Lieutenant? Well, one of you mentioned this in the dining room—probably just to the other. But that's all it took. Everybody in the place knows about it, now. We're frightful gossips here.'' Martinez cocked an eyebrow. "Well," Caledonia went on, "we spend long, boring days here, waiting to die—"

"Cal! Don't say that!"

"—and we are delighted with anything to break the monotony," Caledonia finished, ignoring Angela's protest.

"Almost anything," Angela amended. "I admit we like to talk, and we like spectacular events . . . someone tripping and falling in the dining room, a fender-bender in the street outside . . . We adore being spectators of the unexpected. You can imagine the stir these murders are causing—even if this second one isn't really what you'd call 'ours.' "

"Well," the Lieutenant said, easing himself into a chair and gesturing them to sit down as well, "now I'm not at all sure about that, Mrs. Wingate. Not at all. What kind of odds would you say there are against a person's being murdered? Even an unpopular person like Mrs. Kinseth?"

"Why, I don't know . . ."

"Let me tell you, they're pretty high. The vast majority of people go through life and don't even *meet* someone who gets murdered, let alone getting murdered themselves. Now, how would you like to bet on two individuals—who actually knew one another—each getting murdered separately, by different murderers, for reasons that were totally unrelated?"

"Well, but . . ."

"Mrs. Benbow"—he turned toward her, because it was she who had made the quibbling noises—"if you like to bet on long shots, you go ahead and put your money on two separate murderers having killed Amy Kinseth and Bobby Baird for reasons that have absolutely nothing to do with each other. You'll lose your bet."

"But if there's a connection," Angela said, "what is it?"

"Now that, of course, we don't know yet. Maybe we never will. But that," he went one, gesturing to both of them, "is what you're doing here. Telling me everything about your contacts with Baird . . . because we never know when something—even something small—is going to be meaningful."

And so for upwards of half an hour they sat and went over all they could remember of Baird. Swanson took notes as rapidly as he could. A few times Martinez asked Angela and Caledonia to amplify or explain something, but nothing seemed to have special significance, though the women recalled minute details like the color of Baird's scarf, the embroidery on his jeans, the wallpaper on the walls of each little display corner at his shop, the way he held his pencil as he sketched, and the way his damp hair curled and clung to his forehead. . . . Angela misted up a little when she recalled that. "Such a *nice* young man," she sighed again.

At about the thirty-five-minute mark in their conference, the phone at the far end of the room rang loudly. Swanson unwound himself from his chair and answered it by the second ring. He listened more than he talked and when he hung up and came back, it was obvious he had something to tell his boss. He beckoned conspiratorially.

"Okay," Martinez said. "Ladies, if you'll excuse us a moment . . ." They walked together to the far end of the room, where Swanson whispered awhile, Martinez asked a question or two that Swanson answered briefly, and then they came back.

"I'm going to have to go to the shop, ladies. They have found something I should see. It seems that somebody not only killed Baird, but they took an axe to some of the furniture in the storeroom behind the main part of the shop. I don't know what I'll be able to tell from the splinters—that's what we've got a forensic team for—but I'd better take a look."

"Chopped up his furniture?" Angela marveled. "How mean! Just plain nasty!"

"Well," Martinez said, "that's what murder is. Mean and nasty."

Shorty added his bit: "Reinhart says there's white wood chips everywhere. Whoever did it took a knife to the upholstery, too, and between white kapok stuffing flying around, and blue wool cut up in strings, and everything—"

"Wait a minute," Angela said. "Blue and white . . . I bet that's Amy Kinseth's furniture."

Martinez, who had been heading for the door, turned

around and came back. "Kinseth's furniture? In Baird's shop?"

"Sure. He cleaned out her apartment yesterday. I was in the lobby talking to him about it. He said he hadn't been paid, and you said it was all right, and so did her lawyer . . ."

"That's right." Martinez nodded. "I told him he could move it. We'd looked it all over. We didn't need it any more. I just didn't realize he'd already . . . Listen, would you two know the stuff if you saw it?"

Angela jumped to her feet. "We certainly would, Lieutenant. When we were in there, we took a good look at everything, and . . ."

Caledonia rose quickly and managed to get one large hand onto Angela's little shoulder, exerting a fair amount of pressure. "I'm sure we could identify it, if the pieces that are left are big enough, that is."

Angela bit her lip, looked guilty, and said no more.

Caledonia went on. "We'd be glad to come with you, of course, and tell you if that's her furniture."

"Provided—" Angela interrupted, "I mean, if you've already moved him—I mean, if Mr. Baird isn't there . . ."

Martinez shook his head. "The body's been gone for some time now, Mrs. Benbow. Well, I'd be grateful if you would both come with us, then. Shorty, get the car around to the front entrance, will you? The ladies and I will just go down in the elevator." Shorty took off at a run.

Angela's eyes began to sparkle. "You mean, we're actually coming along officially? That we're—part of the team?"

Martinez bowed her out of the room ahead of him. "You can put it that way if you like, certainly. You saw Baird's shop before, as well as Mrs. Kinseth's things, and you'll not only identify the furniture, you'll be able to tell me if you spot anything else unusual or out of place."

Caledonia was, in her own way, equally excited. "Are we actually going to ride in your police car?"

"You surely are," he said, moving them smoothly aboard

the elevator and stepping in after them. "Just don't expect me to use the siren for your amusement."

As they moved across the lobby to the front entrance, a dozen pairs of eyes watched as the three of them swept out the front door and into the waiting police car. You could hear the hiss of indrawn breath, and after that the whispering. . . . "Did you see that . . ." "Well, I never . . ." "What on earth . . ."

Angela preened herself visibly. Despite the circumstances, she just couldn't help it; she was simply delighted to be the center of so much speculation. And Caledonia shared her pleasure, in her own way. "I only wish I'd thought in time," Caledonia said to Martinez with a huge grin. "I'd have had you put handcuffs on me and lead me out at gunpoint. Wouldn't that have had tongues wagging for a week! Then Angela and I would come in at suppertime, and we wouldn't even mention it. They'd have to come up and ask us, or we wouldn't even explain. They'd wriggle and twist with embarrassment. Let's see . . . who'd ask first? Would it be Mary Moffet? Probably."

"Cal," Angela reproved. "You'd cause at least a couple of heart attacks! Handcuffs indeed!" But privately, she was the tiniest bit jealous that she hadn't thought of it herself. That would have popped a few eyes wide open, for sure!

The car drew up in front of Baird's shop, and the women were escorted inside. They moved quickly past the office without entering, but both women saw the chalked outline on the floor, and a flashbulb went off—the forensics crew was still working. Angela and Caledonia were both very curious about the police work, but neither felt like going into the office and stepping over the outline of the body. Shorty was ahead of them, standing at the back of the shop, beyond the office, holding open a door in the back wall, and they hurried toward it. Martinez ushered the ladies through and into the storeroom behind the shop.

"Great heavens above," Caledonia gasped. Angela was silent with surprise.

Everywhere they looked there were loose threads, feathers,

and kapok. Whoever had cut up the upholstery had beaten the cushions until they gave up their contents, then discarded the shredded covers, leaving the filling floating through the air and mounding up on crates and in corners like drifts piling up against a snow fence in a North Dakota blizzard. Clearly visible despite the little mounds of tattered cloth, shredded leather, and various stuffings were splintered boards of various sizes.

"Boy, oh boy, was somebody *mad*," Swanson breathed, awestruck. "I guess we should have come back here right away. We really missed something when we didn't find this! *Gosh!*"

Martinez shook his head. "Well, it waited here for us to find it . . . and now we're here. Better late than never. You're right—it's a mess! Well, ladies?" he turned to them. "Does anything look even vaguely familiar about these—these scraps?"

"Oh yes," Caledonia said. "I see a piece of the molding off her lingerie chest—over there with those boards and splinters. And I recognize the couch from her place, and that chair . . . And I can make out what the upholstery pattern was on this . . ." she lifted with two fingers the shreds of a seat cushion. "It was Kinseth's stuff all right."

"Isn't it strange," Angela said, shaking her head slowly. "Isn't it strange that the couch and the chairs aren't damaged?"

"Aren't damaged!" Caledonia snorted. "I'd hate to try to sit on one of them. It's—it's—" She waved at the curved blond wooden back of the couch frame. "It's like the bones of a beached whale! And about as comfortable now, I'd say, with all the cushions gone."

"Wait," Martinez said. "You're absolutely right. The 'skeletons' of the couches and chairs certainly are intact. The upholstery's been torn up, but the frames aren't damaged. He took an axe to . . ."—he waved a hand—"only to the case furniture. Like that."

"Yes. To her desk . . . to the dressers . . . to the bedside table . . ."

Caledonia looked carefully. "You're right. Anything with drawers and solid sides. But stuff with only a bare frame he left alone."

"He wasn't venting his rage, ladies," Martinez said, nodding in a satisfied way. "This man was looking for something! I'm remembering the torn linings in the suitcases in the basement."

"Oh," Angela breathed. "Of course. The insides—the linings were ripped out! I remember I thought at the time, she could be involved in smuggling. You know, I saw this movie last week . . . They smuggled stolen paintings into the country hidden in secret compartments in their luggage. Well, that's a logical thing to be hidden in that luggage. I mean, it would have to be something sort of flattish—I mean, something that wouldn't be more than an inch or so thick, so you could put it maybe behind a sheet of cardboard and stick the lining down to the cardboard. Nobody would really notice the case was shallower than it should be. In the movie, they used to make a trip to Europe every . . ."

Martinez nodded. "Shorty!"

"Sir?"

"Get the crew in here right away. Have them go over this stuff with a magnifying glass. Find anything that's stuck to it—any packing material, any dust or powder, any fibers, any hairs, human or otherwise—*anything*. And I want to know about it fast."

"Lieutenant, if it was smuggling—well, would you find any traces of—of whatever it was? Of course, if it was drugs, you might find . . . well, something like a white powder, right?"

"I really doubt, Mrs. Benbow, that it was the smuggling of stolen art or of drugs. I could be wrong. But where, for example, would your Mrs. Kinseth get hold of them? She hadn't been out of the country for years—we checked. It's not impossible, of course. There were those two innocent-looking suburban housewives, just a few years ago, who made a fortune running drugs into the country."

At that moment, Swanson came back with two of the crew,

who carried with them various bags and boxes of equipment, or so Angela and Caledonia presumed, since they were not in a position to find out for sure what the men were carrying. Martinez eased them from the storeroom so smoothly they hardly had time to protest. Before they knew it he had them in his car, heading up the little hill toward the old hotel.

"Lieutenant," Angela protested, "we really deserve to know what you find, don't you think? I mean . . . we did think of the smuggling."

"I told you, Mrs. Benbow, that smuggling is highly unlikely."

"But not impossible," Angela said hopefully, reluctant to give up on her first and most glamorous guess. "So we want to hear about this. I think you owe it to us."

Martinez nodded. "All right, I'll make you one promise. You'll hear about it from me personally before the newspapers get it, if possible, and certainly before I tell anybody else—any other civilian, I mean. I have to tell my boss, of course," he corrected himself. "But I'm not going to do what you'd like me to. You'd like it if I reported to you periodically to tell you how I'm getting along. And you know I'm not going to do that."

Angela pulled herself upright into what the Admiral always called her "attack position" and opened her mouth to speak, but Martinez stopped her by bringing out a folded paper from his inside coat pocket and handing it across to her. "Let me leave you with this," he said.

"What is it?"

"Baird's plan for redecorating your apartment. I thought you'd be interested," he said. "We found it earlier today— on Baird's desk at the shop. It was in a folder marked with your name, so I was curious and I read it. And then as soon as I was sure there was nothing about it that could remotely be connected with his murder, I brought it along for you."

"Why, thank you, Lieutenant." Angela was surprised and rather pleased. "That's very nice of you, really it is."

"I'd have given it to you earlier," he apologized, "but

with everything else, I just forgot. Well, we'll undoubtedly see you later . . ."

And the two ladies stood watching as the police car, still without flashing lights or wailing sirens, moved off in the direction of Baird's shop.

"Come on, girl," Caledonia said. "Let's go to my place and take a look at the decorating scheme he's drawn up. Maybe you'll be glad, after you do, that someone disposed of him!"

"Cal, that's an awful thing to say! Oh, good afternoon, Mr. Grogan," Angela called, as Grogan oozed around a corner, his chin sunk down onto his chest, his eyes peering up from under his brows over the deepening bags that puffed out his lower lids. "How are you feeling today, Mr. Grogan?"

"Mmmmph," he groaned. "Like death—and not even death warmed over!"

"Another hangover?" Caledonia asked.

"No such thing. Just the opposite. I'm bone dry—have been ever since you ladies gave me that talking to."

"Oh, Mr. Grogan. How marvelous!"

"Marvelous is not the word I'd be using, Mrs. Benbow. Stupid . . . pigheaded maybe . . . ill-considered surely . . . But I decided, you see, that you had a point. And I decided to give sobriety a try."

"Mr. Grogan," Caledonia boomed, "I congratulate you."

"Stow it," he snarled. "Sorry, Mrs. Wingate, but I've never been so sick and so unhappy in all me mortal days! Man wasn't meant to look at life without something to draw a veil between him and reality. Trust me, Mrs. Wingate, I have never needed a drink so badly in all my life! But I promised . . ."

"You promised *us*, Mr. Grogan," Angela caroled.

"No!" he barked. "Myself! I promised myself. And that's even more important. If a man can't keep his word to himself, what the hell good is he!"

"There's no need to be rude," Angela said. "No need to curse!"

"Who's cursing! I'm just damn well saying what I think, that's all. Now let me pass in my misery. You don't know what you've done to me. You just don't know," and he hunched even further down between his shoulders, shoving one hand, doubled into a fist, into his jacket pocket. The other clutched his cane, which he swung in a wide arc like a scythe, slashing right and left as he shuffled off down the walk—though whether he intended to make a therapeutic circuit of the building or to hunt down and decapitate a few flowers, it was hard to say.

Back in Caledonia's apartment, the ladies sat down over a small sherry. It was a half hour early, but as Caledonia pointed out, they had earned a little leeway in time for their evening relaxation: they had both suffered a shock over the news of Baird's death, they had traveled to Baird's shop to help the police, they had suffered the rudeness of a recovering and cold-sober Grogan—it was time for a thimbleful of liquid fire to warm the inner woman.

"Now," Caledonia said, settling herself on the end of the couch closest to Angela's chair. "I shouldn't speak ill of the dead, but I'm not the type who appreciates interior decorators. I regard them with deep suspicion. So before you open that paper—let me guess Baird's great plan for your apartment. Let's see—I'm going to bet he'd decided to turn your place into a Moorish harem, complete with wrought iron at the windows, satin cushions on the floor, and swinging bead curtains."

Angela did not grace the whimsy with a reply. Instead, she opened the folded sheet of paper. It was not a long note—typewritten paragraphs with a handwritten signature—and as she read them, her eyes filled with tears. "Oh, Caledonia. Listen," she said with a tiny snuffle. "Listen to this . . ."

The report was in the form of a letter. It ran:

Dear Mrs. Benbow:

You have excellent taste, such beautiful furnishings, and the arrangement of your things suits you very well as it is.

Please forgive me, but I'm going to make only one recommendation. If I were you, I'd hire some painters to redo those cream walls—make them bright white to lighten your place up a little. But other than that, well, you've been your own decorator and you've done the job to perfection. I would change absolutely nothing else.

Incidentally, there'll be no fee for this advice.

Affectionately,
Bobby

"Oh, Cal," Angela sighed. "That *nice* young man!"

Chapter 11

O<small>N THE</small> following day, Grogan stopped by Angela's table at lunch, his face etched with the same lines of misery and puzzled despair that one can see in the eyes of a cocker spaniel locked inside the family car to wait while its humans have gone shopping. You can read in those eyes the pain of abandonment. The dog, Fluffy, can remember the past, but he lives in the present because he has no imagination. And because he cannot imagine the future, there is no future (so far as he knows).

And what one could read on Grogan's face was like Fluffy's stoic perception of an empty present, Fluffy's inability to see beyond the aching sense that this is all there is to life. Life is the here and now—and the here and now *stinks!*

"I want to apologize, Mrs. Benbow. I think I was rude to you yesterday. I felt pretty bad and I spoke before I thought. I know you meant well, and I—I'm sorry."

Angela chose to be gracious. "No problem, Mr. Grogan, no problem. You might take time to say the same to Caledonia when she comes, of course. She'll be here directly, no doubt. She'd appreciate the apology. You were pretty rough, you know."

Grogan hunched his shoulders, and his expression of abasement and sorrow deepened. "Oh, I know what I'm like when I'm feeling mean, Mrs. B. I guess I'm just no good, and that's the truth. No good at all. I shall try to watch my tongue in the future—*what the bloody hell!*"

"Mr. Grogan! Your language!" But Angela's reaction was

152

automatic. She was as startled as Grogan was. Their ears had been blasted by the high-pitched electronic squeal of the public address system coming to life.

Trinita Stainsbury was at it again, standing by the amplifier equipment waiting for the assembled diners to quiet down and listen to her latest bit of wonderful news. Today her entire outfit was bright rose, matching the frames on her new glasses and the new dye she'd had applied to her silvery hair. She swung the microphone loosely in one hand, smiling patiently.

Angela turned to Grogan again, but he had stumped off, muttering terrible things under his breath and slamming out of the double entrance doors by pushing one open with his elbow, both hands being occupied with stopping up his ears against the sound of the loudspeakers. "Can't use a gawdam mike, shouldn't be allowed to have one. Silly-ass female with her silly-ass puce hair talking about her silly-ass programs . . ."

Fortunately, almost nobody understood a word he said, so universally sub-par was the hearing of the residents. Even Angela, who had been closest to him as the tirade began, had not caught more than half of the first phrase as he had whirled away from her and started for the door at once, trying to escape before the Stainsbury Pronouncement began.

"Ladies and gentlemen, they're supposed to have this system fixed (*WHEEK*)—I'll try to get through my notes in a hurry before it decides to (*SQUEAL*) act up too badly. The third grade from Camden Elementary School (*SNAP-SCRAPE-POP*) will be here in the lobby this afternoon to entertain us. These darling children have a musical program and some guessing games, and they want us to join them (*SHRIEK*). I'm sure you'll enjoy spending forty-five minutes of song . . ."

"I'd rather be rolled in Shake-and-Bake and put into a moderate oven for the same length of time!"

Angela turned around in her chair toward Caledonia's baritone growl. Her friend had entered while Angela was looking over one shoulder at Trinita. The public address system roared with sound again, and Angela turned her back on Caledonia once more, to catch the last of Trinita Stainsbury's words.

". . . and the one with the funniest hat will win a prize," Trinita was warbling cheerfully. "So use your imagination, ladies—create, create, create! (*CRACKLE*) And may the best hat win." She laughed cheerily at her own wit, and Angela was reminded strongly of a TV quiz master. "Now, let us bow our heads for a word of grace. Father, thou art ever with me . . ."

"Oh, great! I got here just in time for the public 'Holier-Than-Thou Hour'!" Caledonia complained. But she bowed her head dutifully. She might feel that prayer was a private matter between herself and her God, and she might claim that public opinion didn't bother her, and she might be brave in the face of all kinds of dangers—but she had never dared to refuse to bow her head in a prescribed grace before the meal.

Angela saw nothing at all unusual about public prayer, having spent many years of her married life in the South when her husband Douglas was stationed at Pensacola, at Charleston, and at Newport News. She grew quite used to being asked to pray in public at all sorts of occasions—college football games, the opening of the State Employees' picnic, the dedication of a new bridge, the premier showing at a drive-in movie theater. All the same, Angela objected to what she called Trinita Stainsbury's "smarmy familiarity with the Deity."

"She acts like she could talk directly to Him on a first-name basis," Angela had said privately to Caledonia once, "and when He finally meets me, He'll have to call me 'Mrs. Benbow,' because we're not really well acquainted! She acts as though I'll be kneeling before the throne—and she'll be sitting at a steno table up on the dais taking minutes for Him, fetching Him coffee, and calling Him by His initials! 'A little cream with that, J.C.?' " Angela could do an almost perfect imitation of Trinita's slightly lisping, high-pitched voice.

"Well," Caledonia said, reaching for the basket where

she spied some fresh-baked, crusty French bread, "at least we have one thing to be thankful for—no more Elroy Carmichael this week."

It was really amazing how many times within a two-day span Caledonia's pronouncements had been wrong, for the very next day, Elroy was indeed the program. Trinita announced him with the same bubbly pleasure in her tone that she had used for the third-graders' choir and the hat contest. In fact, Trinita used the same affected enthusiasm throughout the year to announce all the programs the committee secured for the residents' diversion—the tap-dancing dog; the sisters who played the musical saw and the Jew's harp; the man who folded paper hats and whistled "O Solo Mio"; the three-evening festival of William Lundigan movies; and the ten-year-old magician. The latter had at least stirred interest among the residents when he dropped and broke the watch he borrowed before he could make it "disappear," and when he tossed an egg into an expensive, pearl gray fedora. The egg was supposed to turn into a live chicken but it broke instead, leaving the lining of the hat soaked and slimy. The residents in the audience were numb with dismay until they learned that both the watch and the hat were loaned for the show by Torgeson, whose nephew the young magician had been. The opinion throughout Camden the next day was that the magician had been one of their more satisfying entertainments.

"I really don't think I can sit through Elroy today," Caledonia said to Angela, over a lunch of tiny lamb chops. "Pass the mint sauce, will you? No, I think I'll skip over Elroy."

"I don't think I can sit through any program, Cal," Angela said. "I just feel so—frustrated, somehow. This whole business is on my mind constantly, and I feel as though there's something I should understand about it—but it keeps hiding from me."

Caledonia speared a tiny new potato. "Maybe if we talked about it . . ."

"Yes, please," Angela said. "When I talk to the Lieutenant, I'm always thinking about what *not* to say. Like—I don't want him scolding us for going into Amy's apartment to search.''

"Now, he's not that bad . . . he didn't scold you for going into the basement to hunt through her things, did he? I thought he'd give you 'what for' because you hadn't just gone and fetched him to do the searching. But he complimented you for finding those things . . .''

"Are you going to have dessert, Cal?''

"What kind of question is that? I love prune whip, and we almost never have it . . .''

"Well, I just thought we could get started.''

Caledonia sighed. "Tell you what . . . I'll take my dish and a spoon along with me, and we can go to your room and talk awhile. Later, when I go back to my own place, I'll drop off the empty dish in the dining room on my way.''

"They don't like you to take dishes away.''

"I'm not hurting anything. Here, wait—'' Angela had jumped up from her place and started out. "Come back. Aren't you going to take any dessert along?''

Angela shook her head. "I don't mind if you do, but I'm not that crazy about prune whip.''

"Then take a dish for me, girl. Don't be so thoughtless. Just pick up your dish . . .''

Thus it was that Caledonia sat, back at Angela's apartment, soulfully spooning prune whip into her mouth, while Angela paced and talked.

"Now, let me think. When she first moved in, I thought Amy Kinseth was going to be a good addition here. But you had that funny run-in with her about bridge. Did you ever find out who she was meeting on Beach Lane, by the way?''

"Never did. Boy, this is good. Angela, are you absolutely sure you don't want yours? Because I'm ready to start on my second dish, if you don't stop me . . . once I start, it's going to be too late.''

Angela crossed the room to her tiny desk and pulled out several sheets of paper and a pen. She folded the paper double, to make a pad about the size of a stenographer's notebook, and started making notes on her first page. "Okay, that's the first question we need answered. Whom did she meet on Beach Lane?''

"It may not be important. And she may not have met anybody at all . . . she may just have wanted an excuse to get out of the bridge game, you know.''

"Of course. But we ought to try to find out.''

Caledonia shrugged. "I don't see how we can.''

Angela sat down near a little table, which she could use as a writing surface. "What was next, now? Her fight with Baird?''

"Yes, I suppose so. No, wait—first came her accusations against Lola.''

"Right. We ought to talk to Lola, I think. That was a mighty strange business.'' Angela wrote busily. "Then there was the fight with Baird and the redecoration of her apartment . . .''

Caledonia scraped up the last bit of prune whip and stared regretfully at her half-filled spoon. "Well, it doesn't sound like much to me.'' She slid the spoon into her mouth and savored. "Mmmmm . . . this is great stuff! How does Mrs. Schmitt do it, day after day? I never cooked this well on my best day!''

Angela ignored her. "And the furniture all chopped up . . . we must ask the Lieutenant about that, I suppose. They'll know if anything was found. I still think it was stolen art or drug smuggling.''

Caledonia snorted. "I agree with the Lieutenant. That's not very likely. I mean, a drug smuggler in a retirement home?''

Angela tossed her head the way Scarlett O'Hara did the time she wore the green velvet drape, remade into a smart gown, to try to talk Rhett Butler into giving her the money to save Tara. Angela and Scarlett could be equally determined. "Well, you notice he didn't throw the idea out completely. And you know perfectly well we've had some mighty strange people in this place over the years. Cal, you talk just like a teenager . . . as though all old people were sweet little grannies, as though as soon as their hair turned white, they turned into angels no matter what they were like when they were young. Look around you at the people you know . . .''

Caledonia nodded. There was really no reason at all that a sweet-faced gentle old man might not have been a member of the maquis in his youth, or that a lady who now did nothing more violent than set her bridge opponents two tricks might not once have hunted big game in Africa and still be a crack shot.

''You know, you might have something, Angela,'' Caledonia said. ''Nobody would ever suspect a little old lady in a retirement home—of *anything*! People suppose that if you *look* old and gentle and harmless, you *are* old and gentle and harmless. We know better, don't we?'' She laughed out loud. ''Well, one thing's for sure, nobody is ever going to imagine you and I are like that. Old, sure. Gentle and harmless? Not in a million years.''

''I wonder if that lipstick Lola had was stolen goods?''

''What?''

''I'm back at Lola and the lipstick again, Cal. Look—suppose, just suppose, that Mrs. Kinseth told Lola to take a lipstick, and Lola took the wrong one. Suppose that expensive case was part of some smuggled goods and Mrs. Kinseth was trying to get it back before Lola showed it to anyone. Suppose . . .''

''Oh, I don't know, Angela. If you were trying to hide the fact that you had smuggled something into the country, would you raise such an almighty fuss about it that everybody noticed it? All that commotion just called attention to the lipstick! Besides, since when do people smuggle lipsticks into the country?''

''Well, why don't we just talk to Lola?'' Angela suggested.

''Okay,'' Caledonia said. ''I think she's working in the wheelchair wing today. I thought I saw her going in there about the time we were leaving the dining room. Tell you what—I'll go get her and I'll leave these dessert dishes in the dining room on my way.'' She headed for the door with her caftan, a rich brocade of several shades of green and gold, belling out behind her.

Angela's apartment was the first on the hall, directly up from the lobby. As Caledonia came down the four little steps, she could hear Elroy Carmichael's voice raised in eloquent recitation.

"I call this one, 'Alone, Without My Love,' " Elroy was saying. He began to pace dramatically, one hand held to his forehead as though it ached.

"O grim-looked night, O night with hue so black,
O night which ever art when day is not,
O night, O night, alack . . .
I fear her promise is forgot!"

"Oh night, oh cripes!" Caledonia muttered to herself, trying not to attract attention as she hurried past the attentive and apparently appreciative audience. She found Lola scrubbing a bathroom floor in one of the apartments in the wheelchair wing. "Sure, Mrs. Wingate. I'll come with you. Glad to take a break from this." Lola gestured with her brush to the spotless white tile. "I was done here anyway."

On the return trip, Caledonia steered away from the lobby and through a backdoor route via the garden, in order to reach Angela's apartment without having to navigate the crowd or listen to more Elroy. It had also occurred to her that someone might ask awkward questions about her bringing Lola along with her. Caledonia was not a secretive person, but there was no point in being too obvious about their investigations, as she told Angela later. "You never know . . . We haven't any idea who killed Amy, do we? And we don't want them knowing we're on the trail . . . so to speak."

As it was, they got to Angela's place without anyone's noticing them. "Do sit down, Lola," Caledonia said, when they had finally closed the door behind them. "Mrs. Benbow wants to ask again about Amy Kinseth."

"I'd rather stand," Lola said.

"As you wish," Angela said. "Now, we know you've told the police over and over about that lipstick . . ."

"Oh, yes, Mrs. Benbow. I sure have."

"And we hate to ask you again—but would you tell us this time? You see," she hurried on, "we know you and they don't. They might think you took something but we know you wouldn't. So we wanted to hear about it from you—not secondhand—and see if we could think of something that would clear you of suspicion."

Tears appeared in Lola's eyes and her pudgy hands began to twist together. "I said it all before . . . she liked my cleaning. You know I always try to clean good," she appealed.

"Of course you do," Caledonia soothed. "You're the best there is. I've always said so."

"Thank you, Mrs. Wingate. And Mrs. Kinseth said I was good, too. I was on my hands and knees with a damp cloth that day, trying to get up some dust from the baseboard. She come into the bedroom and saw me and said something like I worked too hard and why didn't I call that enough. She said I could dust next week, when it was 'big cleaning' day. You know I move the furniture out and get behind it and under it good on 'big cleaning' day . . ."

"Yes, we know," Angela said. "You do a marvelous job." She was straining to understand, for Lola was talking faster and faster, words tumbling out, and though all her English was idiomatic, her pronunciations and her speech rhythms were completely Hispanic. The faster she talked, the more words blended together, and Angela's hearing was not the best. "Slow down, my dear. Take a deep breath. And go on."

Lola inhaled deeply in obedience, and then the words tumbled out again. "I got my bucket and my cleaning rag and my extra roll of toilet paper—you know she used her own brand, but I carried one of ours in, just in case—and I was almost at the door going out when she come after me with that lipstick in her hand. She said something like 'I wonder if you'd like to have this? I don't use it, but it's real pretty. Please take it as a gift.' Something like that. I was happy

. . . you know, once in a while a lady gives me a present, even though they're not supposed to.''

Torgeson had instituted a ''no tipping'' policy as his first order of business when taking over as administrator at Camden, so that all residents would get equal service. He feared that those with more money to tip might get special attention, and that worse, those who never tipped might be neglected. So no tips at all were to be allowed. Just the same, a few of the residents still gave presents for special kindness . . . and the recipients simply said nothing and hoped Torgeson never found out.

''Did she tell you why? I mean, was there a special reason for the gift?'' Angela asked. It all seemed rather odd to her.

Lola shook her head. ''Not really. She said she was sorry she yelled at me about the dusting. But I didn't think she yelled. She just seemed—you know—in a hurry for me to finish and get out of her apartment.''

''Did she say why she wanted you out?'' Angela asked.

Lola shrugged. ''Lots of times, toward the end of my cleaning, I get hustled out. Ladies don't like to go to their bathrooms while I'm in the apartment sometimes, you know. Modest, like. I suppose it was like that. Anyway . . . now Mr. Torgeson, he doesn't believe she gave that lipstick to me. He thinks I stole it. I know he does.''

''Oh, nonsense. Besides, who cares what he thinks? He's not going to fire you, is he?''

''No,'' Lola sniffed, wiping her eyes. ''But he changed my workstation to the first two cottages and the wheelchair wing.''

''And I'm delighted, personally,'' Caledonia said heartily. ''I loved it when you were there before. We got much better service. Nothing against Benjamina . . . she's all right . . . but she's not like you, Lola. I'm glad he changed you over.''

Lola beamed. ''I like working for you, Mrs. Wingate. You're always so nice to me.''

Angela was a bit disappointed with the interview so far. There seemed to be no rhyme or reason to the incident. ''Tell me once more, Lola. Did you see anything unusual in the apartment that day?''

"No ma'am."

"Anything laid out on a table or the desk?'' Lola shook her head. "Anything in one of the wastebaskets?''

"Well, no. I emptied them into my plastic trash bag as soon as I come in. I didn't look at what I was taking out . . . I just took it out!''

"Did you do anything you don't usually do?''

Lola closed her eyes. "Let's see. I come in through the living room door and went straight to the desk and emptied that wastebasket into my trash bag. Then I went into the bedroom and took that wastebasket. It was standing by the skinny dresser . . .''

"The lingerie chest near the bathroom door?''

"Yes. That one. And when I bent over to put the basket back, I saw the baseboard behind the chest was kind of dusty-like. So after I put the new linen on the bed, and after I cleaned the bathroom up, I took a cloth, wet it and wrung it out good, and went back to get up that dust. And that's when she told me I could leave. That's all that happened.''

"I see. Well, there's nothing unusual about all of that, really, is there?'' Caledonia moved again toward the door.

"Lola, we certainly thank you,'' Angela said graciously. "I can't see that we've learned much that's new, but you were nice to come and talk to us.''

Lola smiled, and her pudgy cheeks showed deep dimples. "I don't mind. I got all my work done, and if I take a minute for myself, it serves Mr. Torgeson right!'' She moved out and closed the door behind her.

"Well! That was interesting,'' Angela said. "I wonder if Lieutenant Martinez knows about the dusting of the *seman-ier*.''

"What on earth does it matter? Dust is dust, isn't it? Besides, she says she didn't dust the chest itself.''

"Yes, but she was near it when she was suddenly asked to leave. You see? There's something about that chest—'' Angela jumped up. "I'm going to see the Lieutenant right now.''

She darted for the door, and Caledonia lumbered behind her. There was a side stairway to the second floor near her apartment door, and Angela shot up the steps—or rather, she moved up rapidly. (The day was gone when she could actually "shoot" anywhere, especially if it involved bending her knees, which, she hated to confess, gave her trouble from time to time now.) Taking the elevator, Caledonia arrived a good minute and a half behind her small friend who was pacing impatiently back and forth in the hall waiting for her.

Martinez was not in the second-floor sewing room but Swanson was. He had piles of paper laid out and was adding to them from his little loose-leaf notebook. One page on the first stack . . . another added to the third stack . . . back to the second . . . He was putting notes out according to the person or persons interviewed, rather than according to dates. He looked up when the women came in, and grinned. "Ladies?"

"The Lieutenant's not here?" Angela puffed.

"No, he's off doing his thing. At the decorator's shop, I think. Can I help or take a message?"

Angela sat down on a little chair near him, rather dispiritedly. It was disappointing to come full of news and inquiry, only to meet a complete blank. Then she brightened up. On the other hand, she was thinking, maybe Swanson would tell her more than Martinez would. She bent over toward him at a confidential angle. "We were talking to Lola today—just casually, you know . . ." She didn't want to confess to their deliberate interviewing of the maid. "She mentioned that when she had that argument with Amy Kinseth, it was after she was dusting near that little lingerie chest. Did you know about that?"

"No, she didn't tell us about that. She did say she stopped to dust—that's all. She didn't say where."

"But, you do know there was something unusual about that chest, don't you?"

Swanson cocked his head. "Gosh, Mrs. Benbow, I'm surprised you could see that. It took the guys in forensics all day to find out."

"Find out what?" Caledonia asked.

"Well, you see, when they put all the splinters from the busted furniture back together again, the only thing they had real trouble reconstructing was that little chest. But they finally figured it out." He hitched his chair toward the women and leaned forward. This was information he felt free to share, since Mrs. Benbow had already guessed part of it, he savored his moment on center stage. "They finally figured out the thing had been partly rebuilt. It had two false drawers."

"False drawers?"

"Well, anyhow, false bottoms in two drawers. Kind of crude—just a panel, cut to size and laid into slots cut on the inside. You could take the drawer out and tip the front forward, and there it was . . . a space the size of the drawer and about an inch high. It was really rigged up pretty good, for a homemade carpentry job. It wasn't smooth, but you'd hardly notice."

"We thought somebody had done something to it," Angela said triumphantly. "It was that awful paint job, all drips and blobs . . ."

Shorty smiled. "I used to do that when I was a kid—I'd mess up something I was building in the shop, and then slap thick paint on it and figure nobody'd notice!"

Caledonia nodded. "See if this figures. Amy found Lola fooling around near the chest, bent over close by those drawers with the false bottoms."

"She got excited, thinking Lola might see something, and started yelling," Angela went on. "And she started to hustle Lola out of the apartment fast, before Lola noticed something she shouldn't! But then Amy must have got to thinking Lola would remember a bawling-out—maybe talk about it to the other maids—and it would seem odd. So she gave Lola an apology and the gift of that lipstick."

"Right!" Caledonia said. "But then Amy went back and thought about it some more, and she probably decided that wasn't good enough either. She had to discredit Lola, in case she talked about it! So she accused Lola of stealing the lipstick.''

''I think we've got something, ladies,'' Swanson said cheerfully. ''Listen, I'm real proud of you, and the Lieutenant will be too. That was great . . . and if it's true, it fills in a blank in what the Lieutenant's been able to work out.''

''I'll tell you something else I think,'' Caledonia said. ''I think Amy chose her decorating schemes to fit that white chest. Then she could hang on to it without anybody commenting that it looked out of place.''

''I still can't figure out why she kept that horrid, badly done paint job, though,'' Angela said with distaste. ''She could have had the thing done over in a nice finish—and it would have blended better with the other furniture. As it was, it stuck out like a sore thumb, the very thing she wanted to avoid.''

Caledonia laughed. ''Listen, dearie. I don't think she probably ever saw either the globby paint or the badly fitting drawers. Most of us here have eyesight so bad we can't see things like that. I bet she never even noticed. If she had, she might have thrown the thing away and found some other place to store her—whatever her secrets were. She wasn't the type to keep a lumpy little chest of drawers for sentimental reasons. So I just plain don't think she knew how bad it looked. You and I are just lucky we've got good enough vision to have seen it for ourselves!''

Angela beamed. ''Well, I was right about smuggling, wasn't I? Drugs, right? Or paintings? What else would you want to hide that you could fit into a little space like that?''

Caledonia shook her head. ''It certainly wouldn't hold a stolen *Mona Lisa* or a *Laughing Cavalier*. It was only an inch or two deep, you said.'' Swanson nodded in agreement.

''But it would hold stolen drugs—or stolen diamonds,'' Angela insisted.

''Or secret documents . . . there are such things as spies,'' Caledonia said. ''My vote is for spies.''

''I vote for the drugs,'' Angela said firmly. ''That's the 'in' thing these days to make a fortune with, isn't it?''

Swanson held up his hand. "Let's see what the Lieutenant says, all right? Ladies, if you'll excuse me, I'm going to try to find him and pass this along." He rose and moved down the room to the telephone.

"Come on, Angela, it's teatime," Caledonia rumbled, gathering her green brocade tent about her. "And that means sherry, for me. You coming to my place?"

"Why not to mine today, Cal?" Angela said. Her sense of well-being was almost overwhelming. What a good day's work they had done!

"Because you'd serve that dreadful sweet cream sherry, girl," Caledonia growled, deflating Angela's sense of superiority with a single pinprick. "You simply have no taste when it comes to potables. Come into my place and we'll have a tiny sip of something worth sipping. See you later, Detective Swanson . . ."

Shorty, busy talking on the telephone, only waved as the two made their way out of the room and toward the elevator in the lengthening shadows of late afternoon.

Chapter 12

LIEUTENANT MARTINEZ came to Caledonia's cottage while Angela was still there.

"Join us for a sherry?" Caledonia asked.

He nodded. "You should know I can't say no to your good amontillado. I waited to come here till working hours were officially over—assuming I ever work just an eight-hour day— so I'd be able to say a hearty yes to your invitation."

Caledonia beamed. "Good taste, young man. You've got good taste."

Angela, who enjoyed the amontillado very much herself, was still pouting a bit over yet another dig at her beloved cream sherry. But for once she said nothing.

When he held a glass full of the lovely topaz liquid and inhaled its fragrance and tasted it gently, Martinez sighed. "It's been a busy day, ladies. You've given me a lot to do. I want to thank you for the information about Lola and your reasoning about the little chest of drawers. I think that is probably the explanation of that business with the lipstick. After we talked to her, we couldn't believe she'd stolen it. Frankly, I'm relieved to have that loose end tied up. You two have come up with some good ideas and we've been looking into them."

"Diamond smuggling?"

"Spies and secret papers?"

"Well, I won't say we haven't looked at those possibilities, but they seem highly unlikely to me. And we're looking in another direction now, after our lab men picked up a—a little

167

piece of something—lying among those wood splinters from the lingerie chest.''

"Ooooh," Angela was disappointed about her drug theory, but excited about the possibility of new information. "What, Lieutenant? What was it?"

He sipped and said nothing for a moment, considering. But he had come with a mission and he apparently decided that his impulse to share information was essentially a sound one. "Well, I'll tell you, but only if you agree to a bargain."

"A bargain, Lieutenant?" Caledonia said, levering her bulk upright to a standing position, and rolling across to get the sherry bottle and go around with refills. "Will you settle for more sherry for my half of the deal?"

"Mrs. Wingate, I'm very serious about this. I'm going to ask you to leave this business alone, as of right now."

"But—" Caledonia was dismayed.

"No!" Angela was angered.

"Yes!" Martinez sat back and gazed at his sherry a moment before he said, "I didn't come here officially, you know—I wouldn't be drinking and socializing if I had. I've come as your friend. Because I like you two very much. And I think I should have earned your confidence by now. So that when I tell you it's time you stop playing detective, I want you to trust me. I'm willing to give you an earnest of my sincerity. I'll let you in on a secret you must not—*must not*—share with anyone else. Mustn't even breathe a hint of!"

Caledonia sat back down on her love seat and settled herself to listen. Angela hitched herself forward in her chair. He leaned toward them. "What we found among the splinters of that chest were little shards of dark amber glass."

"Glass?" Angela said, her face falling. "But . . . That's disappointing. I thought it would be . . . I don't know what. But glass. Colored glass?"

"Wait a minute. *Amber* glass?" Caledonia wondered. "That's a bit unusual."

Martinez smiled and sipped his sherry. "It took us a while to find out what it was . . ."

Angela's interest revived a little. "That's true. I suppose

it really isn't all that ordinary. Well, what can it have been? Sun glasses? A camera lens filter?''

Caledonia's patience had run out. "Lieutenant, we're stumped. Obviously you know what it was—so now tell us.''

"The lab men think the bits of glass are the remains of a couple of bottles—small ones—like the kind pharmacists use to store pills. There are traces of plastic, too, that might well have been a bottle cap. The bottles had been smashed to pieces and all mixed up with the splinters of wood—but we were able to put enough together to work out what they'd been.''

"Drugs!" Angela's eyes were shining. "Drugs, after all!''

He nodded. "Maybe. But there were remains from only two bottles—not much of a drug-smuggling operation, would you say? So perhaps they were just her own prescription materials. She may have stored them in that chest.''

"Oh no," Caledonia said. "She didn't." And she stopped abruptly as Angela's foot pinched down on top of her toes. "I mean . . . that isn't a likely place, is it, when you have a big bathroom cabinet?''

"Maybe for security?" Martinez said, ignoring for the moment her obvious cover-up of some concealed truth. It really didn't matter what she had done, provided that she now behaved herself. "Mrs. Kinseth might have used those two false drawers as a kind of private safe, to keep her medicines from being taken, accidentally or otherwise. But it just doesn't seem likely, does it? She could have afforded a commercial safe if she'd really feared theft, couldn't she? It seems to be more probable that those homemade compartments were a hiding place she wanted to keep secret. And if that's so, then there is a lot more I want to know about the lady's background—and that chest—and those medicine bottles.''

"Well, of course!" Angela said, eagerly. "We can ask on your behalf, and . . .''

"No, you can't," Martinez warned. "I'm not joking about this being a secret . . . a deadly secret. Two people have been killed over this.''

"Two? You think—''

"I'm more convinced now that Baird's death was linked to Mrs. Kinseth's. For openers, I think someone ripped her luggage apart looking for those bottles, or at least, for whatever was in them . . . someone you ran into in the basement. I think when you came along, he had just finished searching, and I think you were lucky—very lucky—he acted on impulse and just threw that cloth over your head and ran. You're lucky he didn't find a weapon handy—the way he did when he ran into Baird."

"Ooooh . . ." Angela shivered. "Lieutenant, don't you have any idea yet who that 'someone' might be?"

Martinez paused regretfully. "Not yet . . . no suspects yet. But we're working on it." He continued his story. "I think he would have broken into Mrs. Kinseth's apartment next, except that Baird got there first and took the furniture away before our killer had a chance to search it. The killer then went to Baird's shop, to that storeroom, and took the furniture apart till he found the hidden compartments in that chest. He may have got what he was looking for there, but I'm inclined to think whatever it was was already gone."

"How would you figure that?" Caledonia asked.

"Because there was no need to splinter the chest the way it was torn to shreds. He'd ripped up the other furniture, but only enough to see if anything was hidden inside. He knocked the little desk apart, for instance, but the drawers and top were relatively intact. But when it came to the little chest—well, you saw it. He chopped it into kindling. And I think he took his anger and frustration out on the wood."

Angela and Caledonia looked at each other, and Caledonia shivered hugely. For once, neither had any comment.

Then Angela broke their silence, "You've really nearly finished with all of this, haven't you? I mean, you said that when you found out *why* she was killed, you'd find out *who* killed her. And now you know it might be drugs . . ."

Martinez shook his head. "Saying she was killed because of drugs is like saying airplanes fly because there's air; there has to be more to it than that . . . and the possibilities are endless."

Angela looked disappointed. But Caledonia leaned forward even farther. "I see what you're saying, but if there's still a mystery about all this, can't you still use our help? I mean, at least we could keep asking around here, finding out whether or not residents—or staff—were involved. You once said we were useful to you that way."

"How can I explain this so you'll understand?" Martinez passed a hand over his eyes. "Well, let me say that I wasn't nearly as worried about you when you were looking into a murder that might have been entirely personal. But this, Mrs. Benbow, is a killing over a *thing*. I think Baird got in the killer's way when the killer was searching for the hiding place Mrs. Kinseth used. Whether he had reason to think there was something hidden in the furniture—or just hoped there was— we don't know. We'll probably never know, but if he'd kill to get it, he'd also kill to protect it after he's got it. Do you see the difference? Do you see what I'm saying?"

Caledonia nodded. "I think so. If I set out to kill someone and I succeeded, I'd be through. Unless something unforeseen came up, of course. But with a thing—you might have to go on killing."

"Or feel you had to," Martinez said. "Especially if drugs are involved. Things get pretty nasty when you are working with drugs."

"But I still don't see why that means you don't want us involved any more, Lieutenant," Angela said, her little brow furrowed, her mouth set in stubborn lines of her "mule mouth" again. "I thought we were useful to you."

"Oh, you were. You are. But the killer mustn't perceive you that way! He's killed twice. I don't want you to be numbers three and four. I want you to stay out of this whole thing. I want you to knit. Read. Play bridge. Take long walks."

He looked at the women, and something in their expressions bothered him. He shook his head. "Ladies, you're not listening to me, are you? I came here because I have grown very fond of you. I want to keep you safe. Now, I have only limited personal experience with drug dealers, but I can guarantee you they're not awash with love for their fellow man. You need to stop your investigations immediately—before you get hurt! And while we're at it, let me warn you that I don't take it lightly when a pair of civilians break into the apartment of the deceased . . .''

"We didn't break in! We found a key!" Angela was indignant.

"Uh-oh," Caledonia said. "You blew it, Angela."

"Do you mean to tell me you entered the Kinseth apartment too? I was talking about the last time I came here officially—last year—when, you may remember, I found you in a murder victim's apartment not once but . . .''

"Well, you didn't have a seal on the door, or anything. We knew you'd already collected your evidence, so we didn't think it would matter," Angela defended herself. "Besides, we didn't find anything anyway."

Martinez was nodding, his mind's eye turned inward onto material from his memory's filing cabinets. "I should have known. That's when you spotted the lingerie chest, and took note of the other furnishings well enough so you could identify them for me. Okay, you'd better confess the whole thing."

Rather sheepishly they retold the story of their expedition, this time admitting that the Jackson twins, about whom they had already reported to him, had represented only a detour on the main route.

He listened in awed silence, and at last he said, "Does anybody, anybody at all besides me, know you were in there?"

"Absolutely not. Honestly!"

"Good. Then don't tell anyone. You don't know how crazy and paranoid this killer might be. Don't tempt him. I believe you when you say you didn't find anything special—he might not."

Angela sighed deeply. But it was Caledonia who spoke. "I think we understand, Lieutenant. It's just . . . maybe I should be embarrassed to admit it, but we've both enjoyed the stimulation. The excitement." Angela nodded her agreement, but her expression was wistful.

Martinez smiled gently. "Believe me I sympathize. But this isn't an intellectual puzzle, a word game. Real people are involved—people who can hate and people who can bleed. If I had even the vaguest idea of who to suspect, I'd be more specific. But I haven't a real suspect yet. For now all I can do is caution you generally. Please, ladies. Don't risk your lives just for a temporary diversion from boredom. I want you to promise . . ."

"Promise what?" Angela was slightly petulant, like a child whose favorite toy has been threatened.

"Promise you'll stay as far away from playing detective as you can. Promise you won't interview suspects, won't go to Baird's shop, won't hint to anyone at all about what you know . . ."

"All right. We promise, Lieutenant," Caledonia said. "Don't we, Angela?"

"Well . . ."

"Angela!" Caledonia's voice took on a threatening tone. "Don't fool around. The Lieutenant was nice enough to come here on his own time, to talk to us like grown-ups instead of like little children. So you promise and promise quick!"

"Oh, very well. I do promise, Lieutenant. I'm sorry if I've been acting a bit cross about it. I know you mean only the best for us, and you're trying to be our friend, and I do appreciate that, even if I don't act like it sometimes."

"I know that, Mrs. Benbow. And I'm sorry to spoil your enjoyment. But I'd like to have you around with us a long time. All right? Try some needlework. Play some bridge. Go for a walk on the beach. I'll appreciate your cooperation." The Lieutenant stood up to walk to the door. "Now it's time to head home. Don't see me out, Mrs. Wingate, thank you. Stay comfortable. Thank you for a pleasant break in the day's routine." Through the apartment's view window they watched him walk up the garden toward the lobby entrance.

"Drugs! Maybe even smugglers!" Angela was restored to herself again. "Furniture with secret compartments! Oh, it's all so interesting, Cal!"

Caledonia looked at her with suspicion. Perhaps because

she knew Angela better than the Lieutenant did, she had mistrusted the facile promise from the moment Angela gave it. "Are you going to do what the Lieutenant suggested? What you promised?"

"Absolutely."

"Truly? You wouldn't tell a flat out lie, would you?"

"Absolutely not! Cal, trust me. Now, I better go and get a jacket on before supper—the evenings are chilly by the ocean, you know." And she took herself off, out the door and up the garden path.

And up the garden path, figuratively as well as literally, was exactly where she was leading her friends, for Angela had promised three things: first, not to tell anyone about the things the Lieutenant had shared with them, and that she considered a sensible request and an easy promise to live up to; second, not to go back into Baird's shop, and she had no desire to do that—it seemed to her that avenue was thoroughly covered when the forensics team reconstructed the furniture and vacuumed the storeroom; and third, not to interview any suspects.

But there Angela had found her loophole. For the Lieutenant *had* no suspects—he'd as good as said so himself. So it really didn't matter, she told herself happily, if she just talked to a few people and found out a little more . . . And she fairly skipped along as she went to her room to fetch a wrap.

She put her plan into operation immediately after supper, although the first portion of her scheme would have looked entirely innocent to anyone watching her, even to a suspicious Caledonia. The first stage consisted of trying to recall the list of Amy Kinseth's visitors as detailed by the Jackson sisters.

Of course, Angela reasoned that the killer would most likely be someone Amy knew and therefore probably someone who'd visited the Kinseth apartment. But it was also likely, in her thinking, that if there was some clue on the premises, one of the innocent visitors might have seen it, perhaps without even knowing what they saw. So Angela also reasoned that interviews, even with the innocent, might provide valuable information.

She pulled a sheet of paper from her desk, and while the evening news muttered away in the background on her television, she wrote:

1. Torgeson
2. Baird
3. Janice Felton
4. Carolyn Roberts
5. the nursing staff, various members
6. the Jackson sisters, both
7. Elroy Carmichael
8. . . .

She X-ed out Baird's name ("Being dead surely ought to clear him as a suspect," she muttered) and then hesitated. It seemed to her that the Jacksons had said "about a dozen" or "ten or so" or something like that. But she couldn't seem to think of any of the others. Well, maybe she should separate the Jackson twins—count them as two . . . Oh, of course. How silly. Hazel Hanson about the bridge game. That made eight. She thought a while longer. Diet! The Jacksons said something about diet and Mrs. Schmitt. She wrote "Schmitt" by number 9. She scratched her ear with the pencil-eraser. There had been another name, she was sure of it. But the memory wouldn't come. She got up and walked around her room. That usually cleared the cobwebs . . . nothing.

"Well," she said to herself cheerfully. "A little walk along the sand wouldn't hurt. I could go down on the beach, get a little fresh air, and maybe I'd think of it then."

But high tide was in, covering the hard-packed sand that would have made walking easy. After fifteen minutes of trudging through the deeper, softer sands above the tide line, her thigh muscles ached and her brains seemed to be stuck in neutral. Wearily, she clambered up the worn railway-tie steps to street level, holding the railing for dear life, painfully aware of the slippery surfaces under the soles of the tennis shoes she'd substituted for her dress pumps.

She was walking up the garden, head down, going over her list, when fingers reached out and touched her arm, and Angela jumped as though she'd been touched by a live wire!

"Oh, Angela, I'm sorry," Tootsie Armstrong said, "I should have said something. But you were walking with your head down, headed straight for me . . ."

"You scared me out of a year's growth! I had no idea you were there!"

Tootsie smiled an embarrassed little grin. "I always walk softly, Angela. You know that. I was just out in the garden for a breath of air after supper . . . I thought the spareribs were a bit greasy, didn't you? And the sauerkraut was just too much . . . so hearty and Teutonic! The last time we had ribs, Mrs. Schmitt put caraway seed into the sauerkraut, and I hated that. Mrs. Kinseth said it was authentic, that without it you didn't have a real German dish. But I thought . . ."

"Oh! Of course. You were the one! Why couldn't I remember that?"

"The one who what?"

"The one who called on Amy in her apartment."

"Oh, dear. Yes. I did. She invited me in for about three whole minutes. And then she stood up and walked me to the door. Why, we hadn't even gotten well started talking. And she never offered me anything like a soft drink or a cup of coffee. Of course, I realize she didn't have a kitchen in there, so she had no stove or refrigerator of her own. But we all keep some in the community kitchen on our floor, you know. It seemed to me she wasn't very friendly!"

Angela was all smiles. Tootsie might have given her a gift, she was so pleased to remember at last the final name for her list. "Why did you go to see her, Tootsie?" she asked. "You didn't care much for her, did you?"

"Well," Tootsie sighed. "I thought I'd done something— or said something—that upset her the day we played bridge. I mean, she left so abruptly. I was sure it was because I played badly . . . or . . . I don't know. She said it wasn't. I mean, I tried to apologize to her, you see, but she just said there was no need. And then she sort of stood up—and that was it.''

"Nothing else?''

"No, not really. Why?''

"Oh, just curious.'' For once in her life, Angela decided on magnanimity. "You know neither Caledonia nor I was ever invited inside her apartment at all. She must have liked you, to have let you in. I understand not many people were let past the door!''

Tootsie beamed. "Really? I didn't know that, Angela. Well. Fancy that.'' Then a thought struck her. "Oh dear! And I—I've been so unpleasant about her . . . Oh *dear*! Some of the things I've said . . .'' Tootsie moved off, trailing her remorse behind her like a veil. And Angela went back and wrote "Tootsie Armstrong'' on her list, then put a check mark beside the entry (for "done'' or "attended to'') and a note—"No additional information.'' And after a moment, she also wrote "Not a suspect.''

She checked her watch. It was still only seven-thirty— surely Janice Felton wouldn't be in bed yet. Angela went down the hallway, past the Jacksons' door, and knocked at the Felton apartment.

"Why Angela. Come on in.'' Janice had a single room facing the gardens. She kept her windows open summer and winter—one of the few residents whose blood seemed to circulate sufficiently well that she didn't feel the chill. The windows stood open now to the June twilight, and the drapes stirred in the evening breeze that swept in every night from the sea, cleaning the air of the day's scents and sounds, bringing quiet and a sense of calm.

"Oh, my goodness,'' Angela said, hugging her arms around herself. "You do like it cold, don't you?'' Janice obliged by sliding the windows shut.

"Sit down,'' she said. "I don't know when you last came calling, Angela—not since I first moved in two years ago, I think.''

"Well, I was feeling lonely,'' Angela improvised. "It's

all this—all these—you know—the killings. I needed someone to talk to.''

Janice seemed amused. "Why me! I'd have thought you
and Caledonia . . .''

"Well, why not you?" Angela rejoined a bit sharply. "I
mean, you're close at hand . . . Actually," she said, drawing inspiration from the pencil-scribbled date book that lay
open on the desk, with the heading "Programs for July"—
"Actually, I thought it might be kind of interesting to find
out what's coming up from the entertainment committee."

"Angela, you almost never come to the programs we ar-
range."

"Well, maybe I will—if they're interesting. Besides, it's
something to take my mind off . . . you know . . . all this."

Janice went to the desk and picked up the book. "Actually,
we're not set on a couple of dates. But so far we have a
speaker on Honduras—I hear he has some wonderful slides.
A man who collects rare butterflies. The children from the I
Think That My Redeemer Liveth Baptist Church are coming
to do a Fourth of July program . . . so sweet," she beamed,
unaware of Angela's involuntary expression of distaste.

"Then there's the lady who carves faces onto coconut
shells . . . and there's a puppeteer—he does the cutest little
talking turtles made of pot-lids and washcloths, with drain-
stoppers for eyes. . . . Oh, and we decided to do one mock
quiz show. We'd do 'Dating Game,' but Mr. Bowman refused . . . he was angry because Mrs. Bowman didn't choose
him last time we did this. And there just aren't that many
men who'll cooperate and do the show. So we decided to do
'Wheel of Fortune' instead. Jake the handyman says he can
fix us an old truck wheel and make it spin . . . it's going to
be rather fun." She said the last a bit defensively, for Angela
had yawned—quite inadvertently.

"Oh, sorry," Angela apologized. "That was just—it's
been a long day, you see."

"No offense taken where none is intended," Janice smiled
tolerantly. "That's about the end of the list we have set for
July anyway. We don't do as many programs in the summer,

because so many residents go off on vacation and to visit relatives.''

"I suppose more people will be leaving early this year to visit family," Angela said, seizing the opportunity to shift the conversation back around to her interests. "Because of all this unpleasantness. The murder and all. You know," she went on, still steering her way back to the point, "I thought that was one of the saddest things about Mrs. Kinseth. That she had no family, did you know? I mean, nobody really cared when she died."

"Oh, we all cared, Angela. That isn't fair. It upset everyone around here. Of course . . ." Janice started a sentence and then choked it off.

"Of course what, Janice? You were going to say something."

"Oh, just that with someone so unpopular, we couldn't exactly take up a collection for a wreath, could we? There's caring and there's caring . . . I'd cry for most of our residents, but I never shed a tear for her!"

"Did you and she have a run-in?"

"Of course not. We hardly spoke. Well, once . . . after she'd been so awful to Mr. Brighton. She saw me in the hall one day and she asked me into her place. She said something like 'Time we got to know each other.' She was all sunny and friendly. But when I did come in, it was like she couldn't think of a thing to say. And she started to get uneasy . . . and pretty soon—oh, it wasn't five minutes—she stood up and said something like 'Well, this has been very pleasant, but I'm sure you've got things to do,' and she eased me out the door again."

"Imagine! How very odd. Why do you suppose she had you in there in the first place?"

"Well," Janice said, "I decided she wanted to make up for looking so bad before. She just wanted to make me think she was a nice person."

"Then why didn't she? I mean, why did she turn around and just get rid of you?"

"Well, we had absolutely nothing to talk about, you see.

I asked her opinion about the weather—the meals here—I asked what she thought of sports, and movies, and television, and politics . . . she didn't seem to be interested in any of those things, or to know anything about them. It was like I was supposed to do the talking and she was just going to listen! So we ran out of conversation in about three minutes flat! And after that," Janice smiled ruefully, "it was all downhill."

"Did you ever try to find out more about her? To sort of—oh, I don't know—break through that barrier she put up?" Angela asked.

"No, I think I had her figured out the minute she yelled at Mr. Brighton. That was a mean, hateful way to act. And when she tried to make it up to me—and couldn't—I knew everything I needed to know. She was made of ice, that woman . . . solid ice. I'm sorry she's dead—that was pretty awful. But one try at being friendly was enough. I didn't have to get frostbite trying again."

Angela excused herself and went back to her own apartment. There she picked up her list and put a second check mark on her list, this one beside Janice Felton's name. She wrote—"No information." Then, after a moment's thought, "Not a likely suspect."

The next morning, Angela was able to enter two more check marks. The first was next to Hazel Hanson's name. Since Caledonia didn't come to breakfast, Angela often dined alone. And she preferred it that way. But this morning she hunted out Hazel, who sat on the opposite side of the room and who was also alone at her table at the moment. "May I join you?" Angela said, sliding into the spare seat without waiting for a response.

"I've been thinking," she began, between bites of buttered toast. "You got to know Mrs. Kinseth pretty well, and I was wondering . . ."

"Angela, whatever gave you that idea? I hardly ever spoke to the woman. I mean, I stopped by after she had been here part of a week and asked her if she played bridge. She was gracious enough, I suppose—though a bit cold, I thought. I mean, she let me in the door, but she didn't even ask me to sit down! She said she'd play bridge, but when she got to my place, she didn't stay but maybe forty-five minutes altogether . . . she just got up and left, with some flimsy excuse, and I was really annoyed. I mean, I'd asked her as a substitute for Jenny Walker, who had the flu. I could have asked anybody else; I would have loved to have had you, for example," she said insincerely. Hazel was another one whom Angela scared to death at the bridge table. "But I was trying to be nice to the newcomer."

"And she wasn't very nice in return, I agree," Angela soothed.

"I don't mind telling you," Hazel sniffed, "I was offended, and I never even bothered to ask her why she behaved that way. I made the first move with that invitation, but she made no move at all! She didn't even speak to me when she passed in the lobby or the garden. It was as though she'd never been to my place at all. And you can be sure I never went near her place again, either."

Useless for further information and, at least to Angela's thinking, innocent of any involvement, Hazel went down as another check on Angela's list.

To Angela's regret, so did Torgeson. She dreaded talking to him, and as it turned out, she didn't have to. She was getting her mail from Clara near lunchtime, when Torgeson marched out of his office and across the lobby, head down, his stride purposeful. "There he goes to make our new residents welcome," Clara said with amusement. "Mr. and Mrs. Wilson moved in yesterday. He's making his usual call. He fusses over them . . . asks if everything's all right with the apartment . . . pretends to make a list of things they want fixed . . . and as soon as he comes back here, he files the list and forgets it."

Angela was running out of subterfuge, and besides, directness seemed to get good results. "Is that all he calls on new residents for? To get a list of problems with the apartments? I mean, why did he call on Mrs. Kinseth?"

Clara grinned and leaned forward across the desk, dropping her voice. "After the way she treated him that first day, you'd have thought he'd stay as far from her as possible."

She was in full swing with her story, the mail forgotten in her hand. "As it was, it took him a full fifteen minutes to get his nerve up to go. He'd start out the door . . . and then he'd come back with some excuse like he forgot his key. He'd go into his own office—and in a couple of minutes he was back out. He'd say, 'I'm off for Mrs. Kinseth's apartment, if anyone calls.' And he'd start for the door . . . and then he'd turn around again and make another excuse like 'I mustn't forget to bring a pen, of course. To make notes.' And he'd go back into his own office. You ask me—I think he was taking a little nip each time he went back. To get his courage up."

"Oh, Clara. No!"

"Oh, yes! He keeps a bottle back there in the safe behind the picture. He thinks we don't know about it, the staff. Shoot, Mrs. B., everybody who works here knows about his little bottle. Not that he's a drinker under normal circumstances. I got to be fair about it. He doesn't often take that bottle out. It's there for what you'd call emergencies."

Clara was positively gleeful. "By the last time, when he finally went, his face was beet red and he was sweating. He had a hangover the next day, too. Sick? Lordy, Mrs. B, we had to tiptoe around him all day long. No wonder he never went near her place again."

When Angela returned to her apartment, she marked a check by Torgeson's name. "Too bad," she sighed. "It would have been so nice to have The Toad be a material witness. He'd have been apoplectic! Oh well—five down and five to go."

She picked up the list. The names without a check mark stood out:

4. Carolyn Roberts
5. the nursing staff, various members
6. the Jackson sisters, both

7. Elroy Carmichael
8. Mrs. Schmitt

"I must get started on these right away," she told herself. "I'll just sit a moment and let my lunch settle, then I'll get moving." And she promptly drifted off in her chair, taking her afternoon nap as usual, but sitting bolt upright, her television going full blast. For a woman of seventy-odd years, it had been an exhausting morning.

Chapter 13

THE REMAINDER of the afternoon and the evening of that day were intensely frustrating and a complete waste of time, as far as Angela was concerned. When she waked from her nap, feeling much brighter than before lunch, she had gone to the kitchen; but Mrs. Schmitt was up to her elbows in a giant bowl of dough—kneading and pummeling. "I have no time to talk," she said. "Perhaps tomorrow. Sometimes in the morning I get a few minutes . . ."

Angela went over to the health facility across the street. She didn't know the little nurse who was sitting behind the main desk, a mere child in Angela's eyes. Wages for the nurses were so low that there was a constant turnover. Only a small corps of old regulars stayed, year in and year out. Heaven only knew why they did.

This was another new one, a girl barely into her twenties with a Dorothy Hamill haircut, a turned-up nose, and lovely blue eyes. "Nurse, where is Aretha Thomas today?" Angela asked. She was rather fond of the head nurse, who often manned the desk herself.

"Is that the head nurse?" the girl asked blankly. Angela was distressed to notice that the child was chewing gum. "I only started about three weeks ago. If that's who you mean, it's her day off, I think."

"Well, how about Mary Washington?" Angela felt even more comfortable with Mary, who had the reputation of being the nicest of all their nurses.

"She's back there, in the ward. It's bath time around here.

She's busy.'' The gum popped noisily against the tiny gap in the girl's front teeth.

"Well, how about Connie Maddox?" Angela hated to ask. She disliked "Monstrous Maddox" as much as the other residents did. When Angela was sick, she wanted to be soothed, not scolded—petted, not manhandled.

The girl shrugged. "I dunno." She popped her gum loudly. "Might be her day over in y'all's duty office. Try the main building. You are from the"—she jerked a thumb in the direction of the old hotel—"you know, from the home?"

"The home?"

"Yeah. The home for the aged."

Angela bristled. "Young lady, we call it a 'retirement center.' Not a 'home for the aged'! Yes, I'm from Camden."

"Thought so," the girl grinned and popped her gum again. Angela shuddered.

"Do you know anything about the duty rosters for the last few weeks?" she said, trying to ignore the gum.

"What about 'em?"

"I mean, who did the blood pressures and took temperatures and gave ear drops—you know, that kind of thing—over in the main building?"

"I did, sometimes. Sometimes one of the others."

"Well," Angela persisted. "Do you know who did what, when? Is there a list?"

"I'spose. Somewhere."

"Would it be possible for me to see it?"

"Sure. I guess so anyhow."

"Can you," Angela said, drawing herself up as tall as she could, "can you find that list for me?"

"Nope. Not supposed to leave the desk." The gum popped loudly.

Angela waited for a moment, then realized the girl was finished with her utterance. "Well, you might at least say you're sorry."

"Why? Gosh, you old people have some funny ideas." Oblivious to the effect she was having, the little nurse picked up a copy of *People* magazine and began to read.

"Hopeless! Absolutely hopeless," Angela exclaimed to herself as she left the health facility. "Oh, I wish Cal was here!" Caledonia wouldn't approve of what she was doing, perhaps, but Caledonia was comforting to have around. "Of course, I really don't dare let Cal in on my scheme. She'd only scold. Though, if you look at it right, I'm not actually breaking my promise," she reasoned. But she knew at the same time that Caledonia would say she was bending it awfully hard.

At supper that night, she was meek and sweet and agreeable to Caledonia. It was her conscience that moved her. Caledonia was pleasantly surprised.

"You're certainly taking this tamely."

"This what?" Angela said sweetly.

"This—you know—this inactivity. This lack of involvement. I thought you'd be tearing the wallpaper off. But you seem perfectly content. Don't tell me you finally decided to take someone's advice and like it!"

Angela smiled innocently. "I suppose that's about it," she said. "Now if you'll excuse me, I want to get an early start tomorrow. You know something, Cal, I was thinking about you just this afternoon and wishing you were with me. I really do miss you when you're not around." Slightly embarrassed, she pushed her chair back and got to her feet. "Now, I'm off."

Back in her own apartment, however, her malaise grew. It just didn't feel right—all this looking into things without Caledonia. At last she made a decision. In the morning she'd go to Caledonia and explain everything. If Cal wanted to scold, she'd argue right back. "I'll tell her she can't boss me," Angela argued, talking aloud. "Oh, I hope I'm doing the right thing."

That night, she slept soundly. There is nothing like a clean conscience—or a decision to come clean—to give you a good rest.

It was very early when Angela woke. The clock near her bed showed five-thirty in its oversized red numerals—it was the kind of clock even the elderly can read with sleep-dimmed eyes before they put their glasses on. Angela rolled over to try to sleep another hour. The dining room didn't even open till seven, and it would take her only about twenty minutes to bathe, dress, and walk across the lobby. Caledonia wouldn't be up and around till well after breakfast anyway. Might as well sleep . . .

But she could not. The list she'd made out kept appearing and reappearing before her mind's eye. "Maybe I should get started on the rest of the list before I tell Caledonia," she told herself aloud. "That way, I'll have it nearly all done, and if she does talk me out of it, there'll be less I missed."

"I suppose," she said, getting up and starting toward her bathroom, "I suppose I should try for Mrs. Schmitt first. She'll be at work already. Maybe if I get ready for breakfast a little early, I can finish up quickly and get into the kitchen before she gets started on the lunch."

"There's just no point," she said, sliding on a shower cap and turning on the hot water, "no point in going in there before breakfast, of course. She'd be busy with the baking and all. No, I'll go right after breakfast before she starts lunch. That's the ticket. Ouch!" The water hit maximum heat—far too hot without adding some cold—and she had to give the taps her full concentration for a while to find a mixture she could tolerate.

The advantage of taking morning showers, besides one's feeling clean and virtuous all day, was that one had all the hot water one wanted. Wait till evening to take a shower, and every other apartment in the building was running the hot water as well. Now she luxuriated under steaming water, letting the prickling drops jump-start her circulatory system. She felt thoroughly awake by the time she toweled off, ready for an explorer's hearty breakfast and a day of discovery.

"Mrs. Schmitt," she reminded herself. "Mrs. Schmitt. But first a walk, and then breakfast," she said as she stepped outside the door—and straight into Elroy Carmichael. There was a double "Oof"—one in Angela's little-girl squeak, and another in Elroy's husky tenor. "Oh, I'm *so* sorry, Mr. Carmichael!"

"Mrs. Ah—Mrs. Ah . . . Forgive me, I can't seem to . . . I'm really so sorry . . ." Each assumed the fault, each apologized, and simultaneously with their apologies, each turned and reached out to steady the other. There they stood, he clutching her shoulders, she clutching his waist . . .

"It's Mrs. Benbow," Angela said, recovering first. "Janice Felton introduced us after your Eliot reading a while back."

"Oh. Oh yes, of course." He took his hands from her shoulders and passed a hand over his forehead, as though to wipe off perspiration. It was only a reflex action—the chill of morning was still in the air. "I really must apologize. I wasn't watching—I was in something of a hurry. I'm supposed to meet the Mesdames Jackson . . ."

"Meet Dora and Donna? For pity sakes, why?" Angela privately noted that either Elroy didn't know that both the twins were still "*Miss* Jackson," or else his knowledge of French was faulty.

"We are to have breakfast together. It's to be a morning of creation . . . they have written verses that they want me to go over with them, you see. . . . I couldn't refuse."

I'll bet you couldn't, Angela said silently. She had marked him down as an opportunist. But aloud, she said, "Tell me, do you always come calling before six-thirty?"

"Never. That would be most unsuitable. I . . . what do you mean 'before six-thirty'?" Elroy looked a bit alarmed. "What is the time?"

"Just what I said. Just before six-thirty," Angela said, holding her left wrist up at an awkward crook, so that her watch was turned toward him.

Elroy craned his neck and squinted. Then, in disbelief, he grabbed hold of her wrist and looked closer. "It *is* six-thirty!"

"Yes, it is. Just what did you think?"

He passed a limp hand over his brow again. "I thought . . . well, you see, I got up early to watch the dawn. I didn't look at a clock. I just—just watched the sky, you see. All the colors . . ." He waved his hand vaguely toward the south and east, already pale gold and blue, the brilliant rose and violet shades washed away with the flood of bright light. "So, I saw it. Dawn. Very lovely. And then I was hungry, so I walked over here from my apartment. It isn't far, you know. I assumed . . . I assumed it would be breakfast-time by the time I arrived." He sounded positively outraged and betrayed.

"I'm afraid," Angela said, amused, "that the Jackson girls won't be presentable yet. They usually get out into the lobby exactly at seven, when the dining room doors open."

"Perhaps," he said looking hopefully down the hall, "they'd be ready early today, because they know I'm joining them?"

"I doubt it. It's not easy to get dressed when two people have to share one bathroom. And you better not go down to their room. They'd be in such a panic."

"Oh," he said, rather vaguely, peering around at the gloomy lobby behind them. "But then, I wonder . . ." he shrugged. "I suppose I could just sit out here and wait, couldn't I?"

"Certainly. They'll be out as soon as they're ready. And they always come down this hall—you'll see them right away. But I tell you what—why not come into the garden? I'm headed that way for a little stroll before breakfast. It's lovely and," she lied craftily, "I've wanted the chance to ask you about your verse."

His rather gloomy expression brightened. "Did you attend the reading I gave this week, dear madam? I rather thought your face was familiar." He peered through his glasses with such a myopic-looking squint that Angela doubted his words. "A walk sounds very pleasant, actually. Yes, I should enjoy a stroll in the garden."

Mentally, Angela congratulated herself on her ability to come up with a plan so quickly. She made a note to herself to tell Caledonia how flexible she was.

Aloud she said, "Oh, I beg your pardon, I was daydreaming. What was that?"

"You're right about the garden," Elroy was babbling. "It

certainly is lovely. I've spent most of my time here inside the building, of course . . . giving my programs, visiting my special friends . . ."

"Yes, you do have a lot of friends, it would seem," Angela primed the pump. "Of course you have many fans—that's only natural, with your talent." She was amused to see him simper and twist in an attempt to show modesty. "But you seem to have people who feel closer than that to you. There are the Jacksons, of course . . ."

"Dear ladies, both of them," he nodded with enthusiasm.

"Yes, yes . . . they speak highly of you. So does Janice." The cat was inching forward, belly down in the grass, approaching the bird.

"Mrs. Felton? Oh, yes—she's been so helpful, too, scheduling me in here so I could have an audience hear my work. It would be best if it were published, naturally, and one could ask the readers their impressions . . . that is the way my poetry is meant to be experienced. But alas, you may have heard, I have had a setback in my plans for publication. And until the time that my poems are in print, I will have to read my work aloud."

"I understand Mrs. Kinseth intended to help you with the printing of your book." Angela floated a trial balloon.

For once Elroy's empty babble stopped completely. He even stopped walking. He stood totally still—a statue in the morning garden, albeit an odd, balding statue with buckteeth. Finally he moved forward again, walking very slowly. "Wherever did you get that idea?"

"Why Dora Lee—or Donna Dee—one of the Jacksons. They said you mentioned it to them."

"I mentioned my book to them, that's true. But I did *not* tell them Mrs. Kinseth had offered to help me. Quite the opposite. I dropped in on Mrs. Kinseth one time after our first meeting," Elroy said sadly. He had clutched his hands behind his back as he walked, and that somehow forced his head forward, so that he bobbed as he walked. "I came at her invitation, of course. The invitation made me hopeful that perhaps she might be willing to help me publish. But such was not the case . . . she did not appear even to be interested in the verses. My manuscript lay on her desk—and she didn't even look at it! I don't really know why she asked me to come at all!''

"But didn't you—didn't you try reciting your verses for her?''

"Certainly not,'' Elroy said coldly. "If she wasn't gracious enough to read my written material, I would hardly demean myself by performing for her.'' He sighed deeply. "I really think she invited me there to have the pleasure of mocking me. And when she dismissed me—which she did within a very few minutes—I was convinced she would not change her mind.''

Angela felt a bit muddled. Her very clear image of his visit to Amy—as described by the Jacksons—was getting blurred. But then, of course, much that the Jacksons did had about it an aura of mental fuzz . . .

I'll think about that later—after breakfast, Angela told herself, following the great tradition of Scarlett O'Hara. Aloud she said, "Well, I do believe it's nearly breakfast-time.''

"Ah!'' Elroy brightened up. "Perhaps the Jacksons will be up and about.''

"We'll see. Tell me, Mr. Carmichael, did you ever go back and talk to Mrs. Kinseth again? I mean, she didn't give you a real chance that first time, did she?''

"No, I did not go back. I wish I had—the book should have come first. I should have begged her . . . I should have gotten down on my knees . . .'' He stopped himself short. "But I have my pride,'' he said, drawing his lips down tight over his bunny-teeth. "Oh, Mrs. Benbow, I've so enjoyed our little talk. Do you have any poetry you want me to look at, by the way? You might enjoy joining the Jacksons and me this morning.''

Angela was alarmed. He seemed to be measuring her. More like weighing my pocketbook, she thought. Aloud she said only, "Well, no, actually . . . I don't write myself, though I did major in English literature in college, many years ago. What I do is appreciate the work of others.''

Elroy took that as a personal compliment. "Thank you, thank you," he beamed. "And dare I hope that when I read my newest verses for the group next week you'll be in the audience?"

She smiled and nodded and kept her mouth tightly closed.

As they turned back toward the lobby, the Jackson twins were just emerging from the doorway. This morning the twins were dressed in pink cotton pinafores. Each had a pink velvet bow pinned into her iron gray hair, and each was wearing (Angela gulped) pink and white saddle shoes! Wait till I tell Caledonia, she thought.

"Oh, Angela, how nice of you to entertain Elroy till we could get here," Dora Lee trilled.

"Yes," Donna Dee said, "we wondered what he'd do if he arrived early. So prompt for his appointments . . ."

"Will he be hungry for his breakfast now, do you suppose?" Dora Lee asked, looking sideways at Elroy while addressing her sister.

"Oh, I should think so, dear," her sister answered, beckoning to him.

"Ladies . . ." Elroy moved forward to step between them. Each took possessive hold of one of his arms. "I am yours," he announced grandly, and sailed off with them toward the dining room.

After breakfast, Angela detoured to the kitchen, an area she had visited as seldom as she had the basement furnace room. There a grudging Mrs. Schmitt, already busy mixing meat, egg, chopped onion, milk, and bread crumbs—along with several unnamed spices and quite a lot of stewed tomato—agreed to answer a few questions. She kept on working in the giant, stainless steel mixing bowl, her bare hands stained with tomato as far as her elbows.

Angela thought she had never seen anything so disgusting in her life as the mush oozing between Mrs. Schmitt's strong fingers, slimy egg and pulpy tomato squirting upward, lumps of onion and bread rising and falling on the tide of raw meat loaf. She tried to keep her eyes on Mrs. Schmitt's face, as red with exertion as her hands and arms were red with tomato pulp.

"I wanted to know about your visit to Mrs. Kinseth," she said. "The time you came to her apartment."

There was, Angela decided, no use beating around the bush; Angela could not imagine Mrs. Schmitt involved in anything subtle and secret, let alone hidden drugs and murder. She had the strength in those big arms to kill with a club and with a sword-cane, but why on earth would she do it? Besides, Mrs. Schmitt was known as a lady of placid and imperturbable nature. She even looked a bit like one of the cows from her native Switzerland, Angela thought—big brown eyes, pink flat nose . . .

Angela recalled the day Mrs. Schmitt's young assistant had dropped the giant kettle full of chili, only half an hour before it was to be the only main dish for lunch. "I'd have killed him," Angela had said at the time. Now she remembered that Mrs. Schmitt had only sighed deeply and begun to scramble 200 eggs for 120 individual Western omelettes, while her assistant wept and scooped chili off the floor into the garbage containers.

Now Mrs. Schmitt only said, rather indifferently, never stopping her work on the ground beef, "I really don't remember. Did I go see Mrs. Kinseth about something?"

"Well, yes," Angela said. "A lot of the staff did. Maybe about her diet?"

"Oh. That. I thought you meant something special. But that was just routine. I visit all the new residents. I visited you when you first came here, Mrs. Benbow, don't you remember?"

Angela was dismayed. "No. Goodness. Did you do that?"

"Sure," Mrs. Schmitt said, starting to form up the loaves of meat-mix, shaping and rolling and finally patting with enthusiastic slaps that rather reminded Angela of that fraternal little pat on the rear professional football players give one another nowadays. "I always check on diets, first thing. We get a lot of diet restrictions in here. Salt-free diets, high potassium diets, low cholesterol diets, reducing diets . . ."

Mrs. Schmitt looked up and took in Angela's square frame. "It wouldn't hurt you to consider reducing, Mrs. Benbow."

Angela thought better of answering back. ("You catch more flies with sugar than you do with vinegar," she told an amused Caledonia when she reported the conversation.) "You may be right," was what Angela actually replied. "Now, is that all you talked to her about?"

Mrs. Schmitt simply ignored any abruptness in the inquiry. "Sure. What would I have to talk to her about? Her and all her gold jewelry. I got better things to do with my time."

"But didn't you go inside for even a minute."

"I did. And I almost had to knock her down to do it. She stood in the doorway. But I was going to make notes of anything she told me, and I was going to do it sitting down. So I just came past her and sat, even if she didn't tell me to."

"Did she have any oddities about her diet?"

"No. Except she was allergic to shrimp. But you know that when we have seafood, I always make a second main dish. We got lots of people can't eat seafood. Mr. Brighton, Mrs. Grant . . . So you get a choice on the nights we have it. That's not often, of course, the little that Mr. Torgeson gives me for the kitchen budget this year. You folks'll be lucky if you get a choice of hot dogs or beans for lunch, one of these fine days. I swear, I don't know how I'm going to keep getting together tasty meals with prices going up and my budget for food going down . . ."

For another five minutes or so, as Mrs. Schmitt dropped her meat loaves into separate pans and lined them up in the huge commercial ovens, Angela listened dutifully to a litany of complaints about the difficulty of making fine menus work with less and less money.

"Make 'em do something about that when the residents' dining room committee meets next month, Mrs. Benbow. They could make Torgeson listen to reason . . ."

Angela promised—and fled, her stomach still queasy from

watching raw meat being mixed and sculpted. And she went straight to Caledonia's apartment to make her grand confession.

Chapter 14

"CAL, ARE you busy right now? I—I have something I need to tell you." Angela barged directly into Caledonia's apartment, knocking but not even waiting for an answer before she opened the door and marched in. "Please, Cal—sit down—and promise not to scold me too much." And Angela began to talk.

She went over first, in great detail and with much self-justification, her decision to interview Amy Kinseth's callers and her reasoning that they weren't really suspects until Martinez said they were, and that therefore she was doing nothing forbidden. Caledonia interrupted only once to exclaim, "Oh, Angela! What happened to your promise!" Angela glared, and Caledonia fell silent and listened.

Angela finished her recitation and waited for the storm to break. She had steeled herself to be reprimanded and she was looking down as she talked, focusing her gaze on her hands, which were twisting together in her lap. Even when she was a little girl, scoldings had been easier if she didn't look directly at the person doing the scolding. She waited. But nothing happened. Silence. She looked up.

Caledonia was grinning like a Halloween jack-o'-lantern. "I don't believe this. I really don't believe this! We've been covering the same territory, girl, practically stepping on each other's heels."

"What do you mean?"

"I mean . . . Do you think I was any happier to be left out than you were? I did the same thing you did . . . almost."

She rose from her chair with the same gigantic upward surge that a hot air balloon has when the fire is lit and it begins to inflate. Her scarlet crinkle-cotton caftan billowed outward as though she, like the balloon, would take off for the cloudless California skies. But Caledonia, once on her feet, moved forward rather than up, across the room to her desk where she picked up a small leather-covered pocket notebook.

"I've been making some notes, and one of the things I wrote down myself was a list of the people who'd been to Kinseth's apartment. But I forgot about Mrs. Schmitt and Janice." She held out a list that read:

Staff	Residents
maids?	Jacksons?
nurses?	Tootsie?
Torgeson?	Hazel?
Outsiders	
Baird?	
Carmichael?	
moving van men?	
her lawyer?	

"See? It's almost identical to yours. And I got a start on my list, too."

"Oh, Cal! Did you? Who have you talked to?" Angela's eyes were glowing. It was marvelous to have someone to share with again.

"Well, first I went back to talk to the Jacksons again. I'll promise you there was nothing, absolutely nothing, more they could have told us. I listened to them recite their whole visit all over again . . . And then all about Elroy's solo visit— as picked up through the wall, of course."

"Oh. Remind me to tell you something about that, when you finish, Cal. But go on."

"I talked to Tootsie . . . Funny she didn't mention you'd asked her anything."

Angela snorted. "She probably didn't remember! That woman has a head full of gray, curly feathers, not brains."

"Don't be catty, Angela. I talked to Trish in the office about Torgeson—didn't want to talk to The Wart Hog myself, you see."

They paused to compare notes and found that Clara's story tallied identically with Trish's and that both members of Torgeson's "loyal staff" had taken the same amount of pleasure in his embarrassment!

"Let's see," Caledonia went on. "Well, I talked to the nursing staff—anyhow, to Our Lady of the Harpoon. I hunted her up in the infirmary office here." Caledonia waved her hand vaguely toward the dining room. The nurses' station for the main building lay beyond it in what had once been the old hotel's gift shop. "Can't say it did a lot of good."

"Did she have an old duty roster? That unpleasant child who's on the desk in the health facility across the street said there was one."

"Really? Maybe we should try to get a look at it. I didn't think to ask about it and Maddox certainly didn't volunteer to tell me. She didn't want to talk to me at all! But eventually she told me they all had evening duty over a four-week period, coming to various residents with medications, taking blood pressures—you know. So half the nursing staff must have been in Kinseth's place not once but several times."

Angela sighed. "Another washout. Like mine. But listen, let me tell you about *my* experience . . ." and she went into detail about the nurse she referred to as "that gum-chewing adolescent."

"There's one consolation," she finished. "That young lady won't last long. She'll quit to go and be a secretary in San Diego in another month, or a clerk at the stationery store, or a waitress at the diner . . ."

"Oh! I just remembered. I saw one other person we can scratch off your list," Caledonia said. "Carolyn Whatsis—you know, the activities director?"

"Oh. Of course. I almost forgot her."

"I had to catch up with her first, of course. That woman is into more . . . They said she was conducting a class in poster making down in the main-floor activities room off the library. There were a lot of residents in there smearing finger paint around on some cardboard . . . no Carolyn. They said she'd gotten them started and then took off.''

"At a run, no doubt," Angela said sourly. "She never walks anywhere."

"Look who's talking," Caledonia retorted. "Somebody said she was out helping to set up tables for the barbecue and square dance evening . . . out on the lawn. But that's been canceled."

"That's because nobody really wanted to square dance," Angela said. "I certainly didn't."

"Then somebody said she was across the street, conducting an aerobics class."

"Aerobics?"

"You know—all that jumping around and waving to music that people do these days to stir the blood? Very popular, I'm told. Well, I went over to the big room off the health facility then . . . you know, where you take your exercise classes."

"Where they found Amy." Angela shuddered.

"Right. And there she was. Carolyn Roberts, I mean. She had three people there and she was giving them *such* a workout. She made each one hang onto the back of a chair and kick one leg, then do it the other way. She had them sit in the chair and lift their legs. She had 'em flinging their arms in big circles. . . . And all the time she was playing a record of some jumpy little song with a lot of drums and tambourines . . . and she was bouncing around herself, shouting things like 'Don't stop moving now, keep the blood going, mustn't stop.' I thought Janice Felton was about exhausted, and she was the youngest of the three victims."

"Well, what happened?"

"Oh, eventually the music ended and the three women dragged themselves back here—to die, I have no doubt—and I got a chance to talk to Carolyn. Sort of."

"Why 'sort of'?"

"Because she wasn't through with her exercises. She kept right on jumping and jogging all the time we talked . . . and moving her arms in circles. . . . She was wearing one of those skintight things in bright colors . . . leotards?'' Angela nodded.

"She's got an incredible figure for a woman in her forties,'' Caledonia went on. "Maybe a bit skinny . . . at least, Herman would have said so. He liked women to look a little soft and feminine. But she looks like she could carry sacks of wheat all day out on the farm and not even feel tired at night! Lots of muscle there, even if her bones do stick out.'' She unconsciously ran a hand down her own overpadded exterior as she talked.

"Well, what did you find out?''

"Nothing much. She says she was trying to get Amy interested in one of the group activities. You know, quilting, or sewing for the fall bazaar, or exercise, or maybe the backgammon contest . . . no luck. Carolyn was a bit ticked at Amy for being so standoffish, but she didn't notice anything unusual. I'd say that was a useless interview for me.''

Angela sighed. "Same here with all of mine. The only one so far I've had even a hint from was Elroy.''

"El Wimpo? Aw, come on, you're kidding!''

"No, truly, Cal. Something he said when we were talking . . .'' and as faithfully as a tape recorder, Angela repeated all that Elroy had said to her that morning, emphasizing how his story differed from the twins' version. "The Jacksons thought she was going to give him money for his book, and he says she refused to consider it. Of course, Elroy was right there in the same room, and the Jacksons had to listen through a few inches of wallboard, so I'd be inclined to say he was more likely to know the straight of things.''

Caledonia's brow was furrowed when Angela finished. "You know, it's like that little chest of drawers in Amy's apartment. Something about all that doesn't quite fit.''

Angela nodded. "But you know, I wonder—could they both be telling the truth? Could it be another book the Jacksons heard him talking about? Does that make sense?''

"And Elroy told you he didn't read his verse, even though the Jacksons told us he was yodeling out his poetry, full volume, because Amy'd gone off to get him a soda . . . Speaking of which, do you want some Coke?''

"No thanks. Not just yet. Too soon after lunch. Well, then—she offered him a soft drink, and . . . Wait a minute! A soft drink! Some Coke! Well, that's it, then!''

"What's it?'' Caledonia demanded.

"Don't you see? She wasn't offering him a soda. She didn't even have a refrigerator! She was offering to get him some *coke*. Don't you get it?''

"Cocaine?''

"Of course!'' Angela was beaming. "I said all along that drugs were involved in this business, didn't I, Cal? Oh, I think we're definitely onto something. Elroy gets a gold star as Suspect Number One, from me.''

"Hold it, just a doggoned minute.'' Caledonia put up a hand like a traffic cop. "In the first place, she didn't offer to get him a 'Coke.' The Jacksons said she offered him a 'soft drink.'

"Well, be reasonable. What else could it be? Other people who visited say she didn't offer hospitality. No coffee, no soft drinks, no cookies . . . why would she offer any to him? She hadn't got a refrigerator at all, so she couldn't get him a soft drink, now could she? It came to me when you said 'coke' that the Jackson girls had simply misunderstood and sort of—well, like translated—what Amy really said. 'Coke' became 'soft drink' when the Jacksons remembered the conversation. Because if you're from the South, having a Coke and having a soft drink are sort of the same thing! Everybody says one and means the other!''

"Well, Elroy's certainly around here all the time, and any real suspect would have to be somebody who knows his way around this place, I should think,'' Caledonia conceded. "He could be the person you ran into searching down in the luggage storage area, all right.''

"I think,'' Angela said, remembering his reedy frame, "he could have lifted that cloth over my head. He's not strong, but he's—well—wiry.'' She was warming up as she talked. "We know he wanted money—so he could publish his poetry. We know that was the most important thing in his whole life. So maybe he got into drugs for the money!''

''I don't say that isn't right,'' Caledonia said. ''But you're moving entirely too fast for me. What makes you think that?''

''Well, he says she wasn't helping him with his publication, but the Jacksons heard him say something like 'I have to take care of this book first.' He says she wouldn't give him the money, but the Jacksons heard her say she'd give him plenty to 'take care of it'—meaning whatever book he was talking about.''

''Suppose for a moment you're right. What about it? What does it mean?''

Angela beamed. ''Don't you think that could mean he was her errand boy? That he was going to 'take care of' deliveries listed in his little black book before he did anything else? And she said she was going to give him enough drugs to do that with?''

''I follow you, girl, but aren't you jumping to a lot of conclusions? As usual, you put two and two together faster than anybody else can, but you sometimes end up with twenty-two instead of four.''

Angela got to her feet and started to pace as she talked, gesturing broadly with both hands. ''Well, look at what we've got. In Elroy we have someone who's around Camden all the time. We have someone who was in Mrs. Kinseth's apartment not once but twice—twice that we know of. Amy hardly asked anybody in, but she asked him. And he admits she didn't invite him because she loved his poetry . . .''

''Who could, for Pete's sake! Angela, you haven't read it. I did. It's awful!''

''Hush, Cal. That's entirely beside the point . . . which is that we have her offering to get him some cocaine.''

Caledonia shook her head. ''Well, you're starting from mighty slim evidence. It'll take more than this to make a believer out of me.''

''The question is,'' Angela said excitedly. ''What do we do about it? What is our next move?''

''Our next move, madam district attorney, is for you to sit

down again and for us to call Lieutenant Martinez. That's what our next move is. Don't get carried away with your own cleverness and think we can go and make an arrest ourselves."

"Oh! But the police will just take over, and we won't ever have a chance—"

"Listen, I vote—no, I take that back—I *insist* we call the Lieutenant."

"But—"

"Angela, *sit*!"

Angela sat, and Caledonia palmed the princess phone from her living room desk. It very nearly disappeared in her large hand. "Oh, hi, Clara. This is Mrs. Wingate. Do you suppose you could locate Lieutenant Martinez for us? This is important. I'd really like to talk to him. Oh, well, that'd be great. Thanks." She put a hand over the mouthpiece. "She's going to ring the sewing room right away. Oh! Hello Lieutenant— oh, Detective Swanson. Is Lieutenant Martinez there? Well, when he gets back, could you have him phone us? I think we may have some information for him. Or at least—at least, a theory. We've asked some questions and we . . . okay, thanks. Thanks a lot." She hung up. "Now, how about a soft drink, Angela? And believe me, I mean a real soft drink!"

A half hour later, there was a knock on the door, and the Lieutenant walked in.

"No point in phoning you . . . not when I'd burn the phone lines if I tried," he said. There was no greeting, no smile, no warmth in his voice. "What did I tell you about not mixing in this thing anymore? And what did you promise me?"

"We're sorry, Lieutenant. Truly. But we sort of happened on this information. . . . We . . . Tell him, Angela." Thus did Caledonia pass the buck. But Angela was equal to the occasion.

"I ran into Elroy Carmichael this morning, Lieutenant. Accidentally but literally. He'd come here to breakfast with the Jackson twins, and he was half an hour too early. So we walked in the garden while we waited for the breakfast bell. And several things he said . . . Go ahead and tell him, Cal,'' Angela said grandly. She hoped she sounded generous, but she was trying to share the blame, in case the Lieutenant was still cross.

''Yes, well, do you remember when we told you about the Jacksons' thin bathroom wall? And how they could eavesdrop on everything that went on near Amy Kinseth's bathroom door . . . and half that went on elsewhere in her living room as well? Do you remember how they said Elroy was one of those invited in, and that Amy gave him a soft drink while he recited poetry to her and then she offered to sponsor his book?''

''Well, she hadn't any refrigerator, Lieutenant,'' Angela interrupted eagerly. ''It came to me when Caledonia asked me to have a soft drink . . . only she said something like 'How about some Coke?' ''

''We realized,'' Caledonia said, ''that Amy never offered anybody else refreshments. She didn't even have a kitchen! And so, Angela believes that what the Jacksons remembered as an offer to give him a soft drink may actually have been her offering to bring him some cocaine. They got 'soft drink' and 'Coke' mixed up in their memories, you see.''

Caledonia and Angela waited expectantly.

''I see,'' Martinez said. ''Well, there has to be something more than that. Half the people in the United States, including Coca Cola's advertising agency, call the drink a 'Coke.' ''

''But she didn't have any. Any soft drinks, I mean,'' Caledonia explained, ''so she couldn't have meant a soda.''

''And you didn't hear my conversation with Elroy today in the garden, Lieutenant,'' Angela said smugly. ''In the first place, the Jacksons say Amy offered to give him 'enough for the book,' and they heard him say that the book had to be taken care of before anything else. But Elroy told me that Amy wasn't interested in sponsoring his publication and didn't want to discuss it. So we think it must have been another kind of book they were talking about—maybe addresses he was supposed to deliver drugs to. We think she stored the drugs and he carried them.''

"I see.'' Martinez got to his feet. "Okay, ladies, I think you've at least convinced me I want to talk to this poet fellow.''

"Poet!'' Caledonia snorted. "Not much of a poet, whatever else he may do. I mean, he writes like a fifth grader! Listen . . .'' she squeezed her eyes shut to help her remember and recited, with remarkable accuracy: " 'Oh night, with hue so black—which ever art when day is not . . . Oh night . . . something . . . something . . . alack, I fear her promise is forgot!' ''

She opened her eyes. "Isn't that the worst tripe! I may have forgotten an 'Oh night' or two—but that's about it. And listen! The one that I found in Mrs. Kinseth's apartment is just as bad . . .'' She shut her eyes again, recalling: " 'Oh woeful, woeful, woeful day . . . Most lamentable day that ever I did see (or something like that) . . . Oh day, oh day, oh hateful day . . .' ''

She could remember no more, and she opened her eyes again. To her surprise, they were both gazing at her with awe. "What's the problem? Cat got your tongue?''

Martinez was standing still, looking faintly amused. Angela's jaw had dropped slightly. "Cal, where did you get those poems?''

"Why, Elroy was spouting the first one out in the lobby. The other was on Amy Kinseth's desk with a whole bunch of others.''

"He didn't actually say these were his, did he?''

"Well, as a matter of fact, he did. The one on the desk had a note saying so. And he said the other was something he wrote called 'Without My Love' or 'My Love Has Gone Away' or something like that.''

"Cal, where did you go to school?'' Angela waved her arms rather theatrically. "Don't you recognize 'This is the silliest stuff that ever I heard'?''

" 'The best in this kind are but shadows, and the worst are no worse, if imagination amend them,' '' Martinez suddenly interjected, in a voice quite different from his own . . . silkier, more dramatic . . .

Angela turned to him. " 'It must be your imagination, then, and not theirs.' " She beamed. "You know, don't you, Lieutenant?"

"My God," he marveled. "The colossal nerve of that Carmichael man! Mrs. Wingate," Martinez was starting to smile broadly, "that terrible poetry you're quoting is not Carmichael. It's Shakespeare."

"Say what?"

"Shakespeare! The 'woeful day' poem is one of the Nurse's speeches from *Romeo and Juliet* . . ."

". . . and the night poem is from *A Midsummer Night's Dream*," Angela finished triumphantly. "So are the things we were quoting. They used to make me memorize poetry, when I went to school. All the kids had to. They don't do that any more—"

"Well, some of us still had to in my day," Lieutenant Martinez conceded. "After all, I went to parochial school— and those sisters believed in the fundamentals. We memorized poetry, we memorized the multiplication tables, we memorized spelling lists—"

"But Elroy's poetry is terrible!" Caledonia protested. "It's gawdawful verse! I thought Shakespeare was supposed to be so great! The king of poets."

Martinez shook his head. "He was. But in those two plays, he was writing poetry for two characters who were terrible writers. Do you see? Their writing had to fit their characters. Like the Nurse—she's an uneducated woman, and when she tries to do a classical Latin mourning verse, she's stumped!"

"That's right," Angela put in. "And Bottom is a simple workman, so when he tries to compose a fancy verse play, it comes out as terrible poetry. Bottom," she added kindly, "is a character in *A Midsummer Night's Dream*. He's writing this verse drama in honor of his king's—"

"Stop! I really don't need you to recite a whole play. I'll take your word for it! Personally, I never could stand Shakespeare, wouldn't read it when it was assigned, fudged my way through the exams later. And I certainly never took a class in it. I mean, I was a business major in college. What would I ever want with English literature?''

Angela shook her head. ''You're hopeless, Cal. Everybody's supposed to know something about Shakespeare!''

''But if everybody did,'' Martinez put in, ''Elroy Carmichael wouldn't have been able to pass Shakespeare's verses off as his own! He must have counted on everybody feeling the way you do, Mrs. Wingate—saying Shakespeare is great but never reading any if they could help it!''

''I wonder why Elroy chose those awful poems, though?'' Angela wondered. ''I mean, there's a lot of very good things in the plays that people wouldn't know.''

''Listen, if he'd picked 'To be or not to be,' even I would have caught on,'' Caledonia protested.

''Exactly,'' Martinez said. ''He must have reached for less identifiable things. But why these? Well, maybe his own taste is so bad he can't tell it's bad poetry. There are a lot of people in the world who think that, if it's Shakespeare, it has to be good.''

Caledonia grinned. ''Like me?''

Martinez started toward the door again. ''I shall take great pleasure in trying to find out how Mr. Carmichael decided to steal from The Bard.''

''Will you come back and tell us? I mean, after all, we did uncover this for you . . .'' Angela was pleading.

''Ladies, if you will promise me once more to stay out of things, not to go looking for trouble, not to hunt down people to interview, not to put yourselves into harm's way—then I'll promise to report back. On everything. Is it a deal?''

Caledonia nodded. ''Deal.''

''Mrs. Benbow.''

''Oh, all right . . .''

''No halfhearted promises now. Mean what you say.''

''All right. It's a deal.''

''Ladies, in that case, I'll be back. Maybe not today—we need to find Mr. Carmichael, we need to ask him a lot of questions, we need to check up on him and his background.

But I will be back, and you are to wait for me and do nothing. *Nothing!* And now—'' with a sudden smile, he backed toward the door and did an exaggerated stage bow, sweeping the floor with a hand that held an imaginary hat that undoubtedly sported a huge white imaginary plume. ''Good night, good night, parting is such sweet sorrow. . . .'' And he backed out the door.

''That's Shakespeare again,'' Angela explained kindly.

''Well, at least I know those lines,'' Caledonia said. ''Good thing Elroy didn't try those!''

Angela sighed. ''The Lieutenant did that exit beautifully, didn't he? He should have been an actor instead of a policeman. He really is the most devastatingly handsome man, Caledonia. And to think—to think we helped him solve this murder. These murders!''

''Well, we did figure out that Elroy was a phony . . .''

''*I* figured it out!''

''All right, then, you figured it out. So I guess maybe you may have helped the Lieutenant wrap it all up.'' Caledonia sighed. ''It is good to think that this whole thing is almost over.''

Once more, the oracle had predicted—and once more the oracle was wrong!

Chapter 15

"On the way to supper that night, Caledonia came across Mr. Grogan sitting on a chair on the patio outside the lobby entrance, his elbows on his knees, his hands cupping his chin, his mournful eyes staring vacantly toward the twilight ocean.

"Evening, Mr. Grogan," Caledonia said.

He scarcely looked up. He did not answer at all.

"I said, good evening," she persisted.

He raised a single finger in salutation and groaned softly—a husky, rasping sort of sound.

"See something interesting out there?" Caledonia insisted.

At last he raised his head. "Shut up, dammit," he snarled. "Leave me alone. Interfering females . . . The head is splitting, the stomach heaves, the eyes don't focus . . . and she says it's a good evening. Get lost, lady, get lost!"

Caledonia was torn between outrage and amusement. "Poor Grogan," she told Angela when they were seated at the dining room table. "He's still suffering withdrawal symptoms. It's like a perpetual hangover, and having had one once myself, I can partially sympathize. I don't suppose you've ever . . ."

"Certainly not!" Angela could be disgustingly self-righteous at times.

"Well, then, just think about the sickest you've ever felt."

"When I had the measles when I was ten, I threw up . . ."

"Thanks, no need to explain it. Just think about it. Then

add to it the most unhappy and discouraged you've ever felt . . . and the angriest you've ever been. Roll 'em all together. There's Grogan . . . to the life. Or rather, to the death. I couldn't be angry with the poor fellow. I know he's going through three kinds of hell. I thought it would be over before now . . . that things would start to improve for him. Well, perhaps soon. I think I'll have double on the zucchini-mushroom casserole, Dolores,'' she added as the waitress sailed in with their salad course. ''That's good stuff.''

"Yes, Dolores," Angela said. "I wonder if you'd double up on the vegetables for me, too? I don't think I'd care for any of the meat loaf tonight.''

"Now, Mrs. Benbow," Dolores scolded. The head waitress took it personally if her charges did not eat properly. "You know you like meat loaf the way Mrs. Schmitt fixes it . . . all crusty with egg and milk . . . a lot of tomatoes and onion . . ."

"Thank you, I just don't . . . maybe next time." Dolores shrugged and went on to the kitchen, having delivered the last of her tray of salads.

"What's the matter, Angela? You usually love the meat loaf. All that tomato—"

"Stop! You didn't have to sit and watch her mix it today. I did—you know, when I questioned her? I had to find her in the kitchen. Yech! I may never eat meat loaf again. Here or anywhere!"

"Well, spare me the details, I— Uh-oh. Get a load of Martinez and his guest!"

Into the dining room strode the Lieutenant. Behind him a few paces was Swanson. And between them, moving along just as fast, but gliding rather than striding, was a gray man—gray hair, gray suit, gray skin—obviously a man who worked behind a desk and got few vacations in the sun. He also seemed the kind of man who would simply disappear into the wallpaper, blending into the background.

"If ever I saw a man who designed himself to be inconspicuous, that is the one," Caledonia marveled. "What would you say he did for a living?"

Angela considered. "I'd say he was a book salesman."

"Bingo!" Caledonia chirped. "Exactly what I'd say. Encyclopedias, probably. Door-to-door, certainly. The kind of salesman you'd find it easy to say no to, right?"

"Absolutely," Angela said.

"So my bet is that he's really a government agent. Didn't you ever notice how much FBI men and treasury agents tend to look like a caricature of the man in the street?" Caledonia said. "Like this fellow. He's the kind of man you'd just forget was there. And you'd keep talking about your private business, and pretty soon he'd know as much about you as you did! I remember the federal agents who used to call on the Admiral about security clearances for our civilian employees on naval bases. . . . They were so ordinary-looking, you could spot them at forty paces!"

The man's name was Anthony Tyrell and Caledonia was exactly right in her description. He was, as she surmised, a government agent; in fact he was an expert on the drug trade in Southern California. He was deliberately inconspicuous, and it was a pose he had cultivated with great care. He was also reasonably intelligent, quite charming, and occasionally witty. And he believed his protective coloration to be impenetrable. Had he overheard Caledonia Wingate's accurate assessment of him, it would have depressed him rather severely. At the moment he was basking in a false sense of security and exercising his charm on Martinez and Swanson, getting to know them before he had to get to work with them. And if you'd asked him, he'd have told you that except for the two policemen who had formally requested his presence and his expertise, there wasn't another soul who could guess who he was and why he was there.

But the entire dining room watched the three men. Any newcomer attracted more than a few stares and, when possible, a little eavesdropping. And there wasn't a resident—except perhaps for Grogan, staring dully at his slice of meat loaf—who didn't realize that Tyrell was some sort of official. That made him even more interesting. So though the diners continued to eat and to finish their meals, they did not leave.

They ordered an extra cup of coffee, they dawdled over their dessert, and all the while, pretending to converse together, they watched Tyrell.

For his part, Tyrell began to feel the solemn, silent observation before he was halfway through dinner, and it made him fidget nervously.

"I feel," he told Martinez, "like I am wearing a big sign that says, 'Look at me, I'm a T-Man!' I don't usually have this problem. Listen, do these people stare at you this way?"

"Most of the time," Martinez was amused. "Don't let it bother you. To them you're just a substitute for 'The Price Is Right' or a rerun of 'Hogan's Heroes.' You're a way to pass a few minutes for folks who are interested in everything— and have nothing much to occupy their attention."

"This place would drive me nuts," Tyrell said. "I hope I die on the job—young . . . or anyhow, before I have to retire to somewhere like . . ." he waved his hand around him.

"Sir," Swanson jumped into the conversation, "you got this place all wrong. It's great—especially for people who can't drive any more, because they get everything they want right here. It's like a vacation all year long . . . people wait on you, people to work for you . . ."

"Imagine you could retire onto a cruise ship," Martinez said. "That's the way they take care of these people . . . like passengers on a cruise ship!"

"And the food is almost as good," Swanson added.

"They make new friends . . . and when they want to visit with one of those friends, they only have to walk down the hall. It's like a very small town."

"Well, maybe," Tyrell said skeptically. "I'll have to take your word for it, because I don't plan to be around here very much. It gives me the creeps, seeing nothing but white hair and wrinkles and hearing aids everywhere I look. Though I'll admit the food is as good as you said it would be. And the service was terrific!" He covered his coffee cup with his hands as Chita Cassidy brought the pot around once more.

"Swan-sohn?" she cajoled. "Just a lee-eetle more?"

"Gee, thanks, Chee, but we've got to get back to work. We've got a pile of stuff . . ."

"Will I see you later? I'm on cleanup tonight, but you know I finish at eight-thirty."

Swanson blushed. "If I'm off. But don't wait for me. We may work late."

"Okay." She shrugged and went cheerfully off to bring coffee to other diners on the station.

"So it's progressed to late dates, has it?" Martinez asked. "Well, Shorty, you could do worse."

"Yessir, I sure could," Swanson said enthusiastically but with obvious embarrassment. "I just wish she hadn't . . ."

"I don't like mixing business with pleasure myself," Tyrell interjected. "It's a bad policy to get involved with any of the staff here, until you've cleared everybody. Kitchen staff, for instance, could easily bring drugs in and out of a place. I remember one time in Malibu there was this guy who was delivering for a dealer who also owned a restaurant. Well, the dealer hired his delivery boy to work as a dishwasher, and every night the dishwasher carried home meat scraps for his dog—in a plastic baggie, you know. But down inside that mess of half-rare meat and lumps of fat and bone, he hid packets of cocaine. Nobody wanted to look too closely at the garbage, so he got away with it for a long time."

"Chita's not carrying drugs in or out of here, either one," Swanson said indignantly.

"Maybe not," Tyrell said. "But until you know that for positive . . ."

"I do! I do know it!" Swanson's voice started to rise in volume and Martinez gestured him with a warning hand.

"Okay, young man," Tyrell said. "Don't get excited. I didn't mean you and that girl anyhow. I meant that as a general rule it's not a good thing to get yourself involved with anybody even remotely connected with a case while it's on. Well, shall we go and hunt up your suspect?"

Angela and Caledonia watched them as they walked from the dining room. "Maybe we'll hear something about Elroy tonight," Angela whispered.

But they did not.

The next morning was Sunday, the one day of the week that provided a change in the routine of the residents' days. On Sunday, residents could breakfast later than usual, which pleased Caledonia in particular. And lunch was delayed until twelve-thirty so that those who attended services in the chapel would have time to go home, remove hats and gloves, tuck away prayer books and purses, and freshen makeup and coiffures before venturing into the dining room.

The truth was that chapel services were thoroughly enjoyed, not so much for their religious content as for their entertainment value. The religious tone varied from one Sunday to the next, depending on which of the pastoral rota was next in the assigned cycle of ministers. But for the residents who attended, it was Something To Do, an event, a change in the routine of their days.

The services also left the congregants feeling virtuous, as though they'd done The Right Thing, thus attaining a bit of one-upmanship over the stubborn holdouts who did not attend at all, either because it was not their sect's day to supervise the service, or because they felt like hypocrites if they pretended to be religious one day a week.

Caledonia was in the latter category, but on special occasions she agreed to attend chapel with Angela who was a regular. Easter and Christmas were two services they both genuinely enjoyed. Memorials for deceased fellow residents were another "must" on both their lists. This Sunday was such a memorial. It had been announced repeatedly—by means of a placard on the desk, a typewritten insert in their dinner menu three days in a row, and an announcement at lunch. (Trinita Stainsbury had, for once, been reasonably solemn and dignified in her use of the public address system.)

Even so, Mary Moffet had forgotten and expressed surprise (in a genteel whisper) to Tootsie Armstrong when she read the notice in the chapel program they were given as they entered. "It doesn't matter," Tootsie assured her kindly. "You are here. That's the important thing."

"But I came for the wrong reasons!" Mary whispered

sadly. "And I'd have worn black, if I'd remembered it was Amy's memorial service."

"Why?" Tootsie said blankly. "You didn't even like her!"

"Well," Mary hissed, "it would just have feel better." She subsided and looked about her. The residents filed in by ones and twos and took their usual places. Part of the fun of Sunday chapel was to notice if anyone was late, to see if anyone had a guest, to speculate in whispers if one of the regulars was absent.

"Look, there's Emma," Mary pointed. "Oh, and Caledonia came with Angela today! My, my . . . that's an event!"

Angela and Caledonia stood in the center aisle at the back, and Angela's face was a study in outrage. "They took my seat! They've taken my place!" she was grumbling to Caledonia in an undertone laced with fury.

"Well, there are plenty of places," Caledonia said reasonably.

"But that's my seat," Angela objected.

Caledonia felt exactly the same about the table they shared at meals. The table had become *theirs* as surely as if it had an engraved brass plaque affixed to it. A couple of years before, Torgeson had suggested that residents change tables every six weeks or so, but the outcry had been overwhelming. For all the fuss, he might have been suggesting they exchange toothbrushes!

Now, however, Caledonia was pretending not to understand Angela's complaint. In Camden's chapel, Angela habitually took the seat closest to the back right-hand corner. Today, the seat was occupied, as were the two nearest to it. Tyrell had chosen her place, and Martinez and Swanson sat beside him. That left two seats in the same half-row on that side of the aisle, but even Mr. Brighton—who, with his arthritis, always chose the aisle seat in that back row so he didn't have to walk any further—even Mr. Brighton had moved to a different row. There was something forbidding about the gray man. Martinez and Swanson, they liked; they were used to those two. Many of the residents even called them "*Our* policemen." But Tyrell . . .

"What's the matter with that one?" Tyrell whispered, leaning over to Martinez and pointing to Angela, who stood in the center aisle glaring daggers down the row at him. "She acts like I took her seat or something!"

Caledonia meanwhile was putting a firm hand under Angela's elbow. "Come on and sit over here," she directed, pulling Angela to the left-hand section of the seats.

"No. That's not right," Angela said stubbornly.

"Come on!" Caledonia gave her a yank that propelled her into the second-to-last row on the left. "Here's a vacant place . . ."

"It doesn't matter to you," Angela hissed as they stumbled into the row and found seats. "You don't come here every week. I do. That's my seat and everyone knows it!"

"Why do you think those policemen are here, anyhow?" Caledonia rumbled, changing the subject.

They were there at Tyrell's request. He wanted an introduction to what he called "the cast of characters," but he wanted to be less conspicuous than he had been in the dining room. He preferred to look at others without their being able to look at him—and the back row corner of the chapel seemed perfect.

But Tyrell was doomed to disappointment. All during the service, the congregation had the policemen squarely in their sights, even if they never seemed to turn their heads in that direction. When Tyrell pulled out his pocket handkerchief to smother a cough, 164 eyes noted the fact. When Martinez flicked a speck of dust from his sleeves, 164 eyes watched it go. (There were 85 people in chapel besides the police—but the pastor had his eyes on his notes, and two residents were legally blind and could not see that far.)

"Well, what a fizzle," Angela said to Caledonia as they walked slowly across the lobby toward the still-closed dining room door. "Nothing. They just sat and watched us watch them! I thought maybe they'd arrest someone or something. . . . And I gave up my favorite seat in church for nothing!"

Caledonia grinned. "Well, better luck at lunch."

But the rest of Sunday passed without incident.

It was near mid-morning on Monday before Martinez sought the two ladies out by phoning their rooms. Each was at home watching television. Each responded at once, heading for the elevator and the second-floor sewing room. Angela, with not so far to go, was there when Caledonia arrived.

"Come in, Mrs. Wingate," Martinez said, "and have a seat."

Caledonia's cerise-and-blue-striped silk caftan fluttered in her self-generated breeze as she walked across the room and plopped onto a straight chair near the table. Angela was already seated in the room's only easy chair, but Caledonia didn't mind, for it was of rather too dainty proportions, and the only time she'd chosen it for herself was at a quilting bee. She'd gotten embarrassingly stuck, and the other women present had to pull her from the chair's embrace.

"Coffee?" Martinez asked. "Shorty will be glad to go and get some from Chita Cassidy for you." Swanson grinned and blushed.

Both women nodded. "Cream and sugar," Angela said. Caledonia ordered hers black—"for my sins of the flesh," she sighed—as Swanson took off, pleased to be sent officially to the one place in the whole building he would most like to be.

"Well, Lieutenant, what's your news?" Caledonia asked, not the least embarrassed at her own curiosity. "Have you arrested Angela's culprit?"

"In a manner of speaking, ladies. We have certainly taken him into custody."

"Wonderful!" Angela said. "Then I was right?"

"Not exactly. When I left you," Martinez said, "I thought Carmichael offered some interesting possibilities for investigation. And he did. But, as it developed, it had nothing to do with the drug trade. Elroy Carmichael is just a slightly weak-wristed con man working on a scam to defraud elderly ladies. Tyrell, our treasury agent, agrees with me on this."

"A con man!" Angela was outraged. "What do you mean?"

"I mean he was trying to promote money out of you—well, perhaps not you personally, although from what you told me, I think he'd started working on you out in the garden Saturday morning."

"But—surely you still suspect Elroy of the murders!"

"No, we don't. Well, of course one can never be a hundred percent sure of anything. But we're pretty sure he had nothing to do with the murders. We called on the eminent poet in his apartment and he came apart at the seams. We didn't even have to accuse him, he just started talking. We barely got him stopped long enough to warn him we might use it all against him later. He's been afraid from the first of being tied in to Amy Kinseth's death."

"A con man? Trying to get money?" Caledonia was still incredulous.

"Yes, and he's done this sort of thing before, apparently. At other retirement centers. We've been checking—and there was a complaint last year from a place in Phoenix. . . . A 'poet' named Bradford Raphael showed up, enchanted all the residents, and they got together a substantial fund to help him put out a book."

"Which was never published?" Angela asked.

"Right. Instead, Raphael disappeared—and so did the publishing fund. A few years ago, it was a retirement community in South Carolina. There a 'poet' named Buford T. Pinckney was going to do a biography of Robert E. Lee in epic verse. He started two funds there, one for the biography, one for a memorial statue. But he put both funds into one pocket, one dark night, and took off."

"And he was doing exactly the same thing here, right?" Caledonia said.

"That's it. He's admitted that he was after the whole program committee—your Mrs. Felton and Mrs. Stainsbury and the Jackson twins—they're the ones who seem to have had the most to do with him personally, and to be the most completely taken in by him. They're the ones who booked him in here for lectures and readings—not once, but over and over again. Of course, he went after everyone. But they were his first targets. He actually had managed to start collecting. He had a couple of checks."

"Who from?" Angela demanded at once.

"That, Mrs. Benbow, I cannot tell you."

"You mean you won't," Caledonia accused.

"All right, if you prefer, Mrs. Wingate. Besides, it isn't relevant. The point is, he never intended to publish a book of any kind. How he worked—he wasn't a writer himself at all . . . He gathered obscure poetry from other writers . . . not all of it was Shakespeare. He let us see that manuscript he circulated among prospective investors. There was a little Sidney, a dollop of Swinburne, just a dash of Lovelace—"

"I suppose he thought they were the ones we'd have been least likely to read," Angela said.

He nodded. "Like most people, he assumed the elderly were all a little simple. He felt confident nobody would catch on. It never occurred to him that anybody—like you, Mrs. Wingate—would be perceptive enough to see it as pure trash. And in his wildest dreams he never expected anyone here to identify it as plagiarized, as you did, Mrs. Benbow."

"Uh-huh! That's what really gets me steamed up, Lieutenant," Caledonia said. "He looked down on our intelligence just because we're old! If he wasn't in trouble already, I'd see he got in trouble!"

"Oh, he's in trouble all right. The problem is—it's nothing to do with the main part of this case. We'll see that he's put out of action, and we'll see the money is returned to those who've already written him a check. But as for arresting him for murder . . ."

"I still don't see why you insisted he's not involved, Lieutenant," Angela argued. She hated giving up her very own suspect. "He's a criminal, and I would think that once a criminal, always a criminal. I mean—if he'd cheat an old lady out of her life savings, he'd do just about anything."

"On the contrary, Mrs. Benbow. It's not 'once a criminal, always a criminal.' It's more like 'once a con man, always a con man.' The arsonist doesn't steal cars . . . the car thief doesn't torch buildings. The fellow who successfully robs a liquor store doesn't suddenly start in on banks. Each person picks something he feels comfortable with, and he sticks to it.''

''You're saying,'' Caledonia interjected, ''that he wouldn't kill someone if he thought he was in danger of being discovered? Of being sent to prison?''

''Well, I suppose he might, if he felt he had to. But so far as we can tell, he didn't have to. He was getting along very well with his schemes. In a small way, of course. He wasn't a very ambitious little crook—less like Ponzi and more like the carnie who makes a modest living on the shell game. He could say he was a success, assuming he wasn't too greedy.''

''Lieutenant, how do you explain the discrepancy in what he says went on in Amy's apartment and what the Jackson sisters heard through the wall?'' Caledonia protested. ''The Jacksons thought Amy did give him money. He told Angela the opposite.''

''He's telling a different story now,'' Martinez smiled. ''Mrs. Benbow, he didn't want to admit to you that Mrs. Kinseth had agreed to help him get that book of poetry published. He thought that implicated him in her murder, and he was scared to death. When you asked, he pretended she'd turned him down. But she hadn't.''

Angela shook her head as though to clear cobwebs. ''But what about her offering to get him some cocaine? Some coke?''

''The Jackson sisters had the right version of what happened, after all. They said that what Amy offered Elroy was just a soft drink, nothing more—and he agrees. You didn't ask him about that, when you had him out in the garden, did you?''

''Well, no, but . . .''

''Here's how he tells it, and you can see the Jacksons heard correctly. He came to ask for money for his poetry book. Amy acted interested and asked him to recite for her, but then she just turned her back and walked out, down the hall to the community kitchen to the big refrigerator there, and came back with a chilled can of root beer for him.''

"You mean she just walked out of the room and left him bawling his verses? She couldn't have been more insulting to him if she tried," Caledonia marveled. "It's a wonder he didn't up and hit her with something right then!"

"But why did she agree to help him with his publication," Angela asked, "if she didn't really like his poetry?"

"I'll bet," Caledonia said, "that in a few days, when he was really convinced he was getting a lot of money from her, she'd have called him in, told him she'd changed her mind, and watched him come apart. She seems to have taken delight in making people unhappy."

"Yes, that was something of a specialty with her, I take it, from what people around here have told me," Martinez said. "She really got to your Mr. Torgeson."

Caledonia grinned at the memory of the encounter in the lobby. "Well, to be fair about it, she skewered everybody she could reach, right from the first. She let Connie Maddox have it . . ."

"The nurse," Angela explained, "who was trying to take her blood pressure. A sort of check-in procedure."

Caledonia continued, "She insulted her decorator . . ."

"Poor Bobby Baird," Angela sighed.

"And she went right on making people angry. Everybody who came to her apartment went away in a rage, according to them," Caledonia said.

"Except Mrs. Schmitt," Angela amended. "She doesn't get angry about anything. But Lieutenant, are you saying that there wasn't anything at all to my theory about the cocaine?"

"Apparently not. Though I admit it was ingenious. Oh! Here!" Lieutenant Martinez got to his feet to help Swanson, who was coming through the door with a double-sized tray on which he had four cups of coffee, a creamer and sugar, and two plates of sweet rolls Chita had insisted he take along. The tray wobbled precariously, but for once Swanson set it down without spilling anything.

Angela sighed deeply, her breath across the surface of her coffee setting up a series of wavelets in her cup. "Oh, dear.

My beautiful, my perfect theory! I still can't believe I could be so wrong."

Martinez smiled kindly. "I wish I had a quarter for every time one of my ideas has been wrong. And I've worked some out even tighter than you did that one . . . down to the last detail. Motive, opportunity, psychology, sugar . . ."

"What?"

"Please pass the sugar."

"Oh. I thought you meant . . . never mind, Lieutenant," Angela said.

"Well, Lieutenant, what's the next step?" Caledonia said, rather indistinctly because her mouth was filled with fresh hot roll and almond frosting.

"Nothing that involves you, I'm afraid," Martinez said. "We may have unmasked a con artist and a phony . . ."

"And a simply terrible poet!" Caledonia added, picking up another hot bear claw and reaching for the butter plate.

Martinez grinned. "Remember, that wasn't his own stuff anyhow and there's no law against bad poetry. But don't sidetrack me, because what I'm going to tell you is important. I told you to stay home and stay safe—and now I'm telling you that it's more important than ever for you to do so. If drugs are really involved in this, Tyrell's very presence here may make our killer frantic with fear. You don't know what he may perceive as a threat . . ."

Caledonia nodded. "Uh-huh! We thought this visitor of yours was somebody official. Drug specialist, is he?"

Martinez nodded. "A specialist. Right now, he's working on a theory of his own that has to do with the kitchen staff and drugs. He's giving us a lot to follow up on. But now—about your staying out of this . . ."

"Good advice. And this time, Lieutenant, I propose to take it. Angela?"

Angela sighed and nodded. "I know you mean well for us, Lieutenant. I'll try to behave in a way you'd approve."

"Good. Now ladies, I've paid my debt—I've brought you up-to-date on Elroy and his status . . . I've used about half an hour of my morning schedule in a coffee break Tyrell wouldn't approve . . . the man is a hard worker, I'll say that for him. So I must get back to work myself and justify the tax-payers' faith in me.'' He rose and indicated the door.

The two women rose with reluctance. It was nice to be in the middle of things—to know things—but now, apparently, it was back to the rocking chair.

"Thanks for the brunch, Detective Swanson," Caledonia said, giving her mouth one more swipe before she tossed the napkin aside and followed Angela toward the door. "You tell that Cassidy girl she could do worse—you're a nice young fellow."

The women started talking even before the door swung shut behind them. Caledonia was saying, "That young man is more than half a boy! But he's such a nice boy . . .''

"I like Chita, too. And isn't her father a retired police-man? I think they'd make a good pair, she and young Swanson." Their voices trailed away down the hall, leaving Martinez and a blushing Swanson to prepare themselves for another session of work.

Chapter 16

ANGELA MAY have seemed serene on the surface, but in truth she was keenly disappointed at the loss of Elroy as her Suspect Number One for murder. She had tried not to let Martinez see how much of a letdown it was, because she felt somehow that she should have been able to take it all in stride. But for once, amusement—which would ordinarily have stifled her disappointment—did not seem to come, and she only felt petulant at having been proven wrong. She was mildly surprised at herself.

That evening, she was annoyed again to find she had no appetite. She phoned the desk to say she would not be coming to supper. She no sooner hung up her phone, than it rang again—Caledonia suggesting a drop of sherry before dinner.

To her surprise again, Angela found herself flaring up. "You're getting to be as bad as Grogan, Caledonia. You have sherry every night now, not just on special occasions. You're going to be an alcoholic and end in an early grave!"

Caledonia was amused. "It's far too late for 'an early grave' for me, girl. And you know I never have more than one—well, sometimes two—glasses. And they're tiny glasses at that—liqueur glasses, not real sherry glasses. So I don't know . . ."

"Don't fight with me, Caledonia, I don't feel like it. I'm sorry if I hurt your feelings. Incidentally, I won't be coming down to supper. Goodnight." And Angela hung up the phone abruptly. And just as abruptly, she burst into tears.

All night long, she tossed and turned and had bad dreams.

224

She was an author with a book of poetry, and Caledonia handed back her manuscript and said the poems were awful . . . Didn't even rhyme. Angela wept in her dream, and woke wringing wet. She went to the bathroom and got a glass of water, for her throat was dry. "Sleeping with my mouth open again," she thought, and stumbled back to bed. It was a tangled mess of lumps and ridges.

Grumpily she got back up and smoothed the sheets and the thin blanket. How hard it had been, when she first moved to Southern California, to believe she would never need the Hudson's Bay blankets she'd brought with her. Even now she hated to give them up, and two five-stripe blankets were folded into plastic bags at the back of her highest closet shelf. She lay back down and felt a little better for smooth sheets. "But I'm still upset. I probably won't get to sleep at all," she told herself, just before she drifted off to another round of nightmares and disturbingly active slumber.

It had been years since she'd had to set the alarm; habit roused her daily, usually close to six o'clock—or when she was excited or happy, somewhat earlier. This morning she was jolted to see, when she finally woke, that it was nearly seven. She had been in a deep slumber, having another bad dream that teased at her memory but eluded her.

Her morning shower made her feel somewhat better, and she dressed and headed for the dining room. But when she was seated at her table, and her waitress—Dolores again this morning—came to take her order, she found she was no longer interested. "I think I'll just have some fruit juice, please," she said.

"You didn't eat your meat loaf the other night," Dolores scolded. "Now you're going light on breakfast. . . . That's just not good for you."

"Oh, leave me alone, can't you?" Angela said grouchily. Then, because she really liked Dolores, who was looking pained, she said, "I'm sorry, Dolores. All right, bring me some toast too, then. But I'm really not hungry and I don't"— she was surprised suddenly at the truth of her excuse—"I don't really feel all that well."

"You haven't got the flu, too, have you?" Dolores asked, concerned. "Once it starts around a place like this, it really gallops. Mrs. Hanson and Mrs. Dougherty had it last week, and Mr. Singleton and his wife are both down with it. Geraldine Williams, down in the cottages . . . and one of the new couples who just moved in last week . . . I forgot their name . . . you know . . ."

Angela was staring down at her plate and hardly listening. She only nodded.

"Did you get your flu shot last fall the way you were supposed to?" Dolores asked.

"I never take a flu shot," Angela said. "I never get the flu."

"Everybody was supposed to."

"Besides, I hate taking shots. And I thought you only got the flu in the winter," Angela protested.

"Maybe that's what you're supposed to do—but people here don't seem to know that. We sure have had a lot of it . . ." and Dolores trotted off. When she came back with juice and toast, Angela had gone.

Back in her room, Angela conceded that something was wrong. Of course, it couldn't be the flu. She never got the flu. But it was something! She felt perfectly terrible.

She turned on the television, then stretched out on her couch and pulled an afghan up over herself. She drifted in and out of sleep, while some doctor on a talk show declaimed about Southern California's outbreak of the flu—so unusual for late in the year.

About an hour later Caledonia phoned to see how Angela was doing. Angela was a bit groggy and disoriented when the phone woke her, and her ears seemed to be ringing. She couldn't quite hear Caledonia's questions, and she had a feeling her answers weren't quite on track with what was asked. Caledonia was sure they were not, and without asking Angela, she phoned the nurses' station.

"I think you've got a very sick lady—Mrs. Benbow—first floor hallway. Might be the flu everybody's got . . ."

The Monstrous Maddox groaned. "Don't tell me . . . another . . . We've got three new cases on the second floor today, one new one in the cottage apartments, and now one on the first floor. We've got seventeen in various stages of recovery. Mrs. Wingate, did you take your shots this fall?''

"You bet," Caledonia assured her. "Never miss. I forgot one year, but I don't skip 'em on purpose.''

"Good. I wish everybody did that. Well, I'll check in on Mrs. Benbow for you as soon as I get done with Mr. and Mrs. Peabody here. They've come in to get their ears cleaned out—so they can be fitted for hearing aids this afternoon. Won't take me a minute.''

The Monstrous Maddox might not be a popular nurse, but she did her job thoroughly. It was a half hour before she could get down to Angela's apartment. Angela woke halfway as the nurse entered. All she could make out at first was a blurry white figure coming through her outside door.

"Who is it? Didn't I lock the door?"

"It's Connie Maddox, Mrs. Benbow. I used the master key because I didn't want to disturb you. Now, how are you feeling?''

Efficiently, if not gently, Maddox took her pulse and got a reading on her temperature—"You've got nearly three degrees, Mrs. Benbow"—and checked her over for other aches and pains. "I think it's just the flu," she finally said. "But Doc Carter better come across here when he gets done with his rounds and take a look.''

"Don't bother him . . ." Angela began. She hated all the medical fuss.

"Get on a clean nightie and get into your bed," Maddox said, ignoring Angela's protests. "You're going to have to do that anyhow—might as well do it now.''

Angela nodded wordlessly—a sure sign that she was not herself—and staggered up from the couch. She tottered on into the bedroom without even pausing to fold up the afghan she'd been using—another sure sign that something was amiss; ordinarily, even a Kleenex drooping from its box gave her a sense of disorder. Now she left things where they fell, including the clothes she removed in the bedroom. She collapsed into the bed and gave in to weakness and aching muscles. And within minutes, she also fell victim to her first attack of nausea—her first of many through the two days that followed.

In the acute stage of her illness, which Dr. Carter did indeed diagnose as flu, Angela cared little that she was isolated, allowed no visitors. The nursing staff and the doctor came and went. They brought thermometers, took her pulse, tried to get her to drink fluids . . . and she neither knew nor cared.

But on Thursday morning, the third day after she fell ill, Angela sat up in bed, and when Mary Washington came in with a thermometer and breakfast tray of several juices and a slice of dry toast, Angela bit her head off. "Put the tray where I can reach it, can't you? No use having it down around my ankles. Use your head, Nurse!"

Mary Washington beamed. "That's the way, Mrs. Benbow," she said. "Got your old fighting spirit back! I'll just leave the tray—and you try to eat that toast and drink all the juice. I'm going off duty now, but I'll give orders you're to have some solid food by lunchtime. You'll be weak and we need to try getting some of your strength back."

"Just go away," Angela barked.

By ten o'clock, Angela had taken a sponge bath and changed her nightclothes to dry, clean pajamas. She had even ventured into the living room to look at the mail the nurses had brought each day and left there for her. She wobbled as she walked, but at least she walked.

At twelve-thirty the lunch tray arrived, and with it Thursday's day-duty nurse, The Monstrous Maddox, armed with a pitcher of juice, a small plate of chicken salad and some buttered crescent rolls, a stack of clean towels, and the inevitable thermometer.

"I still feel terrible," Angela complained. "If I'm getting well, why do I feel so weak?"

"You're almost eighty years old and you haven't eaten properly since Sunday," Maddox said, shaking down the glass cylinder. "Open your mouth . . . lift the tongue . . .

thank you. Let's have your wrist so I can take your pulse. You've got to expect that fever will take it out of you, too. At your age—after all, next month you'll be—''

"Be quiet," Angela snapped. "I don't broadcast my age, and I don't want anyone else to, either. You may have to know it because it's on my record. But don't shout it out loud!"

"Nobody can hear," Maddox said, pulling the thermometer. "Ah-ah-ah—you've had your mouth open and this hasn't registered yet. Now, just keep quiet a little while. I'm going to change your towels for you." The maids were instructed not to come by a sickroom—more of the quarantine procedure by which the medical staff tried to keep in-house epidemics from taking hold—and the nurses obliged by changing linens and doing a little minor straightening up whenever a resident was ill.

"That's why they can hear . . . the bathroom door is open!" Angela said, raising her voice slightly as the nurse disappeared around the corner. "That bathroom wall is like paper. Ask the Jackson twins if you don't believe me. They heard every word from next door, right through their bathroom wall!"

"Oh, I believe you," Maddox said, coming out with the old towels and dumping them beside the breakfast tray. "But your next-door neighbor is as deaf as a post. I'd have to yell awfully loud for her to find out that you'll be seventy-eight next month!" Maddox grinned wickedly. "My, my— seventy-eight!" She repeated clearly.

"I told you not to say my age out loud!" Angela grumbled. "And you don't have to be so gleeful about it. I think you enjoy—"

Maddox paid absolutely no attention. She merely pulled the thermometer from Angela's mouth and held it up in the light. "Uh-huh. That's better. You're right at 98.4. The worst is over. I think you should try to get up tomorrow, Mrs. Benbow. The sooner you walk a little—go to the dining room, try to get your strength back—the better."

And she scooped up the used towels, hoisted the breakfast

tray, and left. Angela could hear the outside door slam vigorously as she departed. "I won't wait till tomorrow—I'll get up and walk around today," she told herself. But by the time she'd gotten only as far as the bathroom door, she was shaking. So she took one more nap before she roused herself to dress and phone Caledonia.

"Ah, great to hear from you," Caledonia rumbled into the phone. "You know I wanted to come by, but Carter's strict about quarantine for things like colds and the flu. He says we're all so old we have no immunity left, and we catch everything anybody else gets. The only way to stay healthy is to stay away. Feeling better?"

"Terribly weak," Angela complained. "Because when I wasn't asleep, I was throwing up and that's the truth!"

"Didn't they give you shots to settle your stomach?"

"All the time! But it took them a while to work each day . . . so mornings were rough. But I'm supposed to try going to the dining room."

"Tell you what," Caledonia said. "I'll come by your room to pick you up. You'll need support—literally."

Promptly at five-fifty that evening, Caledonia knocked on her door. "Convoy's here to take you to dinner," she announced. "Gosh, I missed you, girl." And she beamed as she put her big arm out for Angela to lean on.

In the dining room, people made a gratifying fuss. Emma Grant came by, Tootsie Armstrong came by twice, and so did Mary Moffet—even Mr. Grogan did.

"I suppose I should say I'm glad to see you, but seeing you reminds me of my own problems. Still—it's nice to have familiar faces around. Welcome back." And he stumped off, looking glum.

"I think he's getting a little better, Cal," Angela said. "He's not acting nearly so hung over."

From the far corner of the room, Dora Lee Jackson came, her angora sweater glowing rose and shedding profusely with her every move, her azalea pink cotton skirt swirling in unpressed pleats around her knees. "I tell you what it is," Caledonia muttered, before Dora Lee got into earshot.

"Those Jacksons are caught in a time warp. They're back in the fifties—when girls wore those fuzzy sweaters with pearls and big circular skirts . . ."

"And pink saddle shoes?"

"Hah! Nobody but the Jacksons ever wore pink ones. Hello, Dora . . ."

"Hi there, Caledonia. Oh Angela, I'm so glad you're back here with us. 'Course you still look a little peaked . . . you feeling better?"

"Yes, but weak."

"Well, at least you're on the mend. I know Donna Dee would welcome you too, if she was here. She came down with the flu this afternoon."

"Oh, dear. I'm sorry to hear that," Caledonia said. "But, how about you? Should you be out here? Surely you may be coming down with it."

"Well, I hope not. Nurse Maddox said it was probably all right—unless I start feeling icky-sicky . . ."

"Icky-sicky!" said Caledonia incredulously. "Icky-sicky?"

"You know," Dora Lee simpered. "Woopsy. Up-chucky."

Caledonia closed her eyes. "Please don't go on. We are trying to eat dinner, you know." Angela, eyeing her first full meal somewhat dubiously, had already started to push it aside with distaste.

"Oh, I'm sorry, but that's what we girls always call it when we throw u—"

"*Please!*" Angela pushed the plate farther away and turned her head to look out the window, away from the food.

"Oh, dear, is something wrong? Mama always said I was the one with the strong stomach, of course. Donna Dee was always the first to get sick, but I could hold out for ages. And nothing upsets me enough that I can't eat. I could always eat . . ."

"Yes! Well, that's wonderful," Caledonia said hastily. "We certainly hope Donna feels better soon. And that you don't come down with it."

"Oh, I'm sure I won't, now that I'll be getting my flu shot this evening. Better late than never, I always say."

"Very original," Angela muttered, still looking out at the garden.

"It doesn't seem to have helped Donna Dee, of course. Nurse Maddox warned us she might be too late giving us the shots. But we thought we better have them anyway. We were alarmed when you came down with flu—with us living so close to you and all. We didn't take the shot last fall, you see . . ."

"Everyone was supposed to," Caledonia said. "I took mine."

Dora Lee twisted her hands together apologetically. "I'm such a coward about things like that. Really . . . But this afternoon, when they started giving shots on our hallway—well, we told Nurse Maddox to go ahead. Donna's brave—she took hers right away, though it obviously didn't help much. This evening I'll try to be a brave girl and take mine, too—and hope it does better for me than—well, I don't want to bore you with our problems."

She fluttered her eyelashes coyly, waiting for someone to say, "Oh, you're not boring us." No one did. Angela and Caledonia sat absolutely silent, gazing at her. "Well, I just wanted to say it's a pleasure to have you up and about," she finally said, with a small and rather pinched smile, and she flounced off out of the room, a cloud of angora fuzz floating behind her, presumably to go back to her ailing sister.

"Well, well," Caledonia said, "so now the doctors aren't waiting till you go to them—they're delivering right to your door! I wonder if I should take another shot? To sort of increase my immunity. I hate being sick."

"Nobody likes it," Angela snapped. "You know, I think I really have eaten all I can manage."

Caledonia grinned. "Yeah, the dinner table conversation did get a little too much there for a while. That woman has no sense of delicacy, has she?"

"Well, not just that. I feel a little woozy. After all, it is my first time out this week. How about helping me get home?''

Her knees did wobble noticeably as she walked across the lobby, but she made it back and to her pleasure was not suffering at all from a queasy feeling as she might have been the day before. Caledonia helped with the door key and kept her arm steady, and Angela leaned on it as she would on a walker, till they were inside the apartment. "Stay a minute, Cal," Angela said. "I'm certainly not sleepy—I did nothing else much but sleep for three days. And I'm not really sick any more—I just need to sit down. I hope this weakness doesn't last. . . . Anyway, I'm lonely and I could stand the company. Besides I want to hear the news. . . ."

"There isn't any news." Caledonia helped Angela into a chair and plopped herself down on the couch. "At least, not that I've been told. That government agent—his name turns out to be Tyrell, did you know?"

"Yes, I heard that somewhere—before I got sick."

"Tyrell seems to be busy. He pokes around everywhere. I saw him out in the trash barrels the other day. . . . He has some of Martinez's policemen assigned to him, and three of them—Tyrell included—had wilted lettuce and crumpled paper strewn all over the sidewalk behind the kitchen. I'm not sure what they were looking for, but it was a sight, something that would definitely put you off your feed—as bad as Dora Lee talking about her sister being sick!"

Angela grinned ruefully. "I wasn't doing too well even before she got started. But after . . . I'm sorry their flu shots didn't help them, but I just didn't feel like hearing about every nauseating moment."

"You know," Caledonia mused, "flu shots used to take a couple of weeks minimum to take effect. I remember last fall, when they were giving 'em out . . . We had to line up in the corridor and wait, but nobody had remembered to put out chairs, and some of the people with canes and walkers just couldn't stay in the line. . . . It was pretty bad."

"That's another reason I skipped it!" Angela said.

"Well, anyhow, they came up and down the line with a little printed sheet and they read it to us . . ."

"Typical," Angela grumped. "They always assume we can't read for ourselves. They treat us like . . ."

"The leaflet said that we should try to stay away from crowds and take plenty of vitamin C for a couple of weeks, because the point of the shot is to get your body's defenses working, and it takes a while for them to get up to speed. But I guess now, apparently, the shot takes effect immediately."

Angela furrowed her little brow. "What makes you think so?"

"Well, didn't Dora Lee say they were giving shots up and down the hallway today? I mean, what's the point of giving shots right in the middle of an epidemic, if they don't take effect for weeks?"

Angela bit her lip and then reached over and dragged the phone toward her. "Under the table, Cal—there on the shelf—hand me the building phone directory."

"Who are you calling?"

"Janice Felton. Down the hall. It seems to me that . . . Ah, Janice. Hello. This is Angela Benbow. . . . Much better, thank you. A little weak, but—well, that isn't why I called. Janice, did you take a flu shot last fall? . . . Well, neither did I. I regret it now, of course. But what I wanted to say was—did you take one when they came by giving them today? . . . This afternoon, I understood . . . Oh, I see. Well, maybe I was mistaken. Thanks. I was just curious . . ." There was a considerable pause while Angela listened—and listened. Finally she said, "Oh, my goodness, yes, I'll look forward to that. Provided I feel strong enough, of course. 'Bye now." She hung up and made a face.

"Janice wants me to come to a program tomorrow afternoon in the chapel—some man has a chicken that plays the piano. A toy piano, I suppose, but no thanks, all the same. Let's see . . . Sadie Mandelbaum—Mandelbaum—Mandel . . ." She ran her finger down one page of the directory and up the next.

"Angela, what are you up to?"

But Angela was dialing again. "Oh—hello, Sadie? It's Angela. Angela Benbow. . . . No, Sadie, I know you're not Angela. *I'm* Angela! . . . Yes, that's right. How are you? . . . *I said*"—she raised her voice again—*"How are you?"*

She covered the mouthpiece and whispered, "Why the woman won't use that voice amplifier her nephew bought for her . . . *That's good, glad to hear that*, Sadie . . . Listen, Sadie, do you think you could plug in the amplifier? . . . I said, *plug in the amplifier*!"

The hand went over the mouthpiece again. "Thank goodness!" Angela hissed. "She said she couldn't hear very well and to wait while she got the amplifier. . . . There, now, is that better? Good. Sadie, I think you know I've had the flu . . . Oh, I'm better, thank you. I was wondering if you took your flu shot last fall? . . . Uh-huh. Well, then, did you take one today when they came around in this hall? . . . Yes, they did. . . . No, I don't think they just skipped you."

The hand went over the mouthpiece again. "She's perfectly paranoid," Angela whispered to Caledonia. "She always thinks people are talking about her or plotting to leave her out of things." Then aloud she said into the phone, "Well, certainly, I think I'd ask at the infirmary. Better late than never—ha-ha-ha-ha . . ." Her laugh had an artificial sound that made Caledonia wince. "Thanks, then. And 'bye now, Sadie." She hung up and sat looking at the phone, a puzzled frown on her face.

"All right, Angela. What was that all about?" Caledonia said.

"Well, didn't Dora Lee say she and her sister got flu shots because everybody on this hall was getting them today?"

"I think so. Something like that."

"Nobody else got them. Nobody was even offered one. At least not Sadie or Janice. . . . Now, don't you think that's a little strange?"

"I guess so. But talk about paranoia . . . Sadie's not the only one. What makes you so sure there's something odd about the shots?"

"You. Saying they must give instant immunity. Because I was watching television Monday morning, and there was this doctor on the 'Phil Donahue Show.' I was pretty groggy—going in and out—because I had a fever. But one thing I do remember. He was warning that it took two to four weeks for the shot to take effect."

"That's what I said," Caledonia was puzzled. "That's what it used to be."

"But it must still be so, or why would he talk about it?"

Caledonia nodded. "Of course! And if that's so, who told the Jacksons they'd have instant immunity?"

"And why give them a shot at all? And why only them?"

Caledonia grabbed the phone. "Clara?" she shouted. "Clara, find that policeman, Lieutenant Whatsis-face . . . Martinez . . . and get him to come to the phone, will you? . . . Oh? Well, when you find him . . . Thanks."

Angela nodded. "I think it's worth telling him anyhow, Cal. It may be nothing . . ."

The phone rang within minutes and Angela answered and started her story without any preamble. "I didn't have the shot, you see, but Cal did and they told her—and it said on the 'Phil Donahue Show,' too—that it wouldn't take effect. Not right away, you see. But the Jacksons think it will, and the nurse told them she was giving the shot to everyone on the hall. Donna Dee is very sick already. I don't know . . ."

Whatever Martinez understood of the jumble, it was sufficiently interesting to him to bring him to Angela's apartment within another few minutes, Swanson behind him. "Slow down, Mrs. Benbow, and tell us about this."

Caledonia held up her hand. "Let me try. I stammer less. Donna Dee Jackson is terribly ill, according to her sister. And she got sick today after she had a shot to prevent her getting the flu. Dora Lee said she was nervous about shots, but she'd take one herself, later this evening."

"All right. I understand that much. Now, what about it?"

"Well, it's crazy," Angela interrupted. "Flu shots don't take effect for days and days—a couple of weeks even. Why would they give the Jacksons a shot in the middle of an epidemic when it's too late for it to help them?''

Martinez was not especially perturbed. "Perhaps they're traveling later on. Like maybe next month. They'd want to be sure they didn't get sick then, while they're on the road. I took my own flu shot this year late—but in time to keep me from being susceptible on my vacation.''

"They're not going anywhere. They don't have the money to travel," Angela protested.

"There are a lot of reasons," Martinez soothed. "Maybe they just insisted. You could have the shot if you wanted it, even if it was useless—couldn't you?''

"Oh, I suppose so," Angela said. "I didn't think about that.''

"But Lieutenant," Caledonia said, "the girls were told that everyone, up and down the hall, was being offered a shot. But that isn't true. Angela called two of the residents on the hall—Janice Felton and Sadie Mandelbaum—and neither of them was offered a shot, even though neither of them had taken a shot earlier this year. So they probably should have been on a list to be immunized, if this was legit.''

"Who's giving these shots?" Martinez was on his feet.

"Nurse Ratched," Caledonia said.

"Who?" Martinez asked.

"You know—The Monstrous Maddox," Angela said. "Connie Maddox.''

Martinez and Swanson looked at each other. "I tell you, Mrs. Benbow, Mrs. Wingate. I think we will just look into this. The Jacksons live down the hall, don't they?" Martinez said, moving smoothly toward the door.

"Just beyond Amy's apartment. You remember—I was telling you about how much they heard through the bathroom wall . . .''

Swanson and Martinez exchanged another glance. "Mention this to anyone else, did you, Mrs. Benbow?" Martinez asked.

Angela thought for a moment. "I think I did. To the nurse,

this morning. To—'' her voice got faint. ''To Nurse Maddox.''

Both men turned, hit the door—not running but moving very fast—and went to the left, up the hallway toward the Jacksons. After that, there was a while when nothing happened—as far as Angela and Caledonia were concerned. Then suddenly there was a confusion of noises.

First two nurses passed the door, heading toward the Jacksons. Angela and Caledonia caught the flash of their white uniforms through the door, which still stood ajar. Caledonia had moved to close it after Martinez and Swanson left, but Angela had gestured with a finger to her lips and whispered, ''Leave it, Cal. We may be able to tell what's going on.''

Within a short four minutes, the paramedical emergency team arrived, siren going and lights flashing, parking their truck almost directly opposite Angela's living room windows. Their station was not far from the old hotel building, and they were often summoned to Camden for emergency treatment when Dr. Carter was not available—and to transport patients across the street for fuller treatment. Residents, alerted by the siren, began to gather in the lobby, wild with curiosity to see who had broken a leg or had a heart attack this time. Angela and Caledonia could hear the babble of voices out there, though they could pick up no words.

There was a certain amount of clanking as the emergency team carried their equipment, including a rolling stretcher, into the hallway. Outside in the street, through the open windows of the truck, the radio dispatcher's voice crackled metalically, issuing instructions to other teams. Then the paramedics came back down the hall again, through the lobby and out to the truck, on the double, returning with a second stretcher.

Dr. Carter arrived, and several men neither Angela nor Caledonia recognized . . . and the comings and goings became more and more confused and confusing. But eventually the stretchers rolled out, a recumbent form on each held in with straps and sheets. ''It's the Jacksons,'' Angela said, turning back from the window, where she'd watched the two stretchers lifted into the ambulance. "I saw the pink sweater on one, where the sheet didn't cover." The ambulance roared away.

Caledonia was more cautious. "It was one of the Jacksons. We don't know who was on the other stretcher," she warned. "You ought to have the biggest thigh muscles in California, with all the jumping to conclusions you do."

Then things quieted down. Caledonia ventured into the hallway on the pretext of getting a soft drink from the vending machine that stood in the recreation room of the health facility across the way. She came back with two barely chilled cans of orange soda. "Nothing doing out there. You ought to be able to handle this," she told Angela. "Carbonation is supposed to settle the stomach."

"There's nothing wrong with my stomach now," Angela protested. "In fact, I'm a little hungry."

"You ought to be. You didn't eat any supper. I'll go back and get you some cheese crackers from the machine, if you'll give me a couple of quarters. I used my last ones on these sodas."

"Didn't you see anything going on?"

"Not a thing . . . but maybe I will this trip."

But she was disappointed. All she brought back with her from her second trip was the crackers and a dime in change—no news.

It was nearly ten-thirty when there was a knock at the still-ajar door, and Lieutenant Martinez put his head inside. "Still awake, ladies?" he asked.

Four bright eyes turned to him with wonder. "Still awake!" Angela chirped. "Who could sleep with all the excitement?"

He smiled. "Excitement's been over for a couple of hours, you know. Even the crowd in the lobby gave up and went home."

"Not us. You know us better than that, Lieutenant," Angela said. "Please—you know we're dying to hear . . ."

He came all the way into the room and eased the door shut behind him. "Swanson's taking care of some details and we're on our way down to the office, but I will fill you in a little before we leave. To begin with, you'll be glad to hear we think the Jackson twins are going to come through all right. And we've arrested Nurse Maddox for attempted murder."

"Attempted murder?"

"That's right. We got to the Jacksons just in time to stop her giving a shot to a very sick woman . . ."

"Donna Dee."

"I can't tell them apart," Martinez shrugged.

"Nobody can," Caledonia assured him. "The sick one, though, was Donna. Dora Lee was well enough when we saw her at supper."

"Not by the time I saw her, she wasn't. When we got to their room, they were both down and sick. One was much worse than the other, almost unconscious. And the nurse had a loaded hypo ready for one of them. That room was a shambles and both women were in terrible condition."

"But from flu shots?" Angela said.

"Huh-uh. The lab will tell us exactly, but the medical team told me already they think it's some kind of strong emetic. It would make you very sick to your stomach—but it might not kill you directly."

"What do you mean, 'directly'?" Caledonia asked.

"Poison would kill you more directly," he said. "This would be just as effective in the long run. Two elderly ladies like the Jacksons couldn't stand very many days of being violently sick to their stomachs. They'd become very weak, dehydrated, their body chemistry would be all out of whack, it might affect their hearts. If they had heart attacks and died, nobody would be very surprised."

"Of course! If they didn't have a heart attack all by themselves," Angela said, "they could have been given another shot to speed things up. I mean, the nurses came in here every day to give me a shot to settle my stomach and nobody thought anything of it."

Martinez smiled. "I said before—I'll say it again—you'd have made a marvelous criminal, Mrs. Benbow. A first-class murderer. That's exactly right . . . and that's exactly what your friend Nurse Maddox thought.''

"Oh, yes . . . Maddox. Why? I mean, why would she want to kill the Jacksons?'' Caledonia asked.

"Because she killed two people before, and she was covering her tracks. Or trying to. Until you told her, Mrs. Benbow, she had no idea that everything said in Amy Kinseth's apartment could be heard through the wall. She thought she'd better be certain nothing damaging had been picked up. And the Jacksons were her biggest danger. She's the one, all right . . . and it's all over but finding out the details, I think.'' He rose and started for the door.

"But why did she kill Amy Kinseth? And Bobby Baird?'' Angela said. "You can't just leave the story in the middle like that.''

"Oh yes I can. Because everything I have right now is only guesswork. I can't really even be a hundred percent sure about Nurse Maddox killing Kinseth and Baird. You'll notice I said we'd charged her with *attempted* murder. Trying to shoot the Jackson twins full of something harmful will be enough to hold her till we're positive about the rest.''

"You'll tell us?''

He bowed. "I'll tell you. You earned that and more, when you got the notion there was something wrong and called us about the Jacksons. You two have probably saved their lives.''

"Oh, Lord,'' Caledonia said. "Do us one favor, Lieutenant. Never, *never* tell them that! I don't want two grateful Jackson twins pouring me mint tea every day from here on in. Just pretend you worked it out by yourself.''

"But come back. Soon. Don't make us wait,'' Angela pleaded.

"Soon,'' he promised, and left.

"Oh, Cal, how exciting!'' Angela jumped to her feet . . . and her knees sagged. "Oh, dear! I—I'm afraid I'm not quite back to normal yet. I feel—''

"Here," Caledonia said, putting an arm around her friend's shoulder. "Let me see you in to bed. We'll talk tomorrow."

"I know I won't be able to sleep," Angela said. "It's all too thrilling. I may be weak, but my mind is going a mile a minute!"

Once more, the oracle was wrong. Angela slept like a baby—and a happy baby at that.

Chapter 17

I̴T̴ WAS Sunday evening, after supper, when Lieutenant Martinez returned to Camden. He had phoned in advance and both Angela and Caledonia were waiting—dressed in their best—in Caledonia's apartment. Angela had decided on a turquoise two-piece suit with a long jacket that hid—to some degree—the failure of her waistline to indent more than an inch or two inside her hipline. Caledonia had settled for a burnt orange caftan shot with bronze threads marking a floral pattern.

The Lieutenant afforded himself the time to kiss each lady's hand and to compliment her attire. Someone else might have found it amusing that they took such pleasure in his small attentions. He did not. He found it charming.

"You're off duty, Lieutenant, I hope?" Caledonia said, waving a hand toward her liquor cabinet. "May I offer you a little after-dinner something-or-other?"

"Ah, certainly. We only work seven days a week when we absolutely have to. And after supper when we cannot avoid it. This is Sunday evening, and even I have time off when a case is complete. I'd be delighted with a tiny Cointreau, if you have it."

"Of course." She moved to the bar. "Did you mean what you said about the case being complete?"

"Yes, I did. And you'll both feel happier to know that the Jacksons are going to be up and around and back here from the hospital next week. I checked once more before I came just to be sure. It was nip and tuck with the one—Donna

243

Dee, I believe. Her sister Dora Lee says that when—ah, thank
you, Mrs. Wingate." He took the liqueur glass and waited
while Caledonia served Angela, took her own, and seated
herself. "To your very good health, my friends. Now, where
was I?"

Angela supplied the nudge. "You said Donna Dee was
sicker than Dora Lee. We know that, of course, because
Dora Lee was still walking around at suppertime Thursday
evening. And she told us how sick her sister was after the
shot."

"Yes, it must have affected Donna almost at once. Nurse
Maddox apparently realized it might look very odd if they
got ill at exactly the same time—being twins doesn't go that
far! So she injected one first—"

"Donna Dee?"

"Exactly. Then when she came to give Donna her second
shot, she also gave one to Dora Lee. Apomorphine."

"Beg pardon?"

"Apomorphine. A hospital facility like yours undoubtedly
had it on hand somewhere or other. It's a cousin to morphine,
but it has rather different results. It affects the nausea centers
of the brain and it's supposed to be given in very small doses.
If they had been given large doses, the Jacksons would certainly have died quickly. Maddox gave them tiny doses,
counting on their getting repeatedly and terribly sick until
the nausea and its results killed them—so she didn't have to.
Not directly. She probably would have given them a shot or
two every day till they died of dehydration, convulsions, a
heart attack, or just general weakness—all the things a violent bout of nausea can bring on in an eighty-year-old woman.
As I think I told you before."

"Well," Angela prodded him, "so she tried to kill them
both to be sure they couldn't ever tell anything they'd heard.
But what had they heard?"

"They heard her coming and going from Amy Kinseth's
apartment at all hours, even when she wasn't officially on
duty. Kinseth wasn't sick, she didn't welcome physicals, they
weren't friends, and everyone knew that. So what were all

those visits about? The Jackson twins were her only danger, because only the Jacksons knew that every single time she came into that hallway, she ended up coming to Kinseth. And they might have commented on it to someone.''

"Nobody would have paid the slightest attention if they had,'' Caledonia said. ''They generally talked such awful nonsense.''

"Maddox didn't know that, though. At least, she couldn't take the chance.''

"But Lieutenant,'' Angela said, ''what did she do when she got to Amy's apartment?''

"Delivered stolen jewelry. Mrs. Kinseth was her fence— and Maddox had a thriving little business going here to supplement her salary. She took and she passed along odds and ends of jewelry she picked up in residents' apartments.''

Angela said, ''I don't understand. Jewelry? Things Nurse Maddox stole from us?''

"That's right. You told me little things were always disappearing around here . . . and everyone assumes the residents have merely lost or misplaced their possessions. It's the perfect setup for any thief, you know. And as for a nurse— well, who else has immediate access to all the residents' rooms at all hours? Who else comes and goes as she likes— and with a pass key at that? Who else could be there unwatched in the apartment while the resident is asleep or even perhaps unconscious . . . without anyone suspecting anything wrong?''

"It wasn't drugs? It was jewelry?'' Angela was still taken aback by the change of direction. This was not at all what she'd set herself to hear.

"What about the amber glass, Lieutenant?'' Caledonia put in. ''The glass from the pill bottle?''

"Well, that was part of the cleverness of Nurse Maddox. She always carried a thermometer and a stethoscope and a pill tray—the tools of her trade. And she put a few empty pill bottles in among the full ones on the tray. Then if she found a little bauble as she ministered to her charges—say a platinum chain or perhaps a pair of pearl earrings—she just slid her find into an empty pill bottle standing among the others. You can't see much through that amber glass, and who's going to poke around among the several bottles on the pill tray anyhow?''

"I see—I see—'' Angela was now hot on the scent. "And then when she went to see Amy Kinseth, she simply carried the loot''—Lieutenant Martinez gallantly stifled a grin—"in with the pill tray and left the bottle and all with Amy!''

"How on earth did Amy ever get involved with all this?'' Caledonia marveled.

"She kind of inherited the business, we're told. I better start at the beginning.'' He settled himself in his chair more comfortably.

"Amy's husband was a fence. Not a big, important one. But that's how he and Amy got to live so well—with the money he made after hours! His legitimate business was insurance. We figure he got to know thieves and even some of the big operators who melt the metals and break up big stones—maybe through insurance claims he had to investigate. Anyway, he wasn't very successful as an insurance man, so he decided to supplement his income, and he developed quite a neat little business on the side. In fact, he amassed a tidy little fortune.''

"So rabbity little Gordon Kinseth was a fence!'' Angela said, rolling the word in her mouth. "I saw his picture, and you'd never have thought he was a criminal king . . .''

"He was hardly that,'' Martinez said. "In fact, the reason he stayed safe and kept working over several years was because he was so modest in his ambitions. He never dealt with the really sleazy types, and he never did business on a very large scale—which is probably why we never caught on to him. He kept his purchases and his sales modest and inconspicuous . . . but steady. He just plodded along his cautious, illegal way making a lot of money and living well. Then one day, he died. He popped over with a heart attack one morning when he was out jogging.''

"Well,'' Caledonia said, "why on earth did Amy get involved? She obviously had plenty to live on.''

"Ah, but she was also greedy," Martinez said. "We believe Amy knew all about Gordon's sideline. At least, she deliberately hung on to that little chest, which we believe he'd rigged up himself as a sort of 'holding cupboard' to hide his purchases till he could pass them along. We think she hoped somehow to start his business up again. She certainly seems to have known a couple of his big-time buyers who would take things off her hands. But if she meant to start business for herself, she had a problem. She didn't know Gordon's suppliers—the thieves from whom he'd bought things. They came to him secretly and at night, Maddox tells us—and Amy probably never even saw them. So she was stumped about how to make contact, at least she was till Maddox recognized and contacted her!

"Nurse Maddox—who is singing like a little bird, by the way—Nurse Maddox used to be one of Gordon's little circle of men and women who brought in stolen goods. When she saw the name 'Mrs. Gordon Kinseth' on the roster of new residents, she knew who that was—so Maddox contacted Amy the very first day she arrived."

"Of course!" Caledonia said. "The day she came up to Kinseth and took her blood pressure there in the lobby—the very day Amy moved in!"

"I thought that was odd at the time," Angela said. "Nobody did that for me when I moved in!"

"Maddox was taking something of a chance, I suppose. Someone might have pointed out that it was unusual to do a physical right in the lobby. On the other hand, we take for granted familiar people doing familiar things . . ."

"Well, we certainly did in that case! Nobody even asked about it," Caledonia said. "Imagine the brass of the woman! The nerve!"

"She wanted the chance to make contact. Amy was rude and dismissed her, but not before Maddox had asked Amy for a meeting . . ."

"Down on Beach Lane, I bet," Caledonia said.

"Of course," Angela agreed. "When Amy left your bridge

party so abruptly! But Lieutenant, what went wrong? Why did Maddox kill Amy?''

''Amy was a greedy woman,'' Martinez said. ''Maddox was the only person Amy Kinseth was fencing for—and that didn't make her the kind of profits Gordon used to drag in. But Amy simply wouldn't acknowledge that she'd have to spread out—make more contacts, and thereby take more risks—if she wanted a bigger profit. She started to pressure Maddox to bring her more things . . . but Maddox wasn't anxious to take any of the three apparent alternatives.''

''Three alternatives, Lieutenant?''

''Three I can think of. First, of course, she could have actually done as Amy asked—and increased the rate of theft. But that would have been very dangerous. While the occasional missing ring or necklace could be dismissed as the owner's carelessness, increased stealing would surely draw unwelcome attention—the police might be called in, she might be found out. Second, she could try to find a new fence. But that's not so easy. I don't think she had any contacts in the criminal world.''

''But she got to know Gordon Kinseth . . .''

''According to Maddox, she got acquainted with him legitimately. She was one of his insurance clients. I am not sure how they turned their business relationship into one of fence-and-thief. Maddox says their conversations turned to speculation about how easy theft would be from a retirement home—and then to Gordon's suggesting he could be of help. She's not really sure how, but she became aware of what she calls 'a marvelous opportunity.' No, she wouldn't have known where to begin to find another fence to take her things.''

''Well, what was her third option, Lieutenant?''

''Her third option was to quit stealing! One disadvantage to that option was the loss of the additional income. You say the salaries here aren't big—and she'd gotten used to having some of the nicer things. You should see the car she drives, for instance. A foreign sports car . . .''

"Maddox?" Angela was incredulous. "Stuffy dried-up stick-in-the-mud Maddox?"

"Not so stuffy—not so dried up. She was a successful thief and a murderer, after all. The other problem about quitting is the chance that the fence may get angry at you for trying to stop your business arrangement, and he may, in revenge, sell you out to the police."

"Seems to me," Caledonia rumbled, "there must be a fourth alternative you didn't mention. To kill off the fence! You get out of the trap, and you protect yourself against being sold out at the same time. Is that why she did it, Lieutenant? Is that why she killed Amy?"

"Partly, I suppose. But it seems to have been mainly rage. Maddox tells us Amy called her in or made a date to meet her early in the morning or late at night three times, and every time she pressured Maddox to step up the rate and volume of her stealing. Every time Maddox tried to explain the dangers—but Amy wouldn't listen. And she was quite nasty about it—"

Caledonia nodded. "Oh yes, she had a nasty tongue, that woman."

"Well, the third time was the time Amy met Maddox late at night over at the community center. That time Amy suggested that if Maddox didn't want to steal more jewelry, she might consider supplementing her income by stealing drugs from Camden's medical supplies. And at that point, Maddox just plain lost her temper!"

"Why?" Angela asked. "If she stole jewelry, what was wrong with stealing drugs?"

"Was it because she was a nurse and it went against the grain, Lieutenant?" Caledonia suggested. "It would be against everything she'd been trained for, which was the saving of lives."

"Oh, I don't think that crossed her mind for a moment," Martinez said. "She tried to kill two of her charges by making them so sick they'd die naturally, didn't she? You can't say she was too concerned about the Jackson twins. No, she says that going into drugs was just plain too dangerous. Drugs are the Big Time these days, and the people you end up dealing with aren't exactly warm and cuddly types, not to mention that falsifying drug records isn't all that easy to get away with, even in a place like this where record-keeping isn't very strict. The law might get onto any substantial shortages in the drug cabinets.

"But Amy kept pushing and pushing, urging and threatening, doing a little name-calling . . . and Maddox got angry. Very angry. She lashed out—hit Amy with the first thing that came to hand, one of those sticks someone left there after an exercise class. And then, if you please, she just went coolly along to the health facility where she had night duty and started giving the evening sleeping pills to her patients!"

"Lieutenant," Angela said, "what about poor Bobby Baird? How did he get involved?"

"Maddox decided to retrieve whatever odds and ends were left of what she'd been hiding with Amy—it would be too easy to trace them to her if they were ever found. Those pill bottles she used to carry the jewelry in were an arrow pointing straight to her. She didn't know exactly where Amy kept them, so she searched the basement first—all the boxes, all the luggage. She ripped out the linings just in case there were any baubles concealed in the luggage. Of course she had no luck."

"And that's when I came along, right?" Angela said.

"Right. She's the one who locked you in after throwing that cloth over your head, Mrs. Benbow, so you couldn't get a look at her. We thought it was a man because of the strength it took to lift the heavy material, but Nurse Maddox has arms like steel bands. From there, she went up to Amy's apartment a couple of times to look through her possessions."

"How?" Caledonia asked. "I thought you decided it had to be someone who never had a chance to search the apartment."

"Well, I was wrong. I'm told the nurses keep a master key so they can visit the sick and nobody has to worry about getting out of bed to let them in the door. She says she just let herself in and hunted through Amy's belongings before we took them away. Twice. With no luck.''

"Lieutenant, you thought the killer was upset by Baird's moving the furniture," Angela reminded him.

"I was wrong about that, too," he admitted. "She was delighted! That way she had a chance to take things apart to search thoroughly. It was bound to be a noisy business—too noisy for her to try in an apartment that was supposed to be empty. She went to Baird's shop at night, and unhappily for him, they came face to face. She told us that as she went past his office, he came out of the door. It startled her, and she just grabbed up the cane and hit him. The blow knocked him down and out—and it also broke the halves of the cane apart . . . so she saw the sword.''

"She didn't have to stab him!" Angela said. "I mean, if he was knocked out . . .''

"He might have identified her. She didn't want to take that chance. And she'd already killed one. How was it any worse to kill two?''

"For mine own good, all causes shall give way. I am in blood steeped in so far, that should I wade no more . . . returning were as tedious as to go o'er," Angela said. "Remember, Lieutenant?''

Martinez nodded. "Macbeth said it, didn't he?''

"You two and your Shakespeare. You'll be the death of me with that stuff, if you'll excuse the unfortunate figure of speech," Caledonia said. "Well, what happens now?''

"She goes to prison, of course," Martinez said.

"You know, the oddest part to me is that a nurse did it. I'd really never suspect a nurse," Caledonia said. "Nurses are usually very special people—caring and dedicated—the very last ones, I'd think, to turn to violence.''

"But would you believe it, Tyrell suspected a nurse all along," Martinez said. "Remember, he came here thinking the problem was something based on drugs. And who has constant access to drugs? A nurse. Before long, he'd focused in on Maddox, because she's the nurse who takes inventory and has responsibility for control of supplies.''

"Of course," Angela crowed. "I even saw her once doing a check of supplies."

"How about all that garbage Tyrell went through?" Caledonia asked. "I saw him hip-deep in leftover cornbread and eggshells one day out behind the kitchen."

To his credit, Martinez mastered the impulse to laugh aloud and masked it with a discreet cough. "That was just one angle he was looking into. He ran a check on every one of the staff, including the kitchen staff," Martinez said. "You'll be glad to know they're all just what they seem to be. Except Nurse Maddox. Among other oddities in her background, she had way too much money for what Torgeson was paying her. I told you about the car she drove, for instance. She had a Merrill Lynch Cash Management Account, as well. I understand that requires at least twenty-five thousand dollars in securities for a start—not a fortune, but more than any other nurse on the staff here would have, I think."

"She could have inherited money, couldn't she?" Angela asked.

"She could have, but she didn't. We checked."

"It sounds so—so ordinary, somehow," Caledonia said. "I always think of criminals as living high and spending all the profits!"

Martinez bowed slightly. "And thanks to the good Lord they usually do just that. It helps us solve a lot of crimes. We just sit still and watch for someone to buy himself a diamond ring, a car two blocks long, and a round-the-world cruise. But this time it was different. Maddox wanted to play it safe, so she regularly invested some of her take. Not standard procedure for your average thief, but maybe not too surprising from her. She wanted to have her cake and eat it too, to profit from crime but not to take any chances."

"So you're saying you were already suspicious of her when we phoned you about the Jackson twins?" Caledonia asked.

Martinez nodded. "Well, at least Tyrell had alerted us to watch her especially. She was a bad person, ladies. She killed two people who got in her way—and in the end, she tried to kill two little old ladies for no good reason except that they had an extra-thin bathroom wall."

"Lieutenant," Angela said suddenly, "where is Detective Swanson? We thought he might come with you this evening. Such a nice young man . . ."

Martinez smiled broadly. "Chita Cassidy would agree with you, Mrs. Benbow. Well, he did come with me—as far as the lobby. Then he peeled off to meet Chita. They're going dancing, I believe, after she finishes her stint on cleanup duty in the dining room."

"I hope, Lieutenant," said Caledonia with severity, "that you approve. We think Chita is a lovely child."

"I never approve or disapprove my friends' and associates' social activities, Mrs. Benbow. Any more," he said mischievously, "than you would dream of approving or disapproving what someone here at Camden did with their own time."

That put a complete stop to the conversation for a moment. Neither Angela nor Caledonia could think of an appropriate response, and neither could tell if he was teasing them or not. He, on the other hand, kept a straight face while he finished his Cointreau. "Now I will be going. I'll have to drive myself, of course. Swanson's gone off with Chita in her car. . . . Oh well, I used to do that all the time. It's just that I got used to having a chauffeur."

"Don't wait for another murder to come to visit, Lieutenant," Angela said. "You know we'd be delighted to see you any time."

"I'm going to try. And I know we'll detour in this direction frequently . . . as long as romance holds out," he smiled. "Now, ladies . . ." he moved to each in turn and kissed their hands. "You've made a difficult assignment easier and happier for me."

"Oh, thank you," Angela breathed, as he moved out the door, then up the walk toward the main building.

Without another word, Caledonia and Angela stepped back into the apartment. In the air, almost tangible between them, there was a sense of sadness mingled with satisfaction, the feeling of a job well done, of the book closed on a life, of the law upheld, of friendships renewed . . .

"Angela, do you want another Cointreau?"

"Thank you, Caledonia, I don't think so. That's awfully aromatic—something milder, perhaps."

Caledonia went to the liquor closet and began to rummage around. "Ah, here's something—Chambord. You like this, Angela." She took out two tiny etched glasses. "You know, girl, we haven't done badly for two old war-horses, have we?"

Angela smiled. "Not at all badly. I'm sorry about Bobby Baird, you know—but everything else worked out all right. And it was wonderful to see Lieutenant Martinez again." She walked idly to Caledonia's front window and gazed out. Suddenly she made a strangled, coughing sound, followed by a sort of whoop that made Caledonia turn abruptly to stare at her.

"Cal! Come here! Look! Out there on the lawn!" Angela was pointing frantically out the window. Caledonia billowed over to join her, peering out into the gathering gloom of evening.

The sky was still painted with gold, old ivory, pale silver-blue, and a soft streak of coral that trailed off into purple close to the horizon. But the garden was already wearing its widow's veil of black, and even the path, illuminated by lights held up on foot-high stakes and focused downward at the concrete, looked forbidding. In the middle of a patch of grass that seemed charcoal gray in the gloom, there was a human form, a man's body.

"Ohmygawd," Caledonia exclaimed. "Another one! It's starting all over. Come on, Angela . . ." and the two ladies charged out into the darkness, twin cylinders of very different girth and height, their distinguishing features obscured by the twilight.

Angela reached the figure first and knelt beside it, reaching to turn the recumbent man so she could see his face. "Don't touch him," Caledonia said behind her. "The police will want to see him exactly as he is . . ."

"Police?" said the figure on the lawn. "Now why ever would the police be wanting to see me?"

"Grogan!" Both women recognized him at the same time. "Grogan, are you ill?" Caledonia said.

He sighed deeply, and as the air caught in his throat, he belched—just once.

"Mr. Grogan, have you been drinking again?" Angela scolded. "You promised . . ."

"That I did. And I've been true to my word," he replied, rising onto one elbow to address them. "But it's been absolute hell. Ladies, you may enjoy life sober, but I most distinctly do not. I'm full of pain—in my mind, with my bad memories, and in my body, for I find I'm getting old. I didn't really notice so much when I was drunk half the time. Amazing what a dram of Drambuie will do to damp down the pain of an aching shoulder or a throbbing knee . . ."

"But you told us . . . you *promised* us . . . that you'd stop drinking forever."

"And I've regretted giving my word to such a foolish pledge. But give my word I did, and that's the truth. So . . ." he sighed deeply, "rather than break my word, and rather than live any longer on this 'sterile promontory,' I decided to end it all. I've taken poison."

Both women gasped. "Now see here! When did you take this poison?" Caledonia demanded. "How long ago? And what kind?"

"Ah, ladies, you'll be doing me an eternal kindness if you just belt up for once, you'll excuse me. You know how disagreeable I am sober . . . I don't like people and people don't like me. I'm much nicer drunk—but I smell and I fall over things, and I offend the tight-corseted group in the lobby no end. There's just no place where I fit in, alive. I'm better dead."

Caledonia knelt and placed both huge hands on his shoulders. "Grogan, if you want to have some peace, tell me what you took and how long ago. Or I'll shake it out of you right now. I mean it . . ."

"Awww, Mrs. Wingate . . ."

"The truth . . ."

"Oh, all right. I took the poison the gardeners set out for the snails. I went through the garden emptying the little saucers . . . I think I found every one, just to be sure. It wasn't half bad, you know? Bitter, but not bad . . . about, oh, fifteen minutes ago I finished the last one. And then I lay down here to die under the stars and the open sky. And I'm already feeling a little numb . . . so just let me drift away, will you? There's a good lady . . ." And he fell back, his eyes only half open, his mouth agape, his breathing deep, rattling in his throat.

"Oh, Cal, what are we going to do? We must call for help . . ."

Caledonia levered herself to her feet with difficulty and helped Angela to rise from the damp grass as well. "Come on . . . back to the apartment . . ."

Angela pattered behind her gigantic friend, chattering nervously as they returned to the apartment.

"First the ambulance, I think. Or no, maybe the police . . . But they'd only arrest him. Suicide's a crime, isn't it? I seem to remember hearing . . . Maybe we should call the nurses across the street in the health center. Yes. They'd know what to do. And possibly alert Torgeson . . . No, I hate that—he'd want Mr. Grogan out of here when he recovered. Isn't there something in the lease about not committing suicide? I signed mine so long ago I've forgotten, and I haven't read it since. But it stands to reason that—Cal, where are you going? What are you doing—Cal . . . *Caledonia*!!!"

While Angela dithered, Caledonia closed the door behind them firmly and made her way over to her bar, lifted out the Chambord, and poured two tiny thimbles full of the rich, raspberry red liqueur. She brought one to Angela and took the other herself, lifting it up toward the chandelier in a silent toast, then bringing it to her lips for a blissful sip. "Ahhhh, that's lovely. Take some of yours, Angela. It'll relax you."

"Caledonia Wingate! What on earth . . . You're letting Grogan die?"

"No, I'm not going to let him die."

"Then *do* something, for heaven's sake. Or I'll do something myself. Where's that phone : . . ." Angela put her little glass down and started for the telephone.

"Angela, stop it. Sit down. I'm not letting Grogan die . . . but I'm not calling for help, either. Angela . . . he drank the snail poison. Don't you get it? The *snail poison*!"

Angela stopped, completely bewildered. "I know. That's what he said."

"Well, don't you know how our gardeners kill snails here?"

"I've seen them putting out the saucers of poison every evening, all right . . . and there are dozens of dead snails lying in the saucers every morning . . ."

"They drown."

"What?"

"The snails drown, they don't die of poison."

"But . . ."

"Angela, those are saucers of beer! The snails love it, wade in to drink, get blasted and can't get out of the liquid, and they *drown*!"

"Then Grogan . . ."

"Yup. Grogan has drunk the equivalent of four or five quick bottles of beer . . . and after two weeks of strict sobriety, he's feeling numb after only fifteen minutes, or so he says."

From the grass across the walk, now engulfed in shadows, came a soft voice, singing:

"Oh-ho, I will *ta-hake* you hoooome Kathleen . . .
Across the ocean wi-*hild* and wi-*hide* . . .
To where you something-something been . . .
Since first you were my bonny bri-*hide* . . .
The ro-*hoses* all have something-something . . ."

"Drunk! Grogan's drunk!" Angela stamped her foot in frustrated indignation.

"Yes, drunk, and happy again. We made a mistake, Angela. It's nearly always a mistake to interfere with what someone else has found happiness in.''

"But the drink will kill him!"

"So will old age! So will loneliness . . . so will sorrow . . . and he obviously had all three of those, when he was sober. For Pete's sake, Angela, the man is in his eighties. Let him alone to be happy in his own way. And to choose his own way to die. Besides''—she cocked an ear toward the lawn again—''he doesn't sound much like he's going to die anytime soon, to me.''

"—and far, far away, her warrior gay, had fallen in the fray.
Oh-*ho-oooo*, the moon shines tonight on pretty Red Wing—''

Grogan was in fine voice again, progressing happily through his enormous repertoire.

"And far, far away, her brave lies sleeping . . .
While Red Wing's weeping, her heart away-*hay*!''

"Oh, Caledonia, we're failures.''

"I don't think so. We've had a lot of excitement for a change, and something to do. We revived a friendship with the handsome Lieutenant and his aide-de-camp. We helped, in our own way, to put a murderer behind bars. And we learned not to interfere with other people's happiness, just because it's not our choice for happiness. Didn't we, Angela?'' Angela did not answer, and Caledonia said, more forcefully, "Didn't we?''

Angela was looking wistfully out into the dark, toward the now invisible Grogan. "Well, I suppose . . .''

"We did! And that's all there is to it. Pick up your drink, Angela. I don't believe you've even tasted it!''

And as the ladies sipped, Grogan serenaded them softly through the falling dew.

"Oh Genevieve, sweet Genevie-*heave* . . .
The days may come, the day-*hays* may go-*ho* . . .
But still the hands of mem'ry weave,
The blissful dreams . . . of lo-o-ong ago-*HO-o-o-o-o-OH*!

About the Author

Corrine Holt Sawyer, a former actress and television writer, is Director of Academic Special Projects at Clemson University. She lives in Clemson, South Carolina.

HOUGHTON MURPHY
and
MURDER

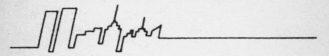

TAKE A PEEK...
IF YOU DARE